VICE, VIRTUE & VIDEO:
Revealed

BIANCA GIOVANNI

OMNIFIC PUBLISHING
LOS ANGELES

Omnific Publishing
1901 Avenue of the Stars, 2nd floor
Los Angeles, CA 90067
www.omnificpublishing.com

First Omnific eBook edition, January 2014
First Omnific trade paperback edition, January 2014

The characters and events in this book are fictitious.
Any similarity to real persons, living or dead,
is coincidental and not intended by the author.

Library of Congress Cataloguing-in-Publication Data

Giovanni, Bianca.
   Vice, Virtue & Video: Revealed / Bianca Giovanni – 1st ed.
   ISBN: 978-1-623420-55-0
   1. Erotic Romance — Fiction. 2. Friendship — Fiction.
   3. Porn Star — Fiction. 4. New Adult — Fiction. I. Title

10 9 8 7 6 5 4 3 2 1

Cover Design by Micha Stone and Amy Brokaw
Interior Book Design by Coreen Montagna

Printed in the United States of America

For MJ

Chapter 1

James

I'm having lunch with my buddy Dave Keegan at The Tap, a.k.a. Tap-a Keg-a Day, everyone's favorite college burger joint. We used to go here when we were in high school to flirt with hot college girls from the state university. Now Keegan's just finished his first year there and I'm living in California making movies, but not the kind you see in theaters. They're mostly of the XXX Internet video variety. I'm back in town to visit my family and my best friend, Lola, who's graduating high school in two weeks.

Lola is a frequent topic of my conversations with Keegan, since he's had a crush on her since she was about thirteen. Not that I blame him. Lola's really pretty, and she always has been. I've been her friend since I was nine and she was six, so I've watched her grow from a scrawny little girl into a full-fledged hottie. In fact, I've spent a lot of energy cock-blocking dudes who've tried to fuck her. She's really special to me—pretty much the only girl in town I haven't slept with—and I don't want some asshole to break her heart.

"I saw her at Genova's Pizza a couple days ago," Keegan says, interrupting my nostalgic moment. "I think her tits are even bigger. And she was wearing these little short-shorts. Fuck, dude!"

"Come on!" I chuckle. "That's Lola, man. How many times do I have to tell you that you shouldn't think about her that way?"

"Whatevs." He smirks. "She's hot as fuck, and you know it. Just because you haven't fucked her doesn't mean no one else should get to."

"That's exactly what it means!" I laugh loudly. "Just focus your horny bullshit on some other chick. There are thousands of them at your school, and I can tell you firsthand that some of them are fuckin' crazy in bed. You've always enjoyed my sloppy seconds," I joke, referencing the zillions of former flings that Keegan swooped in on after I was done with them.

"I know you have a 'special' relationship with Lola, so I promise I won't try to bang her," he teases.

"Fuck you! I do have a special relationship with her, dude. She's so sweet and innocent. She's just, like, this perfect little fairy or something—like a fuckin' Disney princess."

Keegan laughs hard at that description, and I know I sound like a total pussy.

It's hard for me to put my feelings into words when it comes to Lola. I love her a lot, but not in *that* way. I get all weird with her. I don't want guys to look at her, touch her, flirt with her, or fantasize about her. Keegan and my buddy Joey always used to talk about how hot she was, and it made me want to kick their asses. I feel possessive of her. She's my little treasure, and it's like I don't want anyone else to discover her. She's the only girl I know who isn't spreading her legs for just about anybody, and I'd like to keep it that way.

"All right, all right, man," Keegan chuckles. "I won't touch your girl."

"She's not *my* girl…but thanks."

"You worried about prom?" he asks with a smirk.

"Why?" I reply, even though I already know where he's going with this.

"You know, she's gonna go to prom with some dude, and we all know what happens on prom night." He makes that little circle and poking gesture with his hands that symbolizes sex. "You gonna freak when she gets that cherry popped?"

I cringe at the thought. *Not my pristine little angel!* The thought of some dude having awkward, possibly drunken, thoughtless, post-prom sex with Lola is just…unnerving.

"Dude," I whine, "don't say shit like that!"

He laughs loudly and watches me squirm. He knows how psycho I get about Lola having sex. I just can't bear the thought of some asshole using her and dumping her. I know how that goes; I've done it before myself, but at least the girls I was with were all pretty experienced and knew the deal going in. Lola's pure and sweet. She deserves to do it with someone who loves her. I've always felt that way.

"She's not gonna give up her V-card on prom night; she already told me that," I reply to Keegan.

"How do you know?" His lip curls into a smirk, and I can tell he's trying to provoke me, like the little shit-starter that he is.

"She's going with Marcus Montoya," I explain. "She said she's going as his beard because he's not ready to come out to his parents, so she told him she'd pretend to be his date. He's meeting his boyfriend there, so I don't think I have to worry about him."

"What about the other dudes there?" Keegan eggs me on.

"She's only going for, like, twenty minutes. I'm picking her up, and we're gonna hang out because she said she doesn't want to participate in 'that archaic, teenage mating ritual.'" I quote Lola's exact words.

"So she's spending prom night with you?" Keegan gives me a smart-ass glance that carries a big implication.

"Fuck you!" I laugh.

"Hey, I'm just saying, girls get all horny around prom," he teases, "and you're a fuckin' porn star now, so, you know, one thing might lead to another—"

"Not gonna happen." I shake my head.

"You've thought about it, though. Don't try to bullshit me. You know you've thought about fucking her before. Shit, I know I have. I've still got images of her in that little-ass bikini stored in the old spank bank." He grins at me as he taps his temple.

"Dude! That's Lola! Don't jack it to her!"

He smirks and holds up his hands. "All right, all right. I'll take her out of the lineup…for now."

"Good. Stop jerkin' off to my best friend."

"Yeah, yeah." He shrugs and rolls his eyes.

Our leggy, blond waitress comes over and asks us if we'd like another beer. Keegan seems pretty stoked because both he and I are under twenty-one, but the girl never carded us. We tell her yes, and she looks me up and down before she goes to get us two more beers.

"How do you do that shit, man?" Keegan asks me when she's out of earshot.

"Do what?"

"How do you charm the fuck out of girls like that? You've said, like, four words to that girl and she wants to fuck you. How?"

"I don't know. Jedi mind trick?"

"For real, man, how do you make all these girls go crazy for you?"

"Whatever!"

"Okay, first of all," he says like he's getting ready to explain some scientific theory, "that chick's way hot. She looks like she should be working at Hooters and not this place. Second, she's been eye-fucking the shit out of you since we sat down. She gave us free nachos and then she served us beers without checking our IDs."

"Dude, they hardly ever check IDs here." I shrug.

"Bullshit! You've just got it like that, man. Girls just, like, lose their shit around you. You're like Justin Timberlake or something."

I throw my head back and laugh at that one.

"You could totally fuck that girl if you wanted to. She's DTF, dude. She wants you bad."

"Nah, I don't know about that," I modestly reply. It's kind of true though. I probably could hook up with our waitress. She really has been throwing it at me this whole time.

"Here you go, guys." She smiles as she returns with our beers. She gives me a flirty glance as she sets the beers on the table, and I return it with my sexiest smile.

"So what about you, man?" I ask Keegan, who still seems in awe of my interactions with the waitress. "I'm sure freshman year treated you well in the chick department. Those out-of-state girls don't know you're a fuckin' idiot," I tease.

Keegan laughs and nods his head. "I do all right. The Beemer and the Rolex certainly don't hurt."

I snicker. Just like in nature, guys have to use what they've got to get chicks. Keegan's not a bad looking guy, average height with light blond hair and a sort of stocky build, but he plays the "my dad is rich" strategy, which girls seem pretty into. My family's about as middle-income as it gets, but I'm six-foot five, two hundred and ten pounds and girls have always thought I was good looking, so I've been able to get laid even when I was broke as shit.

"But come on," Keegan says, smiling, "nothing I get even compares to what you're getting out there in LA."

A grin spreads across my face. I've been very, let's just say, *fortunate* with California girls. So fortunate, in fact, that I've been able to build an entire career out of having sex with beautiful women.

"You did a movie with that redhead, right? The one who did the webcam stuff?" he asks eagerly.

"Yeah, I had a scene with her." He's talking about Amber Blaze, a starlet who got her start doing cam shows on her website before moving up to the big league.

"She's super famous," Keegan adds.

"She's cool, too," I reply. "And she's smart."

He snickers, probably laughing at the idea that a porn star could be considered smart. Normally, I'd rush to Amber's defense, but I know he doesn't mean it in a dickish way, so I let it slide.

"Does that webcam shit make good money?" he asks. "'Cause I heard that girl has bank."

"It can be really profitable. A lot of it depends on the girl and the show. The crazier the shit they do, the more they make." That's sort of the standard with porn in general.

"When you were doing that show with that blond chick, you were doing okay," he points out.

I sort of fell into porn, as unlikely as that sounds. I was out in LA going on auditions and shit, but I wasn't booking a lot of work. I met this girl who was a stripper-turned-camgirl, and we had a little thing going on. She let me crash at her place for a couple months and pretty soon she asked me to be in her show, since she knew she could make more money for actual fucking as opposed to just her playing with herself. We started doing shows together, and the cash started rolling in. The freakier we got, the more money we made, and she decided she wanted to move up the ranks and try to sign with a real production company. We managed to sneak our way into a party thrown by a major production company, and that was where I met Rick, the owner of Sin Cinema. The rest, as they say, is history, and I booked my first job about a week later.

"You've got some money in your wallet these days, but you still drive around in that piece of shit car." Keegan grins at the thought of my car, making me laugh.

I have enough to buy a decent car, but I love my '96 Honda Civic like a person. "Don't rip on Pansy, dude!" Yes, I've named her Pansy, mostly in an effort to beat my Suburban-driving brother to the punch when it came to making fun of my car.

"I doubt you could sell it anyway. That back seat's got too many different bodily fluids on it," he teases. "If they took a black light to that shit, they'd have to call in a hazmat team."

I crack up, but I have to nod my head because it's true. Pansy's seen a lot of action.

Just then, our waitress comes over again and asks us if we need anything else. I'm anxious to wrap up so I can go see Lola, so I say no. She gives me an ultra-hot smile and hands me the check. When I look down at it, I see that our total is zero and she's written her number and her name, Megan.

"Check it out." I grin as I show Keegan.

"Okay, dude," he exhales with his jaw flapping open in shock. "What. The. Fuck?"

I snicker at his reaction before I shrug my shoulders.

"Can I just be you for, like, one day?" he whines.

I laugh harder. No matter how many times shit like this happens, Keegan's always been in awe of my ability to hook up with girls.

"You're gonna call her, right?" he asks.

"Probably." I shrug. She's cute and she was coming on way strong, so it's basically a sure thing.

"Just promise me something, dude," he says all earnestly. "Promise me you'll ask her if she has a friend for me. Hook me up, dude!"

I laugh hard and nod my head. "It's a deal, man."

Keegan and I finish lunch, and I give Megan a smile as we head out. It's about time for Lola to get out of school, so I say goodbye to him, hop in my car, and head to her house. I pull up in front of the Caraway mailbox and take a quick glance at my house next door. My parents aren't home yet, which gives me some time to hang out with Lola before I have to go over there and do the whole pretending-that-I'm-a-struggling-actor-not-a-porn-star thing.

I walk up to Lola's porch and my heart's racing. I'm already so psyched to see her. I hung out with her almost every day for a little over a decade, and I miss her like crazy now that I'm in California and she's still back here.

I ring the doorbell, and I can hear footsteps inside. I get a fluttery feeling in my chest when the door opens. My beautiful angel! Really, really fuckin' beautiful. Lola's looking straight-up gorgeous, even more than I remember. Her hair's hanging down to her waist in those big, soft curls I've always thought were so pretty. Her honey brown eyes are all wide and sparkly with happiness. Her full, luscious lips are curved into a huge smile. And her body...*wow!* When I left she was wearing kind of baggy clothes, but now she's got on little jean shorts that show off her sexy legs and a white tank top that's clinging to her tits. *Goddamn!* She looks fuckin' amazing!

"Miss me?" I grin at her.

Chapter 2

Lola

"Ah!" I scream when I see James standing on my porch.

"Come here!" He smiles and reaches out, grabbing me around my waist for a huge hug. He twirls me around in a circle and kisses my cheek a bunch of times. I'm smiling so wide my face hurts as I wrap my arms around him tightly. I've missed him so much it's insane!

"You look fuckin' great, Lo," he says fondly when he puts me down.

"You're not looking so bad yourself there, stud," I tease, and he looks down with adorable modesty.

He's looking fantastic, actually. His hair is even longer than it was before—those lustrous, chestnut waves brush his shoulders now. He was usually clean shaven in high school, but he's got a little facial hair going on, and it's drawing major attention to his lips, which have always been one of his best features. His tan makes his hazel eyes look greener, and his arms are more cut than they were the last time I saw him. He's clearly been hitting the gym and enjoying sunny Southern California.

"You've been working out, I see." I give his bicep a little squeeze.

"A little bit." He grins and flexes his muscles. "You're lookin' pretty tight these days too, kid," he teases, playfully patting my butt.

"Yeah, I don't know if you know this, but I'm totally a hot chick now," I pretend to boast.

"I noticed that." He chuckles. "And I'm guessing all the guys in town have noticed it too."

I roll my eyes. "Come on." I motion for him to step inside. "Let's at least get into the living room before you give me the sex lecture."

He laughs and follows me inside.

Before we get past the kitchen, he wraps his arms around me from behind and pulls me close against his chest. I lean into him, and he bends to rest his chin on the top of my head.

"All right, all right," he says, "I won't give you the sex lecture. I know you've heard it a thousand times."

"Good." I smile, resting my arms over his hands on my waist. "I'm a senior in high school, for Christ's sake! Do you know how many health classes and Lifetime movies I've sat through in my life? I don't need to hear about all the pitfalls of teenage sex."

"I know you don't," he says, letting go of me and rotating my shoulders so I face him. "You're the smartest girl I know, and you don't take anybody's shit, so I know you're not gonna let some dude take advantage of you."

I smile proudly. He's battled with it for years, but it seems like he might finally be accepting that I'm growing up. He's been so protective since we were children, and it's sweet, but it can also drive me crazy. He has no qualms about banging anything with tits, yet he constantly tells me not to even make out with anybody. It's hypocrisy, but hypocrisy with the best intentions.

We flop down on the couch in the living room, and I laugh when he turns me sideways so I'm resting against the arm of the couch with my legs over his lap. We always used to sit like this when we'd watch movies late at night in my basement.

"So how's school going, kid?" he asks warmly. "You got finals coming up, right?"

"Yep. Just a couple weeks until I'm officially done with high school."

"Well, finals will be a breeze for you. You were always a good test taker."

"Thanks, James." I smile at the compliment. "I'm not nervous for anything except Spanish. I know there are going to be a lot of subjunctive tense questions, and it's so hard! I know the verbs, but sometimes the conjugations throw me and I second-guess myself."

"Let me help you," he volunteers eagerly. "That was always the only class I was good in."

When James was a little kid, his two best friends, Rueben Medina and Enrique Cortez, both spoke primarily Spanish with their families at home. James used to hang out at their houses a lot, and in addition to learning how to make Abuelita Medina's fresh tortillas, he picked up Spanish very quickly. He's practically fluent now.

"I'm psyched that I get to help you with school shit instead of the other way around. You were responsible for some of my best grades. I remember when you peer-edited my history paper and helped me turn it into something besides a total piece of shit."

I laugh and nod. That paper was pretty bad, but it was only because he didn't put any effort into it. School was never a priority for James. He was always more concerned with girls than grades.

"You pumped for prom?" he asks.

"Eh, kind of." I shrug. "I mean, I'm not really going for real, you know? The whole thing just seems too lame to get excited about, so it totally worked out that Marcus and I made our little arrangement. I feel bad because he keeps saying his parents will freak out if he tells them he's gay, but I keep telling him that they'll love him no matter what and he should just be who he really is. He says he's just not ready yet, and I respect that, so I told him I'd cover for him."

"Mother Theresa," he teases, and I playfully kick him in the shoulder. "You're right, though, he should just tell them. There were so many kids who were out in our school. I don't think his parents would flip their shit over it."

"But, then again," I say, raising an eyebrow, "you're hiding a pretty big secret from your parents, too."

I've known about James's adult film career since he shot his very first sex scene last year. He thought it would totally freak me out when he told me, but I really couldn't give two shits what he does for a job. He's still my best friend, and as long as he's not killing kittens or bombing Planned Parenthood, what he does for work is no big deal to me.

"Yeah, but that's different because doing porn was my choice. Marcus is gay and he's always been gay. I was always kind of...*popular* with girls—" he smirks "—but I opted to do porn, I wasn't born a porn star."

"That's valid. Though, according to legend, you were made for the big screen. The *big*, big screen."

He laughs loudly. "Legend, huh?"

"Legend or myth, I'm not entirely sure which," I tease.

"You wanna find out?" he says, pretending to go for his zipper.

"Ah! No!" I laugh and I can feel the rosy hue spreading across my cheeks.

James pauses for a minute and looks at me with a big, warm smile. "God! I missed you so fuckin' much, Lo!"

He reaches out to me, and I sit up and wrap my arms around him.

"You're the only person who calls me out on my shit and keeps me in check," he says into my hair.

"And that's a twenty-four-hour-a-day job."

"Honestly, I don't know how you have time to study when you're so busy calling me a hypocrite." He snickers.

I sit back, giving him a pretend scowl.

"What?" He grins. "I'm not saying I'm *not* a hypocrite—and actually, it's probably a good thing that you call me out on it."

"Admission is the first step to recovery," I tease.

We playfully bicker like that for a while as if we're making up for lost time. James and I have always challenged each other, which was part of the reason we became such good friends. There's a mutual respect and appreciation that gives us a bond like superglue.

We're watching TV on the couch when my mom comes home from work. She seems a little startled to see James sitting beside me, but maybe her surprise is because he has his arm around me and I'm all cuddled into him. I can't help it; I like being close to him and I always have. Still, she knows his rep as an über-player, and I think it kind of freaks her out to see how affectionate we are with each other. I can't really blame her. I'd probably be a little uneasy if my teenage daughter was so physically affectionate with a guy who's slept with almost every single girl in the tri-county area.

He stands up and goes right over to my mom to give her a big hug. She's little, like me, and she has to stand on her tiptoes to reach him.

"Theresa, it's so awesome to see you!" he says sweetly.

"Aw, thanks, honey. It's good to see you too. I think somebody's been hitting the gym," she teases, standing back to look at him.

He chuckles and gives her that modest smile I like so much.

"How's the whole acting thing going?" she asks. "Booking anything interesting?"

"Auditioning a lot," he lies. "And I've done a few commercials that are airing in, like, Europe and stuff, so I have enough to pay the bills."

I nearly snicker at this cover story.

"Well, that's great," she says, giving him a parental pat on the arm. "You already look like a movie star, kid, so you've got that going for you."

He laughs, and I think maybe, just maybe, he even blushes.

"Now comes the part where you have to start using more than those looks," she teases. "So just work hard and believe in yourself, and you can do it."

My mom and James have always gotten along really well. She thought he was a crack-up when he was younger because all the girls in the neighborhood would go crazy for him like he was Leonardo DiCaprio. Our physical affection isn't really a huge problem for her because she knows how much James puts me on a pedestal. He's been really protective of me since the day I met him, back when I was playing in the front yard while his family was moving into their house next door. He saw me and wandered over. He was nine and I was only six, but he didn't treat me like a baby and said he'd look for arrowheads with me while his parents were dealing with the movers. We were instant best friends, and there's nobody in the world I'm closer to than him. For that reason, my mom has been willing to overlook some of James's "indiscretions" with various girls and unconditionally accept him into our home.

"Can you stay for dinner tonight or are your parents expecting you to have dinner with them?" my mom asks him.

"I'd love to have dinner with you guys! My parents can wait. I'm staying there, so I can go home later tonight."

"Great!" my mom says as she takes a few steps toward the kitchen before turning back to us. "I was going to make stuffed shells. Does that sound good?"

"Of course! Let me help you out," James replies cheerfully.

James is a man of many talents, though none as obvious as his ability to charm the pants off of girls. He's been a phenomenal cook since he was about fourteen, and his recipes have even impressed my Italian grandmother, Nana Lucia.

I sigh and get up, heading to the kitchen to offer assistance, support, words of encouragement, or whatever I can contribute to tonight's meal with my limited culinary skills.

Once dinner is ready, the three of us sit down at the table and catch up some more. My mom seems approving of my plan to make a quick appearance and then bail on prom to hang out with James. She knows all about the Marcus situation and that I don't really want to do the whole prom thing anyway, so she's fine with me passing on all that to spend time with my best friend.

After dinner, James and I retreat to the basement, which was always our domain. We've got the TV on, though neither of us is paying much attention. Instead, we're having a conversation about his movies. He tells me that he went back and forth from Skinemax style soft-core movies to real porn, but settled on the real deal when he saw how much more money he could make.

"I mean, you have actual sex in a lot of those late night movie channel ones too, but they don't show close-ups or penetration," he explains. "I figured there really wasn't that much of a difference, except for the money."

"Was it weird? Doing your first one?"

"Not really." He shrugs. "At first, it's kind of bizarre to have all these people standing around, but I've done it in public before, so it didn't really faze me."

James has done it just about everywhere, but I remember a particularly sordid story about him being fellated by two girls at the same time right in front of everyone at a party. I was about thirteen when he told me, and I thought it was the single most scandalous thing to ever happen in our town. Of course, he shattered whatever scandal record that might have set with some of the crazy stuff he got up to later.

"I did one last week for this series called *Horny Housewives*," he says. "It cracked me up because it was like a fuckin' biography of my life."

"Oh, yeah?" I giggle.

"You remember how I used to do landscaping with my dad?" he asks.

"And you used to bang the housewives or their daughters while your dad and your brother broke their asses out in the yard?" I smirk.

"Exactly!" he laughs. "I was telling Rick about it the other day, and he said he wanted me to do a movie like that. So, in the movie, I play a pool boy who's cleaning this woman's pool. She gets all horny looking at me, and she fires up her vibrator and watches me. Then she takes me inside and offers me a drink, but we end up fucking on the kitchen counter."

"That's just so porno!" I laugh. "Like, 'Oh, hi, you're the pool boy? Can I offer you a glass of lemonade or maybe some pussy?'"

He laughs loudly and nods his head. "That's pretty much the exact plot, yeah."

I smirk and shake my head. *Oh, James, James, James.*

"I did one where I was supposed to be a student failing math and I have this hot teacher, so I bang her to get a better grade."

"Oh, please!" I laugh. "Is this based on Mrs. Peterson?"

"It totally is." He snickers, knowing I've got his number.

For most of his life, there's never been a problem James couldn't fuck his way out of. Getting a bad grade? Romance the teacher until she decides to let you pass. Want to earn money while doing minimal work? Let your brother and your dad do all the work for the family landscaping business while you go inside and screw a bored housewife. His dick has gotten him out of countless tight spots — no pun intended — and he's been able to lead an easy life because of his sexual proficiency.

He ends up chilling out on the couch with me for a couple hours before he decides his parents will get mad at him for not coming home to see them. After all, his car's been out front since about four o'clock and they can clearly see it from their front door.

I walk him out, and he grabs my face and plants a big old kiss on my forehead, which makes me feel warm and adored.

"See you tomorrow, kid." He smiles as he turns to cross the lawn to his house.

I shut the door and go back into my house, feeling content and happy again. When James isn't around, everything feels…off. Now I've got a spring in my step and a twinkle in my eye. My best friend is back, and I want to spend every waking minute with him in case I don't see him again for another big chunk of time.

Chapter 3

James

"Well, I was wondering when you were going to come home!" my mom says with a cheerful smile as she reaches out to hug me. She kisses my cheeks about a zillion times, and I laugh and rock her back and forth. She's five-foot ten so I don't have to bend down as far as I do when I hug Lola and Theresa.

"I missed you, Mom," I admit, feeling like anything but the cool, suave dude I usually am.

"Oh, sweetheart, we missed you so much!" she says warmly, taking my face in her hands and looking at me in that way that always makes me feel like she's proud of me.

When my mom was younger, she could have been a model. She's tall and thin with dark brown hair and light green eyes. My dad said she reminded him of a cross between Lauren Bacall and Sophia Loren, and she literally took his breath away the first time he saw her. She said the same thing about him, and jokes that the reason she likes watching *The Lord of the Rings* is because my dad looks like a brown-eyed Viggo Mortensen.

She holds my hand when she leads me in the house. "Your father will be so happy to see you, and Jonathan's here."

Ugh. I get the honor of being in the presence of my superb, amazing, golden-child brother. Jonathan's four years older than me and everything he does is perfect, according to my dad. Jonathan got good grades, he was captain of the football team, he dated Lisa, the head cheerleader, and he was even prom king. The dude's like something out of a fuckin' high school movie, and he's been pretty cocky about it forever.

After trying to keep up with him for most of my childhood, I just gave up and accepted my role as the black sheep of the family. I got into trouble sometimes, yes, but I know I had more fun than him. Mom and Dad knew I'd never do anything really bad, so they usually laughed it off.

They weren't too keen on me dropping out of college to move to California, but they changed their tunes when they saw that I was making bank. Of course, they had no idea just *how* I was making bank, but I managed to convince them that I was getting some good acting jobs every now and then and not slingin' dick on porn sets all day long.

"Hey, bro," Jonathan says as Mom takes me into the living room.

He gets up from the couch and gives me a hug. I hug him back, but both of us know that this whole brotherly display is mostly a performance for our parents. We're more rivals than brothers. He was always telling me I was a shit-starter and looking down on me when I'd get caught fooling around with girls. He thinks I'm a fuckup—but whatever, because I think he's a Goody-Two-Shoes.

"Son," Dad says as he walks over to me and hugs me, "good to have you home."

"It's good to be home, Dad," I reply.

"Missed having you around." He nods with a smile. "Your mother's been starting all these projects to keep her busy, since you're not around to spend time with her. We've got scrapbooks up to our ears and she's gotten into decoupage now, so there's glue on damn near everything in this house."

Mom rolls her eyes, and I laugh.

I might have been a little shit in school, but I do love my family and I miss them sometimes when I'm by myself in my apartment. There's just something comfortable and soothing about home that makes you feel loved instead of lonely.

"Have you eaten? I could heat you up something," Mom volunteers, coming over to put her arm around me.

"No, thanks. I actually ate over at Lola's," I reply.

"Oh, you did?" she says with a smile. "Couldn't wait to see her, huh?"

"No," I chuckle, and I feel shy all of a sudden.

Mom knows that Lola is special to me, but she also knows that our relationship is platonic. Still, I think both my parents secretly want me to be with someone smart and sweet like her instead of the fast women I hang out with. When I was in school, my mom would say, "I wish you would go out with someone like that Caraway girl. At least she doesn't spend her weekends getting drunk down at the reservoir."

"How's she doing?" Dad asks. "I saw her mother the other day, but I know Lola's got finals coming up, right?"

"Yeah, she and her mom are both great. Theresa got promoted, so she's pretty psyched about that. Lola's doing great in school, as usual, and she's psyched to move out east for college."

"You must have had a nice visit if you didn't stroll over here until ten o'clock," Dad comments with a vaguely snarky tone.

He's annoyed, but I don't really care. He'll just have to chalk this up to another disappointment from his youngest son. He's never really been proud of anything I do, and if I wasn't so successful with women, I'm pretty sure he'd consider me a total failure. He and Jonathan always thought I was a slacker because I didn't want to work for the landscaping company during the summers. When I did go with them on jobs, I laid a lot more than sod and I know they thought I was lazy for spending so much time inside while I was supposed to be working. But both of them can kiss my ass because that was how we got so much repeat business. Shit, we did Mrs. Landry's yard about seven times because she wanted an excuse to fuck me again and again.

"Jon, he was spending time with his friend. He hasn't seen her in a while, and he wanted to visit with her. You know how close they are," Mom defends me. She's usually the one to have my back, and I've always liked her more than my dad.

"All right," Dad says, "but be good, you hear me? That Lola's a good girl and I don't want you distracting her from her schoolwork or getting her into any trouble."

"Jon!" Mom says sternly. "The boy's just come home and you're already accusing him of getting up to something!"

Of course, my perfect-child older brother is sitting here snickering at all this. Jonathan never gets into trouble.

"It's okay, Mom." I smile at her.

"I'm sorry, sweetheart," she says, putting her hands on my shoulders and giving me a big smile. "He's just a cranky old man!" she playfully shouts toward Dad.

"Yeah, yeah," he laughs and waves her comment away.

"Come on with me, honey. I've got you set up in your old room," she says, taking my arm and ushering me down the hallway to the bedrooms.

My family lives in one of the cheaper houses in the neighborhood. When we moved in, it hadn't been remodeled or renovated like the other houses. It was original nineteen seventies, and my dad fixed it up by himself—more of that "honor in a hard day's work" shit. It's a little quirky inside with the past three decades coming together in a slightly awkward mishmash of rooms and furnishings. My room, for example, has wooden paneled walls and shag carpeting, whereas Jonathan's room has this plaid wallpaper and wood trim like some shit a fisherman would have. You'd walk in and expect to see a bass mounted on the wall and a bunch of lures everywhere. Mine was original seventies because I didn't care—I didn't spend a lot of time in my own bed, if you know what I mean. His was remodeled in the nineties after we moved in, and he got to pick everything, so he said he wanted a "manly" design. It was so dumb.

"There are new sheets on the bed, and you can put your suitcase up here on the chair," Mom says, leading me into my old room.

It's pretty much the same, except they painted the wood paneling white, probably a good choice considering how dated it looked. They kept my old furniture, and it's kind of nice to get to sleep in my squeaky-ass wooden bed again. The only thing missing is my posters on the walls. I had one for the *South Park* movie, one of Pam Anderson in that red *Baywatch* swimsuit, and a cool Bob Marley one I got at a garage sale.

"We saved your stuff," she says when she notices me observing the new Diego Rivera prints up on the walls.

I shrug. I figured ol' Pam would have to come down some day.

"Everything's just in the basement, that's all," she adds. "Your father wanted to use this as a guest room for when your aunt and your cousins come to visit."

"It's cool, Mom." I smile at her, brushing it off. "It's your house. You guys do whatever you want."

"Oh, sweetheart," she says, grabbing my face in her hands and giving me one of those smoochy mom kisses. "I'm just so glad you're home. You know I worry about you, and I miss having my baby boy around."

"I miss being around, Mom, and I'm really glad to be home. I missed you guys…even Jonathan."

She chuckles and squeezes my cheeks. Even though I'm taller, I always feel like a little kid when my mom shows me all this warm, motherly affection.

I've always been really close with my mom, and I used to spend a lot of time with her when I was a kid. She used to call me Little Prince Charming when I was in elementary school. Dad, of course, thought this was going to make me effeminate so he said I was a mama's boy. I'm pretty sure he thought I was gay for the first fuckin' decade of my life because I got along with my mom and I hung out almost exclusively with girls. He actually seemed relieved when I got caught with my hand down Brooke Landry's pants the weekend her family invited me on their houseboat in seventh grade. We had a big sex talk, and he practically high-fived me when I told him that I'd already started having sex a few months earlier. He had to pretend to be stern, of course, but he never got all that pissed off when I'd get caught by some girl's parents because she moaned too loud or I'd sneak home at four in the morning after hooking up with a girl at a party. Mom always pretended that kind of shit never happened and that I was still her sweet Little Prince Charming.

"How have you been out there in California, honey?" she asks me, brushing my hair out of my face.

"Really good, Mom. I made, like, two grand for a commercial shoot the other day, but I think it's only airing in Japan and stuff." Actually, it was for a threesome scene with these two hot Japanese girls, but she definitely doesn't need to know that.

"Really?" She smiles proudly. "That's so exciting! My Little Prince Charming's making a name for himself."

I laugh modestly. I'm making a name for myself, except that name is James Langdon and not James Laird. Still, it just feels so awesome when she's proud of me.

"How about girls?" she sweetly asks. "Have you met any nice girls out there?"

I have to chuckle at this. *Oh, Mom, have I ever!* "A few."

"You know, those LA girls are so pretty," she says like it's a scientific fact. "I bet they just love you."

I snicker and shake my head. "There are a few that I like, but none that I'd want to get serious with, you know?"

"Well, that's all right," she says. "You've got a few years still before I'll start bugging you about settling down."

That makes me smile. It would be cool to meet a nice girl and do the whole marriage thing, but I don't know that it's in the cards for me. I like women too much, I think, and I don't know how I'd ever be able to pick just one.

"How are you doing, Mom? You never told me about all these projects that are supposedly taking over the house," I say, referencing my dad's little jab at her earlier.

She laughs and shakes her head. "He thinks I've lost my mind. He always jokes about the scrapbooks, but it's only two boxes in the basement. He acts like he's going to open a closet and a mountain of books are going to crash down on him!"

I chuckle as I picture my dad being buried under an avalanche of sentimental clippings.

"But I really like the decoupage," she says. "I did that little table in the foyer."

"No way! That's really good. I noticed it when I walked in. I can't believe you did that, Mom. It looks awesome." It's a little blue end table and now it's got birds and orange flowers on it. It looks cool and antique-ish.

"Thank you, sweetheart." She beams at the compliment.

"You're artistic, though, so I'm not surprised you did something really cool like that," I say, praising her again.

"You're just too sweet!" she says, holding my face and giving me a huge smile. "Your father can create all kinds of designs for someone's yard, but I'm pretty mean with some glue and cutouts."

I laugh and nod in agreement. She's been an accountant for, like, thirty years, but she's always had a creative side. When I was in middle school, she got into painting, and she was actually pretty good. I have a little one she did of the mountains by our house hanging up in my place back in Cali.

"Well, you're probably tired from your drive," she says sweetly as she brushes her fingers through my hair again like she can't believe I'm standing here with her.

I can tell she missed me a lot. I don't want to say it because I'll feel like a wuss, but I missed her a lot too. There's just something about having your mom around to take care of you that gives you a nice, homey feeling.

"There are fresh towels in the bathroom, and I bought you some of that Crew shampoo you like," she says with a proud grin.

"Aw, thanks, Mom."

"Your dad's going to work early, but I took the week off to spend time with you, so let's you, me, and Jonathan go for breakfast, okay?" she says.

"I'd love to, Mom." I nod, even though this means spending more time with Mr. Perfect himself.

Even though my brother's a douchebag, it's funny how much I missed home. I don't have any unconditional love in my life on a daily basis now, and it can feel kind of empty. I missed hanging out at Genova's Pizza with Keegan and Joey, watching movies in Lola's basement, my mom's homemade baklava, even my dad bitching about me chasing tail instead of doing homework.

By the time I hop in the shower, I feel the best I have in months. I've got my family, I've got my friends, I've got Lola, and everything seems back to normal. It's like I can leave the cameras and come-shots behind and be my old self again. I'm surprised by how much I enjoy that feeling.

Chapter 4

Lola

It's early morning, and my mom just left for work. I'm in the kitchen making myself a cup of coffee in hopes of getting some study time before my test this afternoon. One reason to love finals: you only have to show up for the test, so you get lots of free time. As I'm pouring the water in the coffeemaker, the doorbell rings and I already have a pretty good inkling of who it is.

"Well, hey there, sexy lady," James says in a wildly exaggerated flirty voice.

I laugh and shake my head. "Yeah, *so* sexy." I roll my eyes.

I'm certainly not a vision first thing in the morning. My hair is messed up, I have no makeup on and probably bags under my eyes, I'm in an old tank top that's frayed on the bottom from how many times I've washed it, and my pajama shorts have paint on the right butt cheek from the time I wore them when I helped my mom paint the hallway bathroom.

"You wanna get breakfast?" James says in a tone I recognize too well — the casual, nothing's-wrong tone he uses when his family's stressing him out.

"Right now?"

"Yeah." He nods. "Mom's taking me and Jonathan out to breakfast, and I can't deal with Golden Boy on my own, so I thought maybe you could come too."

"Is that cool with your mom? She doesn't want to have quality time by herself with her Little Prince Charming?" I tease.

He gives me a pretend scowl. "Just come with me, please. I can't sit there and listen to the many accomplishments of The Great Jonathan Laird without puking."

"Yeah, okay," I reply. "Let me get clothes on and brush my teeth."

"Okay," he says, following me into the house.

I ditch the coffee idea and head straight to the bathroom to clean up a bit. James sits on the edge of the bathtub and smiles at me through the mirror.

"This is gonna be a fuckin' scene, man," he says. "He's getting his real estate license, which my dad's thrilled about because it gives him an in to do landscaping for the houses Jonathan sells. I'm sure we'll have to hear all about that *brilliant* idea."

"I'll counter it," I say, looking at him through the mirror. "Let's get a cover story going and I can brag about you."

"Okay." He smiles broadly like he's touched by that plan.

"I can't exactly tell them you're an up-and-*comer* in the porn business," I say, putting extra emphasis on the last word in the term.

He gives me that sweet, modest smile and chuckles as he bash-fully looks down at the ground. I can so rarely get him to be shy like this that I relish every moment of it.

"So what should we go for? How about a pilot for a TV show? Or maybe a workout commercial? You're totally jacked now, so it's believable that you'd be selling Ab Doers and Tae Bo DVDs."

Again, the modest, cute look.

"Oh! Or maybe modeling," I volunteer. "What if you were the face of some new clothing line? We can make up a designer from, like, Germany or something, and we can say that you're going to be in print ads for their fall campaign."

"You think they'd buy that?" he asks.

"Dude, look at you," I say, stopping in the middle of brush-ing my hair to turn and smirk at him. "You're totally male model material—and more than romance novel covers and shit. You're shirtless-dirty-oiled-up-Calvin-Klein-Jeans-ad with that body and that face. Besides, those ads are basically like couture porn anyway. Everybody's half naked and lying on top of each other, kind of like what you really do."

"Kind of." He chuckles. "Except I highly doubt that there's any double penetration going on at high fashion shoots."

I laugh and shrug my shoulders. "You never know," I reply with a playful grin.

He follows me into my room and sits on my bed while I go into my closet to find something that doesn't scream "I just woke up and I don't give a shit how I look." This is breakfast with James's mom and his arrogant brother, so I don't want to look like a total mess. I opt for a casual, white sundress and some espadrilles with a heel, since I'm going to be in the land of the giants with James's tall family.

"Bringing out the big guns, eh?" James smiles when I emerge.

"Huh?"

"If I didn't know better, I'd think you were trying to look hot for Jonathan," he teases.

"Yuck! Your brother's a douche! He would never influence my fashion choices," I say, crinkling my nose at the thought of Jonathan being attracted to me.

James laughs loudly and stands up from the bed. "Well, no matter who it's for, you look gorgeous, kid."

"Aw, you're too kind." I smile up at him as he comes to put his arm around me.

He kisses the side of my head, and then we walk to the door and across the yard. James opens the door to his house and ushers me inside, where his mom and Jonathan are waiting in the front room.

"Oh, Lola, sweetheart, it's so good to see you!" James's mom says as she comes over to hug me. "We don't get to see you enough these days. You know you're always welcome to come over for dinner."

"Thanks, Brenda. It's really nice to see you too."

Jonathan walks over and gives me the kind of obligatory hug normally reserved for an annoying little sister. "How you doing, Lola?"

"Great. How about you?" I ask him as I part from the hug.

"Great, really great. Getting my real estate license, and I've already got an in with Everleigh Real Estate," he says with a cocky smile.

"Oh, that's cool," I politely reply. It's starting already. I can see why James didn't want to deal with this by himself.

"How does Sunnyside Café sound?" James's mom asks, breaking my mild annoyance with The Great Jonathan Laird.

"Sounds great," James and I reply in unison, which draws a subtle eye roll from Jonathan.

When we were kids, Jonathan was a real asshole. He acted like I was delicate and weak, like my smarts and tenacity were adorable instead of admirable—like I was a newborn kitten instead of Rosie the Riveter. He's always been cocky, popular and a little chauvinistic despite his phony politeness to girls. James's father, Jon, and his older brother seem to believe that women are these precious little flowers incapable of existing without the help of men. All the guys in that family have this instinctual compulsion to protect women, which is a respectable quality, but those two treat every girl like she's a damsel in distress in need of constant rescuing. James might treat me like a princess on a pedestal, but he knows I can hold my own and kick a little ass if I need to.

We hop in Brenda's Jeep Cherokee, and James sits in the back seat with me. He puts his hand on my knee, but not in a flirtatious way. Instead, it seems fueled by genuine fondness and appreciation that I agreed to be subjected to Jonathan-Fest. In response, I rest my head on his shoulder. We pull up to the restaurant, and Jonathan opens my door for me, which could be seen as polite, but just seems annoying when it's coming from him. James gives me an eye roll on the sly, and I suppress a snicker.

Our pretty, brunette waitress blatantly scopes James as she takes our drink orders, which seems to annoy Jonathan. That alone amuses me. Jonathan isn't a bad looking guy; the men in that family are all very handsome, but his self-important vibe is an instant turn-off, at least for me.

"So, sweetheart, how has school been?" Brenda warmly asks me. She's always just a ray of sunshine, and being around her will make you smile, even if you're glum.

"Great." I nod as I take a sip of orange juice. "I'm so ready for graduation. Just a few more finals and I'm all done with high school."

"That's wonderful," she replies with a proud smile as she takes my hand and gives it a little squeeze.

"It's not that hard to graduate high school," Jonathan smugly adds. "It's the first year at college that's tough, because you have to have the discipline to go to class and work hard. You're on your own and you have to be a grown-up."

James shoots him a look, and I internalize my mild loathing and give him a false smile.

"I'm really excited about it, actually," I retort. "I think it'll be nice to get a change of pace, be in a real city out east. Plus, my AP stuff will help me get into the upper level classes right out of the gate."

"Just don't get distracted," Jonathan says like he's in Mensa.

You got into the state school with a football scholarship and suddenly you're Stephen Hawking?

"She's not gonna get distracted," James chimes in. "Lola's really smart and she always has been. She's going to a way harder school than you, but I'm sure she's gonna do really great next year."

"I'm sure she will, too." Brenda smiles encouragingly.

"Thanks," I reply.

I notice James glaring at Jonathan out of the corner of my eye. They might be brothers, but they can be like Israel and Palestine sometimes.

"So did James tell you guys that he landed a fashion campaign?" I say, changing the subject.

"Well, you didn't mention that! That sounds so exciting!" Brenda smiles proudly at James.

He gets this wonderful look on his face like he's overjoyed at her reaction.

"It's this designer—Timothy Müller, was his name, right?" I say, pulling that completely out of my ass.

"Yeah. I didn't want to say anything because it's not all the way locked down yet, but it looks like it might be a go." James nods, letting me roll with this lie.

"He's really new. I looked him up and I couldn't find a lot of info about him, but people think he might be the next Karl Lagerfeld." I smile, patting James on the back. James's family isn't too into fashion, but Lagerfeld's enough of a household name for them to understand.

"It's gonna mostly be print ads, but they'll probably only run in the European high-fashion mags," James says, diving right into this cover story with me. "It's great because it pays a lot, and it's one of those things that could really launch your career."

"I always knew you could do fashion." I turn to him and pretend to snap shots like a fashion photographer. "Give me Blue Steel," I joke, giggling when he pulls the classic *Zoolander* face. "How about Ferrari?" He does the same look, perfectly emulating the movie. "Le Tigre. Work it!" He turns his head to the side, but maintains the *Zoolander* pout as I laugh. "So hot right now!"

Brenda chuckles at our playfulness, and Jonathan seems unenthused. *Big surprise.*

"That's wonderful news, honey," Brenda cheerfully praises James.

"Thanks, Mom." He smiles broadly.

"So you're gonna get all primped and pretty for your big photo spread?" Jonathan teases.

"Do I detect a hint of envy? He's already pretty, Jonathan," I reply, shooting him a look that dares him to keep going. *Please, Jonathan, please test me because I would love to go toe-to-toe with you on the subject of your brother.*

I feel James reach for my hand under the table, and he weaves his long fingers into mine. "Thanks, babe." He winks at me.

Brenda seems joyfully amused by our exchange, and she looks from me to James like she's picturing what our children would look like. I know she secretly wishes we were boyfriend and girlfriend so he'd settle down and quit his playboy antics. If she only knew the extent of those antics, she'd realize that this guy has no chance of settling down anytime soon.

I ask Brenda about how things have been going for her and Jon. She's still in accounting, but she says she's planning to retire soon. She's doing all sorts of art projects, which are apparently driving Jon crazy. James tells me she's really good at decoupage, and she says she'll make me something to take with me to college. She tells me that Jon got a big contract with the city and he's doing the landscaping for the justice center and the library, both of which have huge open spaces that he could really go wild with.

Both of James's parents are creative, but in very practical ways. Jon has a real eye for outdoor design, and he can tell you everything there is to know about every species of tree you'd ever want to plant in your yard. He's a genius with horticulture, and he can transform even the smallest back yard into a virtual wonderland of flowers and shrubs. Brenda was always a numbers kind of woman, a total math wiz, but she always liked making things too. She made jewelry when we were kids, and I still have a bracelet she gave me when I was eleven. After that, she got into painting, and she showed some serious talent. She even sold one of her works to a local coffee shop, and they have it hanging on the wall to this day. I think this is why James likes cooking so much. He's genetically predisposed to enjoy preparing something with his hands, and he comes up with his own recipes like a flavor artist.

Jonathan seems bored as we chat about Jon and Brenda's adventures as empty-nesters. She wants to go to Niagara Falls and do a big outdoorsy thing for the Fourth of July with her brother and sister, who live out east. He wants to go to Minnesota to spend the holiday with his younger sister. It's a running argument between them, and it seems cute. She also says she wants to go on a big trip to Aruba or somewhere with sprawling beaches and lots of sun. Jonathan rolls his eyes at this idea, but I tell her I think it's great. She says Jon shares his son's sentiment and thinks they should choose an easier vacation spot, like Cozumel or Cancun.

James's parents bicker, but you can tell they really love each other. I've always liked being around them because they're such a normal, all-American, happy family. My parents got divorced when I was really little, and my dad's a total jerk, so it's cool to have that *Leave It To Beaver* world right next door.

After breakfast, Brenda drives us all home and wishes me luck with my test. Jonathan seems a bit perturbed that he didn't get to elaborate on his many accomplishments, but neither James nor I care to hear more about how wonderful he is and how everybody loves him so much.

James walks me to my door, and I see a big smile on Brenda's face when he brushes my hair behind my ear and takes my face in his hands, planting a big kiss on my forehead. Part of me wishes James and I were together, just to keep that smile on her face forever. I've never had a boyfriend, and though my mom knows James's reputation, I think even she assumes he's the only guy I'll ever be this close with. The moms seem to have these fanciful visions of us becoming a couple and growing into upstanding citizens with two-point-three children and a yellow Lab running around the front yard. I hate to break it to them, but that ain't gonna happen. I care for James to an astronomical extent, but I strongly doubt some nerdy virgin would ever stack up for a guy who just participated in an all-anal MILF gangbang scene a few weeks ago. James fucks a different girl every day, and sometimes multiple girls each day, so we're basically on different planets when it comes to our idea of romance and relationships.

"I'm going to a party tonight, but I'll be over tomorrow afternoon when you're getting ready for prom." He smiles at me as he stands on the porch.

"Okay." I nod, returning the smile with a cheerful grin of my own.

"Bye, kid," he says, giving me one more kiss on the forehead and turning to go home.

I sigh and laugh at myself. I can't believe how much I missed having him around. Something as small as a kiss on the forehead can put a smile on my face for an entire day, and it's only now that I realize how much I yearn for those tiny, inconsequential, but incredibly touching affections.

Chapter 5

James

"No chance! No chance he's gonna make this putt!" my buddy, Joey Corsentino, loudly predicts as Keegan lines up on the green.

Joey and I were really tight in high school, but it's been a while since I got the chance to hang out with him. He's going to school up at the university and working part time in his parents' bakery, so he's been too busy to do anything the past couple times I've visited.

He passes me the huge joint we've all been sharing, and I start cracking up at the way Keegan's concentrating like he's trying to crack a safe.

This ain't the country club. Today, we're golfing on the shitty, run-down course on the outskirts of town. They don't have golf carts, the grass is dry and dying, and one time we almost got attacked by a rabid raccoon out by the sixth hole. But they have no rules, and most people just come here to smoke weed while they play.

"Where'd you get this shit, man?" I ask, taking a big hit off the joint.

"Becky Callahan's brother," he answers with a shrug like it's common knowledge.

"Charlie's selling weed now?" I laugh loudly.

Becky was one of my sort-of girlfriends in high school. Her family was rich and she was all prim and proper in public, but she dug being tied up and spanked in the bedroom. Her younger brother was a little shit-starter, so it's totally fitting that he'd become a drug dealer.

"Kid's a bad motherfucker nowadays." Joey chuckles. "That family better start savin' up some bail money."

I snicker and turn my attention back to Keegan, who's finally decided on the fuckin' putt like this is the goddamn Masters. He hits it, and it drops in the cup. I clap, since both Joey and I were sure he'd miss, and he does one of those Tiger Woods fist pumps, which makes me laugh harder.

"You're up, smart-ass," he says to Joey.

Keegan's wearing golf shorts and a polo shirt, the kind of thing he'd wear when he plays at the country club with his dad, but Joey's opted for an Armani Exchange T-shirt and a gold chain. He fancies himself to be some kind of Guido, even though he's living out here in Middle America and not in Jersey. I'm just wearing some shorts and a T-shirt, keeping it simple. This course has no dress code, so you can pretty much wear anything. I've seen girls out here in bikini tops and booty shorts before.

"If you miss it, you gotta do something fucked up," Keegan says as Joey walks over to the green.

"What is this, truth or dare?" Joey laughs.

"Fuck you!" Keegan chuckles. "You were making me do stupid shit earlier."

A couple holes ago, Joey dared Keegan to take a huge hit off the joint and hold it in the whole time he putted. He did, and for a second, I thought he was going to pass out. Joey's my age and Keegan's two years younger, so they fuck with each other a lot.

"You miss this one and you gotta play the entire next hole with your dick out," Keegan proposes.

"You really wanna see my dick that bad?" Joey teases.

I laugh, which makes me cough as I take another hit.

"Nah, dude, the next hole's the one by the road, so if anybody drives by, they're gonna see your tiny dick, and I'm gonna laugh my ass off," Keegan replies.

"No problem," Joey says, looking down and aligning his shot. "I got this shit."

Sure enough, he misses and Keegan gloats. I pass him the joint and give Joey a shrug. *A bet's a bet.*

Keegan and I are cracking up when Joey drops his pants around his ankles and holds out his arms like he's displaying it for the whole world to see.

"Ladies, I'm open for business!" he yells.

"Pull your shit up and let's get to the next hole." I laugh and shake my head.

When it's my turn at the tee, I manage to hit a pretty long drive. I hate golf, really, but me and the guys used to come out here a lot to hang out and talk shit.

"Same rules as last hole?" Keegan asks when we get nearer to the green.

"If I wanna see this asshole's dick, all I need is Wi-Fi," Joey teases.

I laugh hard at that. My really close friends know about the whole porn thing, but I keep pretty much everybody else in the dark about it.

"You ever do a movie with Tara Morgan?" Joey asks me. "That bitch is hot as fuck. Big ol' titties, man," he adds, holding out his hands to indicate the size of her boobs.

"Last fuckin' week, dude," I say with a cocky grin.

"Bullshit! How was that shit? She seems wild," he asks.

"She's good. Really good blowjobs, and she's all flexible and shit. It was a really fun scene to shoot."

"That's such fuckin' bullshit that you get to fuck girls like that and get paid for it." He laughs and shakes his head. "I could do that shit, yo. 'Yeah, come here, bitch! Get down on your knees and suck that cock!'" He says in this played-up macho way.

I snicker, and Keegan hands me the joint. "It's not really how you think, man. I mean, it's cool to bang hot chicks and all, but you gotta stop for them to take stills, and there's a lot of waiting around and shit. Plus everybody's kinda giving you the stink eye because they just want you to come so they can break for lunch."

Keegan laughs hard at that description.

"Yeah, but you still get to fuck those bitches," Joey says. "You know what I would give to fuck a chick like Tara Morgan? I fucked this high school girl who looked kind of like her the other night at this party, but I bet she's got nothin' on the real thing."

"Dude, you can't be fucking high school girls," I say, shaking my head in disapproval. *Fuckin' Joey*, always doing that kind of borderline sketchy shit.

"Calm down, calm down," he says, laughing. "She was legal, so don't have a shit fit. Besides, I'm guessing some of the chicks in those movies are just barely eighteen, man."

He's got a point. Most of the girls in the industry are young because the market for teen videos is huge. They're all eighteen and up, but some of them do look like they're still in high school. They play high school students all the time, too. Some girls rip on the industry because, by the time they're in their mid-twenties, they're playing MILFs and teachers and shit. I don't mind working on those MILF videos, and I kind of like doing scenes with the older girls. Some of the craziest shit I did was with Mrs. Landry back when I was in school, and I find that the older chicks in the industry don't make all those fake moans the way the new girls do. I'm glad that guys in the business can have careers well into their thirties because I'm making way too much money to stop doing this anytime soon.

"Besides," Joey adds, "your chick is young."

"Who's my chick?" I ask, genuinely confused.

"Lola, man," he says like it's common knowledge.

"Lola's my chick?" I laugh. "I'm *so* sure."

"Now, now," Keegan says, "you know he'd never touch the Virgin Mary herself."

I have to laugh at that. These assholes have been making fun of me for years for how I am with Lola.

"All I'm sayin' is, that bitch is hot as fuck and you know you could hit that," Joey says like he's trying to piss me off.

"Never, dude." I shake my head. "And I'll bust your ass if you call her a bitch again."

"Yo, be honest — " he grins " — you ever seen her titties?"

I don't answer, and I try to suppress a guilty smile.

"Yeah, you have!" He laughs, hitting my arm. "I bet they were nice, too. I remember that time at the pool party when she wore that bikini and her nipples got all hard when she got out of the water."

I continue to keep quiet, doing my best to scowl at him despite the fact that I also noticed her nipples that day and I've stored that memory with me for years now.

"You think she shaves her pussy? Like maybe a landing strip? Or maybe she's gone completely bare. Hairless girls are fuckin' sexy."

"Dude, seriously, I'm about to knock you the fuck out," I reply.

"All I'm saying is, you could find out. I don't know a single guy who's ever even seen her naked, but your ass could do that, no problem."

"Abso-fuckin'-lutely not," I firmly reply.

Joey laughs hard and shakes his head at me like I'm hopeless. I don't give a fuck what these guys think; I'm not laying a fuckin' finger on Lola. Sure, she's hot. She's downright gorgeous, but I'd feel like I was violating her if I fucked her. She's so far above every other girl that I can't even consider trying to sleep with her.

"We still hittin' up that party tonight?" Joey asks.

"Yeah, and I heard there are going to be a bunch of sorority girls there. So that plus alcohol and you should be in business, Keegan," I tease.

"You have your method, I have mine," he says, chuckling.

Joey and I snicker.

"Yeah, Keegan, when was the last time you got laid, man?" he asks, putting his arm around Keegan in that big-brother kind of way.

"Fuck you!" Keegan laughs.

"Me and James are gonna hook you up," he says. "You'll be balls deep in some sorority bitch tonight."

I roll my eyes. Joey talks like this all the time, acting like he's hot shit and every girl in the world is lining up to fuck him. There's a difference between confidence and arrogance, and Joey's off the deep end in the arrogance department. He calls me a pussy for it all the time, but I hate when he calls girls bitches and acts like they only exist to serve him. That shit is lame. I may fuck a lot, but it's because I have a real appreciation for women. Lola used to call me Don Juan DeMarco, since I tend to find something beautiful about every girl I see. I don't know what it is, but I just find something so sexy about a woman's body and I like when girls lose their inhibitions and stop being all self-conscious. Too many of them are neurotic about how they look anyway, and it's stupid because all of them are pretty in one way or another.

"All right, you're up, bro," Keegan says, looking up at me.

I take a deep breath and try to clear my head. Becky's little brother sells some strong-ass weed. The guys are cracking up as I try to pull my shit together for my turn.

I decided to make a run to the thrift store on my way back to my house to get my mom some old nature magazines and illustrated children's books she can use for her decoupage. I stack them up on the kitchen table and write her a note saying that I think she's really good and I hope she'll find some good stuff in these to decorate more things with. I think she'll appreciate it, and I like doing stuff for her.

After that, I hop in the shower and start trying to decide a game plan for this party. A few hours later and me and the guys are pulling up outside this big house just up the mountain from town. There are people everywhere, almost like they're spilling out from the doors and windows. Music is bumping, and Joey and Keegan have their game faces on like men on a mission to get laid.

I'm a jeans and T-shirt kind of guy, and I have to roll my eyes at the Ed Hardy shirt and Sean Paul sunglasses Joey's rocking tonight. What is he, a hip-hop producer? He looks like an Italian Scott Storch. Keegan just looks like every dude in here, that frat boy look that guys like him have from about age fifteen to thirty-five.

We roll in the door, and I swear to God, I think Joey hears theme music. He's walking around like he owns this place, and I'm trying really hard not to laugh. In fairness to him, he does know a lot of people here, but in his mind, he's P. Diddy stepping into the club. I let him run off and do his thing, and I trail behind him slowly to try to get a little distance between me and the hip-hop caricature calling for everyone to do shots.

I lean against the counter in the kitchen area and watch Joey do a body shot off a blond girl with a spray tan. *Oh, yeah, this kid definitely thinks he's the shit right now.* I watch Keegan try to be on cool duty when a drunk brunette comes up and starts flirting with him. Good for him; he could never seal a deal if it weren't for liquored up aggressive chicks. They gravitate to him. He's just got one of those nice-guy faces, and drunk girls want to corrupt him. They come on to him way fuckin' strong every time we go to parties and stuff like this.

I give the guys a nod and decide to take a look around the place to see if there are any hot girls who aren't spray tanned orange and stumbling out of their shoes. I spot a really pretty sandy-blond girl standing by herself over by the staircase. She's got on a green tank top and a short jean skirt that shows off her natural tan — not something out of a bottle like a few of the girls here. She seems shy and timid, but she's a total babe. She's tall and has really long legs, a firm body like she runs or does yoga, nice boobs, blond hair in a ponytail, and light blue eyes like a Siberian husky.

I approach nonchalantly, but I hear Joey's dumb ass yelling something from behind me, and she turns to look right in my direction.

"Yo, you gonna do some fuckin' shots, bro?" Joey asks me way too loud.

"Nah, I'm good, man." I shake my head.

"Everybody's doin' shots tonight, man!" he yells, and a group of over-excited dudes follow him back toward the kitchen.

The pretty blonde gives me a half smile.

"Fuckin' idiot." I shrug, motioning back to Joey.

"Friend of yours?" She smiles and raises an eyebrow.

"Unfortunately, yes. I've basically got tickets to the show tonight, and I get to watch him get hammered and try to hit on the drunkest girl here. Class act, that kid."

She giggles, and I see her check me out. "Well, I'm sure he'll meet my roommate, Jessica," she says, nodding to a curvy brunette dancing a little too hard by the fireplace. "I think she's a contender for drunkest girl here."

I laugh. From the way that girl's dancing, I think she might be right.

"I just hope she doesn't puke in my car later," she says with a sigh.

"Designated driver?" I ask her. She nods. "Yeah, me too."

"Yay, aren't we fun?" she teases.

I laugh and give her a joking nod of agreement. "I'm James." I smile at her.

She looks right in my eyes and smiles back. "I'm Caroline."

"Nice to meet you, Caroline," I say, giving her a nod like some exaggerated gentlemanly gesture. She giggles. "You go to school out here?"

"Yeah. I'm an Art History major."

"Nice. So, are you into, like, classical art or do you like modern stuff?"

"I like the Postimpressionist period the most, but I love surrealism too," she explains. "My parents have an original van Gogh and it's, like, their prized possession. Personally, I've always liked Frida Kahlo, but I think they find her stuff a bit too surreal."

I raise my eyebrows. Pretty and smart. I dig that.

She gives me a flirty smile, and I squint my eyes as I look at her. She looks really familiar, but I don't know from where. I don't think I went to high school with her, but I swear I've seen her before.

"Are you from here, Caroline?" I ask her with a sly smile.

"No, my parents have a big ranch southwest of here," she says like she's hiding some big secret.

"What's your last name?" I playfully squint like I'm trying to crack the case.

"Kentwood," she replies with a giggle.

"Kentwood Motors, right?" I say, placing her right away.

"Yes." She nods shyly. "That's my dad's dealership."

"You used to be in those commercials with him where you rode that pony through the lot." I smile.

"Oh, my God!" She blushes almost fluorescent pink. "I can't believe you remember that!"

I laugh hard at her embarrassment. She looks even cuter when she gets shy like this.

Kentwood Motors is one of the biggest dealerships in the southern part of the state, and Mr. Kentwood always used to put his daughter in the commercials, so I remember seeing her all the time on TV when I was little. Around Christmastime, she'd be dressed as an elf, on Valentine's she'd wear cupid wings, and her Memorial Day costume was a red, white and blue dress and an Uncle Sam hat. I think she was even in a Wonder Woman outfit once when her dad was dressed as Superman.

"And you'd yell 'yee-haw!' at the end," I playfully tease her.

"Oh, no! Of course the cutest guy here has to have seen the commercials I did when I was a kid!" She laughs loudly. "So embarrassing!"

"No way. Those commercials were cute," I assure her. "I used to think you were so pretty too. When I was, like, ten, I thought you were the prettiest girl on TV."

"Oh, stop." She gives me a playful little shove.

"Seriously, I did," I answer honestly. She was that all-American-dream-girl kind of chick, and I really did think she was good-looking.

"You're just trying to make me feel better," she says, batting her eyes at me.

"No way. I even remembered the jingle because you sang it."

"Ah! The jingle was the worst!" She covers her face with her hands and shakes her head.

I start singing the first part of the jingle, and to my pleasant surprise, she sings the second part with me before she bursts into shy laughter and covers her face again.

I think I might like this Caroline Kentwood. She's pretty, she's smart, and she's got that cute, bashful thing I dig.

I hang around flirting with her for almost an hour before she asks me if I want to "get some air" outside with her. Of course, I say yes, and she holds my hand as she leads me out the back door and through the yard to a gazebo that faces the small ridge. Even though it's outside, it's surprisingly private.

"How'd you know this was here?" I ask her as she sits down on the picnic table inside the octagon.

"This is my friend's parents' house," she explains. "They're in Bali for six months, so she's been using it for parties."

"I see." I nod, taking a look around at the expansive view.

"This was always my favorite place on the property, though," she says, her voice turning soft and silky. "It's quiet up here. Nice and private."

With that, she steps closer to me and gives me a sweet little kiss. I like it. It's not one of those sloppy drunk girl kisses. It's classy and elegant, just like her. I kiss her back, and I move my hands to her hips to pull her into me. Her arms wrap around me, and she leans her whole body against me. She's a really good kisser, and I'm really digging this.

"I don't usually do this," she says, giggling. "In fact, I've never met some guy at a party and done this."

"Well then, I'm honored."

"I swear, I'm not slutty like this in real life." She blushes, and I know she's telling the truth. She's a good girl, and I'll bet the angel and the devil on her shoulders are duking it out over whether she should go for it.

"I don't think you're slutty at all," I say, pulling her in and kissing her slowly.

I keep it sensual as my tongue slips into her mouth and starts massaging her tongue. She's way into it, and I can hear her breathing getting deeper. She runs her fingers through my hair and kisses me with a little more passion before she slides her hands down my chest and onto my stomach. She seems to like what she feels because she starts tugging on my shirt so I'll take it off. I pull it over my head and resume kissing her as her hands roam all over my chest.

She leans back and looks right into my eyes with this lusty gaze as she pulls her tank top over her head. No bra. And a very nice set of tits, which look to be real. She giggles when I give her a big smile, and I move close to her so I can kiss her again.

I lift her onto the edge of the picnic table and stand between her legs. She leans back a little when I start kissing her neck. I reach for her ponytail and let her hair down so I can run my fingers through it. It's silky and it smells so fuckin' nice.

I glide my hands down her back as I move on to kiss her pretty breasts. They're not big, probably only a small handful, but they go with her lean body and they're natural, which is a nice change when you're used to fucking porn stars. She's got a little beauty mark near her left nipple that I can see in the moonlight. It's super sexy, and I kiss it for a second before I move on to lightly brush my lips over her nipple, which makes her exhale really deeply like she loves it. I let my tongue flick out a few times, and her nipples get all hard and perky. Shit like this is why I love women. Their arousal isn't as obvious as it is with us, but it's a lot more rewarding to turn a girl on because you get to see all these subtle signs.

"Mmm," she softly moans when I start to suck her just a little bit.

I move back and forth from one nipple to the other, and I can tell she likes it a lot. Her head's tilting back and she's running her fingers through my hair while she makes these quiet moans. I dig this kind of thing, when I can do something so small and a girl can like it so much.

After a few minutes, she's unbuttoning my pants and rubbing my cock over my boxer briefs while we kiss. Her hands are all warm, and it feels really good. She makes a hungry sort of sound through the kiss, and I think she's surprised at how big I am, which makes her stroke me faster.

I take the opportunity to do the same, and my hand slides up her thigh and between her legs. I start out rubbing her over her panties, but I slowly move the fabric to the side and rub her with just my fingertip on her clit. She moans a little louder, which spurs me on. I slide a finger inside her, and I'm impressed with how wet she is. *Fuck!* I love turning girls on like this. I don't go right for her G-spot because I want her to really feel it when I finally do touch it, so I tease her just a little bit first. Once I hit it, she starts rocking her hips and breathing harder.

"Ohhh!" she moans as I slip another finger in.

"Mmm, you like it?" I whisper against her neck.

She nods excitedly.

Her whole body's moving in this sexy wave that goes from her neck all the way down her back. I know a lot of girls who have no idea where their G-spot is and some don't even think they have one, but it's pretty easy to find, if you know where you're going. Maybe it's just because I've had years of practice, but I know the best way to touch it so it feels really good.

"Do you like the way I touch you, baby?" I say between kisses. "You like how it feels?"

"Yes!" she exhales.

"Good girl. Feel it, Caroline," I say softly.

Her hands grab onto the side of the table, and she leans back a little, which gives me another great opportunity to get to her nipples. I wiggle my fingers a little faster, and I bend down to start sucking her titties again. She moans louder. I was going to try to save it for when we were fucking, but I think I'll make her come right now too.

"That's right, baby," I whisper against her nipple. "Just let it go."

"Oh, yes!" she moans. She's getting really close; I can tell from how tight she's getting inside. "That feels so good!" Another little wiggle of my fingers and she whimpers and shivers as she comes.

I kiss her and slide my fingers out of her so I can hold her while she comes down from it. That was only a little one, like a movie trailer that shows you just enough to make you really, really want to see the movie.

She's out of breath when I look down at her and give her a smile. I like that moment after girls come when they're all relaxed and chilled out. That's how they should be all the time, not all insecure like a lot of them are usually.

"Do you have a condom?" she whispers like she can't believe she's about to fuck me out in this gazebo.

"Yeah." I nod, taking one out of my pocket.

"I swear, I never do this," she says, giggling.

"You don't have to convince me, Caroline. I believe you, and you can believe me when I say that I feel pretty fuckin' special about it."

She laughs and hikes her skirt up as she looks right into my eyes. I step closer and hook my thumbs into the waistband of her panties. She gives me a nod, and I slide them down her legs.

I tear open the packet and roll the condom on as I return to her. She looks in my eyes for a moment or two before she kisses me deeply, and I start to ease into her. I always go slow with chicks at first because I tend to be more than most of them can take right off the bat. I've had porn stars tell me I was nearly too big for them, so I know it's a stretch for regular girls. I pay really close attention to her body and her sounds, making sure she doesn't give any indication that it might hurt. Once I'm all the way inside her, I give her a second to adjust and get used to me—like I said, I'm big and it can be painful if you rush it. She looks up at me and then kisses me softly a few times before she starts rocking her hips and signaling that we're good to go.

This is pretty fuckin' hot. We're out here in the middle of nature like this, all by ourselves when there's a house full of people a few yards behind us. We're kissing and she's holding onto my shoulders in this kind of aggressive way. She keeps kissing up and down my neck, too, and I've always liked that a lot. Her moans are pretty, soft and breathy, and I like hearing her pant next to my ear.

Pretty soon, her moans get a little louder and I feel her legs start to tense. She makes that soft, whimpering noise, and she arches her neck back when she trembles. I hold her close and keep going, but just a little slower than before. She's got this great look on her face that perfectly captures her pleasure as I hold her hips and rock her against me so I can get deeper. She moans louder, and I can feel her quivering inside over and over for about three straight minutes. I swear there's nothing better in this whole world than making girls come.

She feels really good inside when she shivers like this, and I let go of my focus and let myself really feel it. I've learned to control shit like this over the last several years. It's an important skill on movies. Sometimes you have less than five minutes to get hard, then you have to stay hard all day and not come until they tell you to. It's like a fuckin' endurance contest, but you can train for it until you're really good. I can come, basically, on command on the set now, but I tend to let my body take over a lot more when it's a real-life situation. My body's definitely taking over with Caroline right now, and I give her a few slow, deep pumps before I come.

She kisses me sweetly afterward, and I stay inside her, just holding her, for a little while. It's totally not the wild, crazy type of thing you'd think of when somebody says they had random sex at a house party, but I like this so much more than those sloppy drunken hookups. I've never liked banging drunk chicks. I like them coherent and conscious. Where's the fun in hooking up with a girl who's too fucked up to turn you down?

"Wow!" she pants as she gives me a big smile.

I smile back and give her a little kiss. She's got this really pretty, soft, just-fucked sheen on her skin, and it looks super sexy in this low light. I pull out of her slowly, and I look into her eyes.

"You look so fuckin' gorgeous right now," I blurt out with honesty as I tuck her hair behind her ear.

She giggles and blushes like she's gone all bashful. It's so cute.

"Please!" she says, smiling. "I look gorgeous? Just look at you!"

I chuckle at her compliment and give her a little kiss.

Just then I hear her phone ring, and she shakes her head like she's trying to get her shit together as she reaches for it on the table. I'm guessing it fell out of her skirt somewhere in the middle of all that. She makes a frustrated scoff when she sees the screen.

"Jessica...no...no, I'm outside. I didn't leave you behind...stop—Jess, stop crying. Stop crying. I'm right outside," she says as she gives me a smile and rolls her eyes. "Are you by the fireplace still?...Okay...okay, Jess—no, calm down. Calm down. I'll be right there."

She hangs up the phone and gives me an apologetic shrug. "Great. A crying drunk, even better," she jokes.

I laugh and hand over her shirt. I put mine back on too while she's pulling up her panties. I toss the condom and zip up as she looks me over with a big smile like she can't believe the crazy, impulsive thing she just did.

We exchange numbers really quick, and I tell her I'll text her. It's not bullshit; I think I really will. She was a cool girl, and she was so smooth and tight. I definitely wouldn't mind hooking up with her again.

I hold her hand as we walk back to the house, and I give her a little kiss when we part ways in the living room by the big staircase. I can see her friend out of the corner of my eye and she's a drunken, emotional mess.

"Good luck with all that!" I tease as Caroline looks up at me.

She laughs loudly. "Oh, yeah, this is just going to be great," she sarcastically jokes.

I give her a smile and tuck her hair behind her ear again before she leans up and gives me a soft kiss.

"I'll text you, okay?" I say.

"Okay." She nods and looks me over one more time before she goes over to Drunky McGee over there.

"No. Fucking. Way!" I hear from behind me.

I turn to see Keegan and Joey staring at me with their mouths open like they're watching a space shuttle launch.

"What?" I ask them.

"You hooked up with that girl?" Keegan says.

"Yeah, dude. She's super nice, really sweet personality."

"Yeah, her *personality* is the sweet part," Joey scoffs. "She's got a really tight, wet *personality*."

"Dude, shut the fuck up." I laugh. "She's a really cool girl. And she does have a nice personality, dumbshit."

"She's, like, the hottest girl here!" Keegan says like he's totally awestruck.

"She's super pretty, right?" I smile and nod. "I love her legs."

"Titties are too small, though," Joey chimes in, giving her a subtle scan.

"Nah, they're nice." I shake my head. "She's natural, you know? That's sexy."

"You see that chick over there?" he says, pointing across the room to the bleached blonde he was doing body shots with earlier.

"Yeah," I say, nodding.

"She sucked my dick in the pantry earlier, so you're not the only one getting action," he says.

Joey always does this shit, pretends like this is all a challenge and we're competing to see who can get the most girls. He doesn't realize that I don't really give a fuck how many girls he gets and that I never have. *It's not a race, man. Nobody has to try to "win" or anything.*

"Well, hey, good for you." I shrug.

"This kid even got somethin'," he says, pointing to Keegan.

"Oh, yeah?" I smile at him.

"This girl gave me a hand job in the bathroom." He nods proudly.

Joey pats him on the back. "She was a fuckin' butterface, but she was down for giving this fool a tug."

"She wasn't a total butterface," Keegan protests. "She was at least a seven or an eight, dude."

"Yeah, okay." Joey rolls his eyes.

"I'm sure she was great," I say, trying to be reassuring to Keegan. "Don't let this fuckin' asshole try to push his bullshit on you. Have you seen the kind of girls he fucks?"

"Hot girls!" Joey says with a cocky grin.

"Drunk girls—girls who need to take Breathalyzers before they're allowed to make any decisions," I joke. "Even this guy looks good when you're too fucked up to see straight."

Keegan laughs, and Joey flips me the bird.

"Yeah, fuck you, Joey," Keegan says to him. "That girl was hot. You don't know shit."

I snicker, but I do my best to hold it back. Keegan's the dude who takes what he can get and he's basically in awe of any girl who will let him touch her. He's actually a good guy, even if he's influenced by Joey's bullshit.

"You guys wanna get out of here? My cousin can get us into the strip club out in the city," Joey offers.

"Nah, dude, I'm tired as hell." I shake my head.

"I'd be tired too after that girl," Keegan says. "She's fuckin' gorgeous, dude."

I chuckle and pat the kid on the back. "And someday you'll get a really gorgeous girl too, my Padawan learner."

Keegan laughs, and though Joey's pretending he's pissed off, he laughs too.

I convince the guys to bail on the strip club idea, since I'm driving and I don't want to cart these assholes all the way to the city just to see some tits. I drop Keegan off at his dorm and Joey off at the apartment he shares with two of his cousins before I head back to my parents' house to crash.

I think I'll text Caroline tomorrow and see if she wants to hang out and do something normal. Girls like that tend to feel weird about spur-of-the-moment fucks during a party, and I don't want her to get all paranoid about it. I wasn't just there to fuck; I was there to hang out and meet some cool girls, which I did.

I flop down on my pillow and make a plan in my head to call her in the morning and see if she wants breakfast. I want to go over to Lola's tomorrow afternoon, and I want to be there when she's getting ready for prom. I don't know why, but I just feel like I should be around when Marcus comes to pick her up. Plus, I really want to see what she's going to wear and how she's going to look—really, super, majorly pretty, I bet. I've never really seen her all dolled up, and she usually doesn't even wear makeup around me, so this should be quite the transformation. I want to do something special for her tomorrow night, since she's ditching prom just to hang out with me. I'm not sure what yet, but I'll come up with something cool for us to do.

I fall asleep pretty fast, determined to get some rest for both Caroline and Lola tomorrow.

Chapter 6

Lola

I'm putting the finishing touches on my makeup as James lies on his side on my bed in a white V-neck T-shirt and worn out old jeans, watching me apply eye shadow. He seems fascinated with the process of lipstick and mascara as he watches my face transform from plain to glamorous. I don't wear a lot of makeup normally, just the occasional eyeliner or lip gloss, but tonight is prom and I want to look glammed up, even if I'm just going as Marcus's beard.

"Wow, Lo," James says, smiling. "I can't believe how pretty your lips look."

"Jeez, thanks." I smile back at him.

"Seriously, you could do a fuckin' lipstick commercial."

I give him an exaggerated supermodel pout and then blow him a kiss. He raises his eyebrows and playfully applauds.

"All right, out." I grin at him as I motion for him to stand up. "I've gotta put my dress on, and you don't need to be in here for that."

"Lo," he says, smirking, "I've seen you in your underwear before. I've seen you naked for fuck's sake."

"Yeah, when I was, like, eight," I scoff. We used to do a little you-show-me-yours-I'll-show-you-mine when we were kids.

"I've seen you in those tiny-ass bikinis you wear, so a bra and panties is nothing to me," he counters.

I pause for a minute and shake my head at him. "Nope, out of here."

"Aw! But I was so comfortable!" he whines with phony exasperation before he grumpily stands up and steps toward the door.

I laugh as I go into the closet and slip on my pale, orange sherbet colored dress. I mostly picked it out because it was on sale, since I'm not *really* doing the whole prom thing, but I do like the way it fits. The top has bunched strips of fabric that go diagonally across my chest to downplay my ginormous boobs. It's fitted through the waist, then it flares out at the hips and becomes silky and flowing, which makes me look taller. I bought it because it was my version of an Oscar-worthy gown—at least as much as a $29.99 T.J.Maxx dress can be Oscar-worthy.

"Need me to zip you up?" James's voice says from behind me.

"Really, dude?" I chuckle. "You really couldn't wait until I was dressed?"

"What?" He flashes me the classic James Laird: Lovable Trouble-maker smile. "You're pretty much dressed. And, like I said, I've seen you in less."

I roll my eyes at him and then lift my hair over my shoulder so he can zip up the back of my dress. Might as well have him do it, since he's standing right here.

"Not used to putting clothes *on* a girl, I bet," I tease.

"Look out!" He laughs. "She's bringin' the sass tonight."

I chuckle and turn around to face him. He gives me a smart-ass grin. I've seen that grin many times, usually when he's gotten his way and convinced me to do something risky. Most of the time, that meant ditching class or staying out late with him. I was quite the Goody-Two-Shoes, so I think he liked getting me into a little bit of trouble every now and then.

"What do you think?" I giggle, doing a little twirl.

"Perfection!" He smiles broadly. "It's too bad Marcus is gay, because that dress makes your tits look amazing. A straight guy would get a boner just looking at you."

"Charming." I roll my eyes.

He laughs loudly and then flops back down on the bed to watch me finish my hair.

I curl the ends so the waves all go the same direction instead of the wild mess that usually sits atop my head. James is quiet as he watches me, occasionally cocking his head to the side to see what I'm doing.

"Enjoying the show?" I smirk.

He nods with a big smile. "You're, like, all womanly now," he murmurs. "I remember when you were scrawny with braces. Now you're, like, this hot chick."

I chuckle and blush. James always compliments me in less-than-eloquent ways. He can be smooth and charming with other girls, but he tends to be very straightforward with me and tell me exactly what's on his mind. For the past few years, he's told me that my tits look big in my tank tops or my ass looks good in my shorts. He never means it in a come-on kind of way, just as an observation. He's slept with nearly every girl in town and he's very familiar with the nuances of the female form, so I take his compliments in stride and appreciate him telling me I look attractive. He's usually the only boy who says it, since he spent so many years terrifying the other guys in school away from flirting with me.

Finally my hair is all done, and I slip on my heels as I await Marcus's arrival. Prom is going to be short and sweet for me. Marcus and I will get in the limo with a few of our friends, take lots of pictures so he can show his parents later, arrive at the dance and quickly part ways so he can spend prom with his boyfriend and I can ditch the teenage cliché soirée altogether. He gets to let his parents go on believing he's straight, I get to make my mom happy by saying I went to this totally lame "milestone" of high school life, and neither of us has to inconvenience ourselves with awkward pretenses and expectations.

"Let me get some pictures of you in your beautiful dress," my mom says when James and I walk into the living room.

"Mom," I whine, rolling my eyes, "this isn't even real."

"I know, I know," she says, "but you still look lovely, and I still want pictures."

My mom knows the deal, that I'm only doing this to cover for Marcus. Still, she seems as excited as if it were the real thing. I think that, deep down, she wishes I had some great boyfriend and I was going to be whisked away to a glorious prom like some kind of fairy tale. I just get the impression that a tiny part of her wants me to be excited for normal high school things like all the rest of the girls.

"She looks totally gorgeous," James says as he stands beside my mom and watches my sarcastic posing.

"Doesn't she!" my mom gushes. "So grown up."

He smiles proudly at me before I whine in protest of this impromptu photo shoot.

"I never went to prom, you know?" he confesses to my mom.

"Get out of here! With all the girlfriends you had, how did you not go to prom?" she asks with surprise.

"I just wasn't feelin' it." He shrugs. "I think I was pretty over high school by that point."

In reality, James didn't go because he'd slept with nearly every single girl in the senior class and he was worried about igniting a riot when it came time to choose a solitary prom date. It would have become like a *Jerry Springer* version of the rose ceremonies in *The Bachelor* complete with hair pulling and a lot of "bitch, he's mine!" posturing. Every girl thought he'd ask her, but he didn't like high school traditions and he wasn't planning to go anyway. Instead, he and I hung out at my house and watched a bunch of *Seinfeld* episodes on the couch in the basement.

"Get in there and let me take some pictures of you guys," my mom says, ushering James over to me.

He looks bashful, and his smile is shy and sweet. This particular smile is my favorite, since he's usually very carefree and cocksure. His shy smile is really endearing and adorable, and it makes me want to give him a big hug.

He puts his arm around me, and I lean into him and rest my head against his chest. *Oh, James.* Tough guy, Casanova, ultra-charmer, but really just a big old sweetheart deep down. A lot of people throw around the term BFF, but he really is my Best Friend Forever.

He turns his head to me and looks in my eyes adoringly for a moment, and I return his gaze with a warm smile. Even though I'm still nearly a foot shorter than him with heels on, this would have made a cute prom photo.

"These are our prom pics." I smile up at him. "Since you didn't go and I'm only going as part of a big charade, tonight is our personal prom."

"I dig that idea, kid." He grins sweetly.

Almost on cue, the doorbell rings, and my mom answers. Marcus steps inside, and he does a double take when he sees James, who looks like he just stepped out of a Calvin Klein ad. Apparently Mr. Laird has that effect on more than just women.

"Hey, man." James nods at him.

"You're back?" Marcus says with a smile.

"Just for a few days to visit her." He points to me.

"That's so sweet," Marcus says.

"Marcus, honey, do you want me to take some pictures to show your parents?" my mom says, giving Marcus a nod that acknowledges she's aware of the situation.

"Sure, that'd be great," he says, smiling.

I want to tell him to stop freaking out about his parents. My mom accepts him, James accepts him, everybody at school accepts him, and I'm sure his parents won't do anything drastic when they find out. They probably already know and they just don't want to put him on the spot.

Marcus stands next to me and puts his arm around my shoulder. I move closer to him, and we pose like we're a couple.

"Put your arm lower," James instructs. "Really sell it."

Marcus smiles at him, and my mom snickers.

"Here," James says, stepping over, "like this."

He stands next to me and puts his arm low around my waist, his hand resting on my hip. He pulls me against his body, and I curve into him like ivy growing on a building.

"Look in her eyes and stuff," James instructs, demonstrating by giving me a flirty glance. "Make it look real."

"Thank you for the notes, Mr. Spielberg." I roll my eyes to Marcus, and he chuckles.

Marcus heeds James's advice, and we look every bit the happy couple. The photos make it seem like we're some couple out of the fifties going steady. He's elated, and I tell him I'll email him the pics so he can show his parents.

"You ready to go?" He smiles at me.

"Sure." I smile back and take his arm.

"Have fun, you guys," my mom says.

"Call me when you want me to come get you," James says.

"Will do," I reply, heading toward the limo.

Inside are a few of our mutual friends and their significant others. My friends Naveen, Jacob and Zoe are there with their dates, and we look like a Benetton commercial, a group of different races all smiling and laughing.

When we finally arrive, we head inside and scope out the surroundings. The popular kids are gathered on one side of the room in a big pod. There are smaller clusters all around, and there are a few kids sitting at tables. My friends are all excited, so I don't want to be Debbie Downer, but it seems pretty lame to me.

"Hey!" says a voice from the side of us.

We turn to see Evan Katz, Marcus's boyfriend, approaching with a big smile.

"Lola, you look gorgeous." Evan takes my hand and gives me a little twirl.

"Why, thank you, Ev," I reply, striking the classic *America's Next Top Model* "broken doll" pose. "I had to be stylish if I was going to be Marcus's date, even though I knew he was totally going to show me up in the looks category."

Marcus nudges me with his hip and gives me a smile.

"Well, you look spectacular," Evan replies kindly. "If I wasn't with my man, I'd ask you to dance right now."

I blush and giggle at the compliment. "Well, I'll turn you over to your date." I grin at Marcus. "Have fun, guys."

"Thank you, sweetie. For everything," Marcus whispers in my ear as he gives me a big hug.

"No problem." I smile at him. I give Evan a hug too, and just like that, my work here is done.

Zoe convinces me to stay for a little while longer, and both Jacob and Naveen ask me to dance. I'm going to miss these guys next year, though we won't be far away. I'm going to school out east and so are they, though we'll be attending different universities. Zoe's going to the School of Visual Arts in New York. Naveen's going to NYU, and Jacob got into MIT. I'm hoping we can still meet up to visit each other, since all of us will be located in the same part of the country.

About a half an hour into this shindig, I'm feeling a little burned-out on it, so I give James a call. He answers right away and tells me he'll be here in five minutes. I tell my friends goodbye, and we all wish each other luck with finals and make plans to hang out after graduation.

Just as I'm leaving the big event hall, I see the welcome sight of James's crappy old Honda Civic pulling up. This car has been like his white horse for all the times he's been my knight in shining armor and swooped in to take me out of some lame situation. He parks at the curb and gets out to open the door for me, which makes me raise my eyebrows at him in surprise.

"Your ride, m'lady," he says with an English accent.

I giggle and get into the car. He comes around the side and puts it in drive as we leave this land of teenage make-believe behind.

"You wanna just chill at my house?" I ask.

"No, no, I've got something planned." The troublemaker smile is back.

"Do you, now?" I can only imagine what he's got up his sleeve for this evening.

"Yep. It's prom night, and I want to do something special for you."

I have to pause for a second to absorb how happy that makes me feel. "You're such a sweetheart," I say fondly.

"That's just how I roll," he says with a cocky twinkle in his eye.

I look out the window as we drive up and away from town. We head up the mountain that overlooks the university area and our neighborhood below, and he drives up the winding road until we're high enough to see the expansive panorama of lights. He pulls off onto a dirt road just past the scenic overlook and continues until we get to a clearing where there's a big, flat rock.

"Come on," he says, putting the car in park and getting out.

I follow him, and he leads me over to the rock. It's large, about the size of a small SUV flattened out like a pancake. There are other big rocks around, but this one looks the most comfortable, so I hike up my dress and climb onto it.

"Oh, let me get it," James says like he's just remembered something.

He darts back to the car and returns with a Whole Foods bag. He joins me on the rock and starts unpacking the contents. First up are three pillar candles, which he lights and places in front us. My stomach growls as I watch him take out containers of pasta salad, bread, some kind of seasoned chicken wings and even a sparkling grape juice.

"Fake champagne, since I didn't want to get you liquored up," he says, holding up the bottle as I snicker.

"You planned this little picnic just for me?"

"Uh-huh. Beats the hell out of prom, right?"

"Definitely," I softly reply.

"So," he says, looking over the food, "we've got tortellini and feta pasta salad, fresh rye, limoncello wings, and I got a tiramisu for dessert. I picked out your faves, since this night is for you."

"I don't even know what to say, this is…thank you." I'm truly awestruck.

"Hey, thank you for being my best friend for all these years." He shrugs like this beautiful spread is no big deal. "What do you want first? I've got some forks here, and there are napkins in the bag. I have plastic cups, too."

I have a smile on my face that shows no signs of fading. I look him over, and I feel so lucky to have him. These sentimental little moments show sides of James's personality that only I get to see. He's usually just flirty and charismatic, but I get a glimpse at what else lies in his heart.

I blink myself out of this supreme appreciation and eye the food. "Um, tortellini first, and then I wanna try some of those wings because they look amazing." I'm practically drooling.

We pass each other the containers and enjoy the delicious food. The view is spectacular, the food is spectacular, and the company is spectacular. This has turned out to be such a wonderful night.

"This was a really fucking awesome idea, James," I say appreciatively, eating my last bite of tiramisu.

"Thanks, kid." He grins proudly.

"This is like…something I'd wish my boyfriend would do. But any guy I'd date probably wouldn't even think of something like this," I add. "This is, like, movie-level sweet."

"This is what you deserve, Lo," he says warmly, "and any guy who wouldn't do something like this for you isn't worth your time."

I don't know how to respond. I can't put my appreciation and gratitude into words. I didn't know he had this kind of pseudo-romantic thoughtfulness in him, let alone that I'd get to see it. I want to hold his hand or jump into his arms like something out of a movie where the music swells and the couple says some cliché romantic tag line to each other.

We blow out the candles and put the empty containers back in the bag, which he puts in his car so as not to attract any wildlife. He knows I've got no chance running from anything in heels, and while he's tough, he's in no position to fight off the sizable black bears that tend to sniff out human food up here.

He comes back onto the rock and sits really close to me, wrapping both his arms around me as a light breeze blows my long hair toward him. I lean my head on his shoulder, and he puts his cheek to my forehead. We stay like that for a while, not saying anything, just looking out at the town below us. Except for my mom, none of those people down there matter to me as much as James does, and I know he feels the same way.

"I missed you a lot, Lola," he whispers to me before he kisses the side of my head.

"I missed you a lot too," I softly reply, curling into him a little more. "Things are just shitty when you're not around."

He looks down at me and gives me a sweet, warm, tender smile. "So tell me, how does some perfect little angel like you decide you want to be best friends with a guy like me?"

"Oh, stop it," I say, giggling. "You're a good guy, and I'm glad that you want to be friends with me. You could have been spending tonight in bed with some sorority chick, but instead you're up here having a picnic with a high schooler in a cheap prom dress."

He laughs and kisses my forehead. "You know I'd rather spend time with you than anybody else," he softly replies.

Again, I'm speechless. He's defied my imagination with these heartfelt proclamations. I always knew our friendship meant a lot to him, but hearing him express it like this is so special that it nearly brings a tear to my eye. I try to find words to tell him that this means just as much to me, but I can't even articulate it. He sees that he's knocked me—a normally very verbose girl—off my axis, and he gives me a grin. He reaches down and holds my hand, weaving his fingers through mine. He knows. I don't have to tell him how much I care because he already knows.

We only return when it starts getting really late. My mom knows I'm safe with James, but she might start to worry if she wakes up in the middle of the night and neither of us are anywhere to be found.

We pull up in front of his parents' house, and he walks me to my door. I unlock it, and I see that my mom has already gone to bed. I turn to say goodbye to James, but I don't want him to go.

"Come in, okay?" I whisper.

He nods and follows me to my bedroom, where I quietly close the door and flick on the lamp on the nightstand. I grab my makeup remover wipes and get the mascara, blush and eye shadow off my face, feeling lighter with each swipe. Nothing makes me feel more gross than sleeping in my makeup, and I'm relieved to take it off because it means that I've survived prom and the next milestone is graduating and getting out of this town.

"I'm gonna get my pajamas on," I whisper. "I'll be right back."

He kicks off his shoes, and he lies back on my bed as I shut my closet door behind me and put on some pajama shorts and a tank top instead of this now-dirty orange gown.

I emerge and crawl under the sheets, flicking off the lamp so the only light coming in the room emanates from the window facing the porch light at James's house next door.

"Do you want me to stay over?" he whispers with surprise as he props himself up on his elbow beside me.

I nod my head. "My mom won't come in without knocking because she'll know I want to sleep in after the late night. I can sneak you out in the morning."

He gives me a grin. He loves getting me into trouble, and he's totally thrilled that I'm taking this risk. In reality, it's hardly a risk at all. I'm sure my mom wouldn't exactly love the idea of James sharing my bed, but I don't think it would start World War III or anything. She knows that nothing's going on between us, so there's no reason to worry.

"Lo," James whispers, "is it gonna freak you out if I take my pants off?"

I cover my mouth to try to stifle my snickering. "Do you have underwear on? Because if you're free ballin' it then yes, that will definitely freak me the fuck out."

"I have underwear on," he says, chuckling quietly. "I just don't want to sleep in my jeans, so I want to take them off and cuddle with you, but I didn't want to make you feel weird about it."

"All right." I giggle.

He unbuttons and unzips his jeans, tossing them over the decorative metal footboard of my bed before he gets under the covers with me. My mom's got the air conditioner blasting, since it gets so hot in the living room when the morning sun pours in, and the vent facing my bed makes it freezing in my room at night. I'm cold, but James scoots up close to me and his body heat warms me. My back is up against his chest as he spoons me and drapes his arm over me. We slept like this a few times when we were little, and it always gives me a subconscious wave of contentment and relaxation, like I'm safe and sound. If I were a cat, I'd start purring and kneading the pillow.

"James," I whisper, turning my head so I can look back at him.

"Yeah, kid," he softly replies.

"Thank you…for making tonight so special for me," I say. "The picnic was really beautiful, and I really appreciated it."

"Anything for you, kid." He smiles warmly and kisses my cheek.

With that, I lie my head down on the pillow and feel calm and content as I fall asleep with James cuddling me.

Chapter 7

James

That early, orangey, sunrise light is just starting to peek into Lola's window when I open my eyes. Everything's quiet this early in the morning on a weekend. My eyes pan from the window to the angelic beauty sleeping beside me. *Whoa!* I spent the night with Lola. It's been years since I've slept in a girl's bed without fucking her first. Last night was one of the best nights I can remember, but I wasn't out getting laid; I was just chillin' with my best friend. It kind of blows my mind that I could enjoy spending the night with such a pretty girl without sex involved.

I stretch, and Lola starts to wake up. She turns so she's on her back, and she looks at me with cute, sleepy eyes and a big smile. She looks down and sees that I have no shirt on, and she gives me a smirk.

"What?" I chuckle quietly. "I got too hot in the middle of the night."

"You just *had* to strip down to almost nothing while you slept in my bed, huh?" she teases.

I did get too warm last night, mostly because I was holding her close and I didn't want to let her go. But I'll admit, part of me did want to make it even better by getting naked with her. I've still got my boxer briefs on, but other than that, I'm in the buff.

"You've got some sort of problem with your best friend being almost naked in your bed?" I joke.

She looks down at my body and pats my abs as she giggles. "Well, not really, I guess."

I chuckle and pull her against me, wrapping my arm around her. We're both on our sides, facing each other, and she's nuzzled under my neck with her arm around me. Our legs are tangled together, and we're about as close as two people can get. It feels oddly romantic. I've never really done this before, just had a cuddle with a girl. My cuddling usually leads to making out, which usually leads to feeling up, which eventually leads to some part of me going inside some part of her, so this tender moment is foreign to me, but I really dig it.

"What time is it?" she yawns, turning toward the clock on her nightstand.

I can see it over her shoulder, so I reply, "It's six thirty-eight."

"It's too early," she sighs and closes her eyes like she's going to go back to sleep.

"You know I have to go back home soon," I say quietly. "What if your mom wakes up? I don't know how she'd feel about this."

I look down at our bodies pressed together, me with no shirt and her in a tiny tank top. If Theresa came in the door, it would look like I was naked and that me and Lola had a lot more than a picnic last night.

"Good point," Lola agrees, giving my body a slightly flirty scan.

She runs her hand from my stomach up my chest and then wraps her arm around my shoulder, pulling me tighter against her. It's a surprising turn of events, and I can tell she's feeling the romantic calm of this morning too.

As I look at her, all sleepy and smiley, I kind of want to kiss her. *What would that be like?* Me and Lola have messed around a little bit in the past, but I've only ever kissed her neck a few times, never actually kissed her for real. It'd probably be too much. We have such a tight bond anyway that, if things did turn sexual, it'd be really intense. She's the kind of girl you fall in love with. If I kissed her, I'd want to have sex with her, but you don't have sex with someone like Lola. You have to make love to a girl like her. It would put us both in a weird situation, since I've been constantly telling her not to sleep with anybody unless she's in love. She'd probably assume it was all a line of bullshit, like some master plan I've carried out for a decade just to try to fuck her. Kissing her would make everything all weird, so I decide to put it out of my head.

I brush her hair behind her ear before I sit up. I put my pants back on and pull my T-shirt back over my head as she reluctantly crawls out from under the covers. Very quietly, we open the bedroom door and creep downstairs to the basement door, the one I always used to sneak in and out of when we were younger.

I reach out to hold Lola's hands for a minute before she stands up on her toes and throws her arms around me.

"That was the best night ever," she sweetly whispers.

"For me too," I quietly reply, wrapping my arms around her little waist and holding her close.

Again, I get that weird desire to kiss her, but I block it out.

"Want to see a movie or something this afternoon?" she asks.

"Totally." I nod before I take a second to look in her eyes. Beautiful. Really beautiful. *Goddamn!* Lola's, like, the most gorgeous girl I know. "All right, kid, I gotta go," I say, trying to shake off this romantic vibe I'm feeling for her. "I'll call you later today."

"Okay," she replies and I can tell she wants to kiss me too.

I can't let it happen, even though my heart's beating a mile a minute right now. There's a slightly awkward pause between us as we both obviously try to squash our feelings.

"See you later, kid," I say softly as I kiss her cheek. I turn toward the door, but then I turn back to her and give her a grin. "Oh, by the way, your tit popped out of your tank top while you were sleeping last night, and I totally saw your nipple." I smile, lightening the mood.

She gasps loudly and grabs her chest. I give her a wink and leave her with that little chestnut as I cross the lawn to my house.

I'm laughing to myself as I reach for the spare key and unlock the basement door at my parents' house. I quietly step inside, being extra careful to silently shut the door behind me. I walk up the stairs as quietly as I can to make my way to my bedroom, but I stop in my tracks when I hear noises coming from the dining room. It sounds like a woman crying, but it takes me a few seconds to realize that it's my mom.

I panic and rush up the stairs. *Is she okay? Is she hurt? Did something happen?* I burst into the kitchen to see Mom crying at the table.

Dad's sitting in front of her holding her hand, and they both turn to look at me when I enter the room. Dad's jaw is clenched and his hands are balled into fists as he scowls at me. Mom starts fully weeping, and Dad reaches for his laptop, which is open on the table. I think I know what's coming. This is not good.

"Do you want to explain this?" he practically growls as he holds the laptop out to me.

There's a porn site up on his browser, and my stomach drops. I feel like I'm going to puke. They've discovered a video clip from a shoot I did about a month ago. It was me and two girls. It was very hardcore. It's basically the worst thing my parents could possibly see.

"How could you?" Mom sobs.

I feel like my legs are going to give out underneath me. My jaw has dropped open, but I can't summon any words. My mouth is dry, and there's this burning sensation spreading all through my chest.

"This is what you're doing out there in California?" Dad shouts. "You went out there to try to be in movies and this is what you became? You had a good life here, but no, no you wanted to show off and move out to Hollywood to become something special. Well, for twenty bucks a month, now everybody can see how special you are."

"Dad, I—" I manage to say before he cuts me off.

"Shut the fuck up, James!" He spits like a cobra. "Don't you say a fucking word!"

"Please, you guys," I start to say, "let me...I can explain."

I look from my dad to my mom, and she holds her head in her hands as she breaks eye contact with me. It cuts me so deep to see her cry like this.

Dad slams the laptop closed so hard that he nearly breaks the screen. He stands from his chair and gets right up in my face like he's going to hit me.

"You're a goddamned disgrace to this family!" he yells, his eyes blazing with anger like I've never seen before. He grabs me by the back of my neck and jerks my head toward him. "Do you hear me? You're a failure!"

My eyes sting and my throat burns and I can feel myself start to cry. *This can't be happening! This has to be some kind of bad dream!*

"Mom, please." My voice trembles as I look to my mom for help.

"Don't you try to get her to sympathize with you!" he shouts right in my face. "You broke your mother's heart, James!"

I swallow hard, and I feel like there's a rock in my stomach. Those words kill me. I broke my mom's heart. Nothing could feel worse.

Dad lunges at me and gives me a shove before he smacks me hard on the side of my head.

"Jon!" Mom screams.

I hold out my arm to block him. My dad's a big dude and he's strong as hell. I'm sure it would hurt if he really did try to punch me, but he's not going full force. Mom stands up from the table and grabs onto him to calm him down. He steps back from me, and he's huffing like he could breathe fire.

"Do you have any idea what an impact this is going to have on this family?" Dad growls, literally shaking with anger. "How are your mother and I supposed to show our faces when everyone knows our son is fucking girls on the Internet for the whole goddamned world to see?"

"Not everyone knows," is the only response I can think of.

"Well, a whole lot of people do know, obviously, because I got emails about it from three of our friends!" he shouts.

I feel bad. I know that had to be so embarrassing for him. And my poor mom! She had to be devastated.

"I've always known you were trouble, but I didn't expect this, James," Dad snarls. "You're a fuckup, you always have been, but this is a new low, even for you."

I'm so upset, but I feel myself getting pissed off too. He's not even giving me a chance to defend myself, to explain. He's saying all these things about me, and he's taking it to the extreme. I wasn't the best kid, but I was never as bad as he's making me seem.

"I have to run a fucking business! Did you ever think of that, you selfish, immature, irresponsible little shit?" The vein in his forehead is bulging, and his face is completely red.

"You're playing pool boys who fuck housewives on the job! What are people going to say when Laird Landscaping comes to do their yards? They're going to think you were fucking their wives while we trimmed their trees!"

"I was, Dad!" I shout back.

"Oh, Jesus!" Mom wails.

"You know that I was, so don't try to act like what I'm doing is a big surprise!" I yell as I stare him down.

"You shut your mouth right now, boy!" he snarls.

"Don't try to act like you never put that together! You didn't think it was weird that I never did any of the work, but I got all the tips?" I snap back. "You knew exactly what I was doing when I went in the house with those women! You had no problem with it because they kept paying us. Fuck, Dad! We did Mrs. Landry's yard seven fuckin' times! You never wondered why she had you trim her fuckin' trees three times in a week?"

"You little—" He lunges at me again, but Mom stands up and pulls him back with all her strength.

"Jon! Stop it!" she hollers. "Hitting him isn't going to make any of this go away!"

"You had no problem letting a sixteen-year-old fuck some house-wives as long as it helped the business," I yell. "And now you have a problem with your twenty-year-old adult son fucking other consenting adults on camera?"

Dad swallows hard and closes his eyes for a minute. He looks like he's going to explode like something out of *Scanners*.

"You listen to me," he says in a gravely whisper, "I want you out of this house. I want you gone, and I don't ever want you to come back."

"Jon, please!" Mom sobs.

"You get your shit, and you get the fuck out," he says. "As far as we're concerned, our youngest son is dead."

His words hurt me emotionally, but now it's like they're causing me real, physical pain. It feels like someone stabbed a knife in my heart and I'm going to die.

"Jon," Mom says in her calmest voice, "why don't you go cool off in the other room."

"You have five fucking minutes!" Dad growls. "If your shit is not out of this house in five fucking minutes, I'll put you out myself."

My dad walks out of the room, leaving me with my weepy mother. I start crying really hard now, and I reach out to hug her. I'm so happy when she hugs me back, and I wish I could just make all this go away.

"Sweetheart—" she sniffles "—that stuff you said, about the women and the landscaping, that wasn't true, right? You were just saying those things, weren't you?"

I can't lie to her, not now. I know this is going to kill her, but I have to shake my head.

"God, no!" she sobs. "Why, baby? Why did you do that?"

"They liked me and they came onto me," I struggle to explain. "I don't know, Mom. I was a teenager and I was horny and they were hot and…I don't know."

She holds my face in her hands and looks at me like she wishes she could make all of this magically disappear. I hate seeing her like this, hate letting her down and making her sad.

"Did they make you do those things? Did Karen or any of the others coerce you or force you?" she says, referencing the aforementioned Mrs. Landry.

"No, Mom." I shake my head. "It wasn't like that. I wanted to, we both did, and they liked it so much that we started doing it on the regular. But Dad got a bunch of repeat customers from it, and he was making money, and I was having fun, so it wasn't hurting anybody. I just…I liked it."

"Oh, God, baby!" she cries. "My special boy, my little sweetheart," she says like I've transformed from that into some monster. "How could you do this? How could you let those women use you? How could you let yourself get exploited on the Internet that way?"

"It's not exploitation, Mom," I say softly, trying to calm her down. "It's just a job. It's something I'm good at and I like it. It pays really good and it's fun."

She wails and grabs onto me like she's trying to pull the old James out.

"I'm sorry, Mom," I whisper as I hold onto her. "I'm so sorry to make you feel like this. I'm so sorry that this hurts you."

"My baby boy," she cries into my shoulder.

"I never, never wanted to hurt you or Dad. I used a different name. I did stuff for smaller production companies because I figured it wouldn't get out that much. I mean, millions of porn movies are shot every year. What are the odds anyone from home would see one of mine?"

"Oh, James," she weeps, holding my face in her hands again. "You were so special, sweetheart. You're such a good boy, and you could have done so much. Why did you let yourself get dragged into all this? You could have been anything, sweetheart. You didn't have to be this."

I hardly ever feel guilty about what I do, but I feel absolutely awful right now. I can't explain to her that I really like what I do and that I'm becoming a real rising star in the business. My success will only make things worse. I just feel an overwhelming sense of anguish.

"I'm so sorry, Mom," I say to her, my voice a tight whisper as I try to hold back the flood of emotion pressing against my throat. "I'm just so sorry. This is the last thing I wanted, to make you cry like this. I just…I'm so, so sorry."

"My beautiful boy," she says tearfully. "You were always my beautiful boy. When you were born and the doctor handed you to me, I thought you were a little angel from heaven."

I start crying now. I can't hold it back anymore. She's taking it from way back, and I know the story ends with her being utterly disappointed in who I've become.

"Where has that little angel gone, James?" she sniffles. "Why, baby? I just can't believe you'd do something like this."

I totally break down. I lean forward and bury my face in her shoulder and weep like a fuckin' baby. It's one of those hard cries where you feel like your whole body is broken. I need my mom. I need her to not feel so disappointed and sad.

"All right, time's up!" Dad's voice says from the hallway. He doesn't look pleased to see my mom comforting me.

"Dad, I'm so sorry. Please, just let's talk about it," I beg.

"No more talking, James," he cuts me off. "Get your shit and get out of this house immediately."

Mom gives me this heartfelt look, and I get the distinct feeling she's saying goodbye. I don't want to leave. I don't want to walk away from her because I'm really starting to feel like this might be the last time I see her, at least for a long while.

Dad watches me like a warden as I go into my room and pack up my suitcase. I'm crying the whole time, but he's all stone-faced, and I know he doesn't care. He's fuming. Totally livid. The truth is, I hate myself way more than he hates me right now. My decisions made my mom cry, and there's nothing worse in the whole world than making your mom cry.

Dad doesn't even walk me to the door, just points to it and gives me this stern look that tells me I better hurry up and get the fuck out before he snaps. I've never been scared of my dad. He was never the kind of guy to hit us or be really abusive to us, but his fuse is beyond lit right now and it's probably best if I go before he goes totally nuclear.

I try to swallow my tears as Mom steps over to me and gives me one last hug.

"Mom, you gotta believe me when I say I never meant to hurt you guys. I'm so, so sorry," I say through my sniffling.

"I know, honey," she whispers to me. It gives me a little shred of hope, but it's a tiny one.

"Out!" Dad yells, interrupting the moment.

I step out onto the porch, and I take a deep breath. *What do I do now? Where do I go?* I'm so shaken up that I'm actually worried about driving home, but I have nowhere to go.

I turn my head and look at Lola's house, thinking about how happy I felt when I woke up with her this morning. I get this sudden urge to see her. It's like I'm actually aching to look in her eyes and be close to her. I need her right now so bad.

I sniffle and wipe my tears off my cheeks as I walk across the lawn to her door.

Chapter 8
Lola

My mom is awake and none the wiser that James slept over last night. We're both tired but in the mood for some breakfast, so we decide to make waffles. We're sitting at the table chatting about Zoe's personally designed prom dress when the doorbell rings.

I set my orange juice down and make my way to the door to answer. My jaw drops when I see James standing there with his suitcase, completely, fully, intensely sobbing. I whip open the door and pull him inside, throwing my arms around him.

My mom hears the commotion, and comes into the front room to see what's wrong.

"They found out," James snivels into my shoulder. "They found out, and they kicked me out."

"Oh, James," I whisper, holding him tighter. "I'm so sorry! It's gonna be okay." I rub his back to soothe him. "It's all right, babe. It'll be okay."

"My dad…he was so harsh," he cries.

"What happened, sweetheart?" my mom says, stepping over to pat his back while I hug him tightly.

"My parents—" He sniffles. "They kicked me out of the house."

"I'm sure they didn't mean it," she says soothingly.

"They did mean it," he sobs. "My dad said I was dead to him."

"Well, jeez, sweetie, what happened?" she asks with her brow furrowed like she can't fathom what would make a parent take such drastic action.

"They found out about my movies." He sniffles. "They found out that…that I was…doing porn."

My mom's eyebrows shoot straight up. "Well, I wasn't expecting that," she whispers.

James cries harder and leans far down as he buries his head in my shoulder.

"It's all right," my mom says as she gives him a comforting side-hug. "They're upset now and they're going to be angry for a little while, but they'll get over it, honey. It'll be okay."

"I don't know what to do," he says. "I didn't know where to go. I'm sorry I just showed up on your doorstep like this."

"Don't apologize," I interject. "You know that I will always be here for you. Always, James. You are my best friend in the world, and I will have your back through anything. I promise you that."

My mom gives me a look that says she's impressed with me. There's really nothing to be impressed about. It's the truth. I'll be by his side through thick and thin.

James is shaking, and I'm worried that he'll have a panic attack. I take his head in my hands and hold his face so he looks at me.

"Breathe, okay?" I whisper. "Breathe with me, James."

I take a few deep breaths, and he follows my lead. He closes his eyes and tries to get his shit together. After a few moments, he's breathing somewhat normally again.

"Come on, honey, let's get out of the doorway. Come on inside and sit down," my mom sweetly offers, ushering him inside.

He takes a seat on the couch, and I hand him a box of Kleenex from the end table. My mom sits in the chair catty-corner to the sofa, and she gives him an Oprah-style sympathetic look. I put my arm around him and rub his back or stroke his hair to help calm him down. I've never seen him so upset, and it rips my heart to shreds to see him hurting like this.

"Okay," my mom says calmly, "what happened? Let's start at the beginning…with the, uh, movies."

"Okay." He sniffles and nods. "When I moved out to LA, I had a hard time finding work. I did some commercials, I modeled for a couple of romance novel covers, but I was still pretty broke."

My mom listens, and I hold James's hand, knowing how hard it is for him to reveal this to someone's mother.

"This girl I was hanging out with at the time said I should go down to the Valley with her because she knew how I could make tons of money, so I decided to give it a shot. It started out like those cheesy late-night movies, but then I started doing…you know, the real thing," James timidly explains.

A tiny, cringing micro-expression comes across my mom's face, but it disappears quickly as she continues listening to James.

"I did my first one and I really dug it. It was really fun, I started making a lot of money, and nobody back home had any idea what I was doing, so everything was awesome," he says. "A couple of my old friends found out, and I guess they told some people who told some other people, and eventually it got around to my parents."

Fucking Keegan! I know this has something to do with him or Joey Dipshit Corsentino! They're way too proud of having a friend who's a porn star, and they haven't kept their damn mouths shut about it since they found out. Joey's been using it to pick up chicks by lying that he's done a couple movies too. What a load of shit! Those two have been living vicariously through James for years, and now their boasting has gotten James into real trouble.

"They won't even let me try to explain." He looks at my mom with sad, broken eyes. "My dad just threw me out and wouldn't let me say anything. He got so mad. I tried to call him on how he's being a hypocrite, but he wouldn't listen."

"You told him about the landscaping stuff?" I gasp, knowing immediately what big guns James brought out against his dad.

"I had to," James says to me. "He was so pissed about it that I had to call him out on all that stuff. He didn't seem to have a problem with me having sex with those women, so why was he flipping his shit now—sorry, Theresa." He smiles shyly to my mom after cursing.

"I'm sorry, what is 'the landscaping stuff'?" she replies cautiously.

"When I was younger and me and Jonathan used to help my dad on jobs, the housewives would flirt with me, and sometimes I'd sleep with them," James confesses. "But it used to benefit my dad because they'd call us back a bunch of times, and they'd used Laird Landscaping year after year because they liked me."

My mom's trying her best not to completely freak out as she murmurs, "My God, when was this, sweetie?"

"It started when I was about sixteen," he admits with shame. "You know Mrs. Landry? She was the first one to, like, actually do something with me. The other women just mostly flirted with me, but Mrs. Landry, she...she wanted more than that."

"And you were only sixteen?" my mom replies, a pained expression on her face. "That woman took advantage of a sixteen-year-old boy?"

"It wasn't her fault. She just wanted me, and I liked that some hot, horny, older chick was coming on to me," he tries to defend it.

"It *was* her fault, James," my mom says, grabbing his hand. "She was a grown woman—hell, she's my age—and she *was* taking advantage of you. If your father knew about that, if he even had a shred of suspicion, and he didn't say anything, he's the real asshole here."

I've been telling James this for years. I was never that freaked out when he hooked up with girls at our school, even if they were a couple grades older than him, but it really freaked me out when he started screwing these housewives. Mrs. Landry was pretty, in that cougar kind of way, but it was really fucked up for a woman in her mid-forties to be screwing a teenager. I think hearing it from my mom has made it sink in more because James looks like he's questioning the decision for the first time.

"Give your parents some time," she says softly. "I think when they calm down, they'll realize that you didn't mean any harm by—"

She's interrupted when the doorbell rings. The three of us get up to answer it. It's Jonathan, and he's got two big taped-up boxes in his arms. He sets them down on the porch and gives us all a grim look.

"Dad wanted me to give you your stuff," he says to James. "They don't want it in the house anymore, and Mom told Dad not to throw it away. Dad doesn't want you back at the house, so they called me and made me bring it."

It's almost like I can hear James's heart shattering as he realizes the severity of his parents' rejection.

"Jonathan, please," James says, his voice strained with anguish, "please just tell them I'm sorry. Tell them I wasn't trying to embarrass them or disappoint them."

"I'll tell them," he says, shrugging, "but they're not hearing it, bro. Dad's really pissed, and I think they're done for good."

James cries, and to my surprise, Jonathan reaches out and gives him a hug. This act of compassion is sweet and unexpected, even though it's also a little awkward.

"Do you think they'll talk to me? Can I just explain it to them?" James pleads.

"I wouldn't talk to them, at least for now," he replies. "Mom's really upset, but Dad…he's past where I've ever seen him before. Give him a couple days to stop going nuclear about this and maybe he'll listen."

"Okay." James nods. "Thanks, Jonathan."

"All right," Jonathan says, "Good luck, buddy." He looks to my mom, then to me, and gives us a subtle smile. "Lola, Theresa," he says as he bids us farewell.

With that, he walks back across the lawn to the Laird house. This is really, really bad. If they called Jonathan to come over from his apartment just to deliver boxes to James, then they really have abjured him. They won't even talk to him. It seems so cruel to me.

"Honey," my mom says softly, putting her hand on James's shoulder and turning him around, "why don't you stay here tonight and try to go over there tomorrow and see if you can talk to them."

"Really?" he says with the smile of a shelter dog that's just been adopted.

"Really." She smiles back and nods. "Give them a little time to calm down and then maybe they'll listen. You can stay here—in the guest bedroom."

I crack a smile, knowing what she's implying. It was one thing when he occasionally crashed in my room before, but now that she knows he's a porn star, I'm guessing she's revising the rules.

"Oh, Theresa!" he says, getting a little choked up. "You have no idea how much this means to me!"

She reaches out and hugs him. "It's gonna be okay, honey," she says as she pats his back. "This has gotta be a very big deal for them, but you're their son and they still love you, even if they're angry with you right now."

He sniffles, and she rubs his back a few times before we all venture back into the kitchen. He cries some more as my mom fixes him some waffles, but I think he starts feeling numb after a while. James is always fun and outgoing, energetic and humorous. He's always got a smile on his face, but that bright light inside him has dimmed to a flicker. It hurts my heart to see him all broken like this.

He spends the next several hours lying on the couch on his side with his head in my lap while I stroke his hair and try to comfort him. At least he's stopped crying. Now he's just silent with the occasional sniffle.

"It's okay," I keep whispering to him. "It'll be all right."

He puts his arm across my knees and holds onto me like I'm the last lifejacket on the *Titanic*. I lean down and put my arm around his shoulder, letting my long hair fall over us like a tent. He takes a couple deep breaths, and I whisper softly to him that everything will be okay and that I'll always be here for him. It seems to reassure him a little bit, and he pulls himself together.

It's mid-afternoon, and James has been wallowing in misery for several hours. I want to get him out of the house. Maybe some fresh air will do him good, plus he won't have to be haunted by the image of his parents' house from the window. I propose that we go for a hike at the park at the foot of the mountain by our neighborhood. He agrees, and we walk up the street and onto the path that leads up to the steeper area where people rock climb. He was happy last night when we were up in the mountains away from everything, so I want to take him someplace similar to help him get centered.

We sit down on a big boulder at the base of the mountain, and I put my arm around him and rub his back softly.

"This day is so fucked up," he says, his voice gravely from crying. "I went from being, like, the happiest I've ever been this morning to feeling like total shit in about five minutes."

I don't want to dwell on the negative, so I sweetly ask, "You were the happiest you've ever been this morning?"

"For sure." He smiles at me. "Last night was so fun, and I really liked sleeping over. We haven't done that in a long time, and I missed that."

"Same." I nod, looking back at him with a warm smile of my own. "I always liked our two-person slumber parties."

"Everything felt good yesterday, like, just really right, you know? And then that whole thing just exploded," he replies.

"It's painful right now," I say in a comforting tone, "but it'll get better. Besides, we're having a sleepover again tonight, so the world hasn't turned to shit entirely, right?"

He laughs lightly, since he's still too hurt to laugh hard, and he gives me a squeeze. "Although," he says with a little glimmer of that smart-ass grin that I love so much, "Theresa doesn't seem too keen on us having slumber parties anymore."

I snicker. "You noticed that, huh?"

"I'm banished to the guest bedroom now," he says with a slight smile. "No more crashing in your room."

"If you found out your teenage daughter was sharing her bed with a charming, sexy porn star, would you believe they were just sleeping?" I counter.

"Good point," he says with a chuckle. "So…do you really think I'm charming and sexy?"

I flush and turn my head to look out at the park below. "Wow, I think I just saw a hawk fly by," I say, very conspicuously changing the subject.

He laughs harder now and gives me a smirk. "You totally do. You *so* totally think I'm hot."

"You *so* totally need to shut up!" I pretend to scowl.

"Hey, it's no big deal," he teases with a shrug. "You can't hate on somebody for telling the truth, right?"

I roll my eyes, and he snickers. He's feeling lighter, and that makes me really happy.

"It's all right," he continues. "You're hot too, so it all works out."

Now I blush and feel bashful. He compliments me all the time, but even though he's joking around right now, it feels really genuine.

"You know Keegan's been jackin' it to you for years?" he throws out like it's nothing.

"What?" I gasp, which makes him laugh heartily.

"Yeah, when I had lunch with him he said he thinks about you when he jacks off," he says with that classic James Laird mischievous grin.

"Dude…gross!" I say, scrunching my nose.

"And I'm guessing a bunch of other dudes do it too," he goads me. "You're so hot that I bet you most of the dudes you see on a daily basis have jerked off thinking about you at one time or another. So, basically, every dude you talk to has probably imagined fucking you at some point. Vividly. We're talking really graphic stuff. Just think about that, huh?" he jokes.

I make a whining sound and slump forward, covering my face with my hands as my cheeks sting with embarrassment.

"I love making you all shy like this." He laughs and pulls me into his chest. I pretend to punch him at first, but I eventually lean in and rest my head on his chiseled pecs.

He's in a much more jovial mood by the time we're ready to walk back to my house, but I can tell there's a huge ocean of pain below the surface. I take extra care to be cheerful and upbeat as I joke around with him to distract him from looking at his parents' house when we get to our block.

We spend the next several hours in the basement as James volunteers to help me study. Putting his mind to a task seems to help because he doesn't look as depressed while he's concentrating on my schoolwork. He's got a proud, accomplished smile on his face by dinner time, and I'm feeling a lot more at ease as I watch him get happier by the hour.

My mom lets him hang out in my room—with the door open—and we watch the *South Park* movie as we lounge on my bed. I nearly laugh every time she sneaks a glance in the room as she's passing through the hallway. My room sits between the hallway bathroom and the guest bedroom, so there's no reason she would need to walk by so many times, but she's nervous about leaving me alone with James, and I know she wants to keep an eye on us. I don't think she would have cared half as much before she found out he was doing porn, but she's trying to be subtle about it and not make him feel bad.

Evening finally arrives, and I'm wiped out. James and I both slept only a few hours yesterday after our late-night, post-prom picnic. I'm sure he's doubly exhausted from the emotionally taxing day he's endured. At around nine o'clock, he decides to get ready for bed. He takes a shower in the hallway bathroom, and I head to my bathroom to brush my teeth.

I'm stopped in the hallway by my mom, whose eyes are darting around suspiciously like we're two spies coordinating on top secret intel.

"Did you know about this porn thing?" she whispers very quietly.

"I knew a little about it," I admit. "I didn't want to tell anybody because I knew this is exactly what would happen."

"I'm going to ask you something, honey, and I want you to be completely honest with me. I won't get mad. I just want the truth," she says dramatically. "Has James ever…done anything to you?"

"No!" I say, laughing quietly at the outrageousness of the question.

A few years ago, he spontaneously felt me up when we had a quick moment alone during a pool party at Keegan's house but that was a rare outlier, not at all the norm.

"You can tell me the truth," she says again, giving me a look like she's an FBI interrogator and she'll be able to detect even the slightest hint of a lie. "Have you guys ever been…intimate? Are you being safe? Please tell me you're using protection."

"Oh, my God, Mom!" I whine. "I've never had sex with James. I've never had sex with anybody," I bashfully reply, which seems to draw a relieved sigh from her. "It's not like that. We're friends, and I know it might seem weird how close we are, but it's not sexual or 'intimate' or however you're thinking of it."

She sighs and pats my shoulders. "You're a good girl, sweetheart," she begins, "and I know that James is a good guy deep down, but he's…fast. He's always had a lot of girls, and I don't want you to end up as another notch on his bedpost."

"Mom!" I whine.

"Shush, I'm just being protective. You're my little girl, and I have the right to be a psycho about stuff like this. I know I can trust you to make the right decisions, but this porn situation was a pretty big bomb to drop, and I think it's totally natural that I'd be a little worried."

"I know, and I completely understand why you feel that way, but you've got nothing to worry about," I explain.

"All right," she says, nodding. "Try to get some sleep. I'm guessing you got in really late last night."

"We were out having fun," I say. "He brought all this food, and we had a picnic up at the overlook. It was really sweet."

"Oh, well, that's lovely," she replies with a smirk. "Sounds like you two had a nice little date."

"Mom!" I laugh.

"I'm just kidding." She smiles and gives me a little wink. "Just, you know, be smart, all right, honey?"

"Yeah, yeah, yeah." I shrug.

She gives me a kiss on the cheek and then goes off to bed.

I'm out of the shower and brushing my teeth when I start trying to think of ways to help James. Maybe I could talk to his parents. They've always liked me and they might be more apt to listen to me than to their "deviant" son. I'd really like to line them both up and yell at them for being so cold to him. What difference does this really make anyway? It was happening yesterday, but they were blissfully unaware of it. Now that they know, they're acting like it's an atrocity, like genocide or something.

I step into the hallway, and I stop in my tracks. I don't want to just go into my room and go to sleep. I want to check on James and see if everything's okay. I don't want him to be alone with his depressing thoughts. Frankly, I just want to be close to him to tell him that life goes on and things will be okay in the end.

Chapter 9

James

I feel really antsy, and I can't sleep. Everything's wrong, and there's not a goddamn thing I can do about it. It's the worst feeling. Helpless. Worthless. It fuckin' sucks. Normally, I'd use sex to feel better, but I'm all by myself in the bedroom. I wish I could just fuck somebody, have that connection for just a few minutes, and then be mellow for a while, but honestly, I feel like nothing's going to cheer me up right now. I don't know what to do about it. Sure, I could probably jerk off, but that's not going to cut it either. I need to feel something more intense to replace this sadness.

My thoughts are interrupted when Lola taps lightly on the door. All this thinking about fucking means I've got a semi-hard-on going, so I throw the blanket over my lower half and whisper for her to come on in.

"Hey," she quietly says as she walks toward the bed.

She's got on a little white tank top that's nearly thin enough to see her nips through the cotton. I definitely notice it. She's also wearing some gray short-shorts, the kind she always likes to sleep in. Even when we were younger, her pajama shorts used to turn me on. I remember falling asleep in her bed one time when I was about sixteen and getting a boner from the feeling of her bare legs tangling up with mine when she cuddled up against me in her sleep. She's older now, and her legs are more shapely and muscular. They're tan and disproportionately long for such a short girl…and I want to see them spread up against my sides while I'm deep inside her.

I shake the thought away as she lies down on top of the sheets next to me. She's propped up on her elbow, and no matter how much I try to look away, I can't help but appreciate the curves of her body as my eyes roam from her shoulder down to her tiny waist, over her hip, and down her sexy legs.

I've always thought she was pretty, but tonight it's like I can't snuff out all these dirty thoughts I'm having about her. I've thought about her before, even imagined fucking her sometimes during my scenes, but I never considered it that big of a deal. They were just fantasies, and I could brush them off. A whole bunch of shit pops into your head when you're trying to come on command, so dreaming of Lola riding my dick isn't anything to see a therapist about. Right now, though, I can't think of anything but those sexy fantasies, and I'm having a hard time even concentrating.

"Are you okay?" she sweetly asks.

"Uh-huh." I nod, trying to pretend like I'm not imagining her with her clothes off.

"You can tell me for real," she says, reaching out to touch my cheek with the palm of her hand. It's warm and soft, and it makes me relax.

"I just have no idea what I'm gonna do," I admit. "I don't know how to make this better. I don't even know if I can."

"You can. You have to give it some time. Your dad's a real hard-ass, so you have to let him just stew in this for a while, but he'll come around. Your parents aren't total dicks like my dad," she says, "so eventually everything will work out."

Lola's parents went through an ugly divorce when she was a baby, and her relationship with her dad is strained, to say the least. She told me that he basically gave her and her mom the house and started a new family in Michigan. She tries to talk to him on the phone sometimes and have some kind of relationship with him, but they're just on way different pages. Personally, I don't like her dad because he always seems to make her cry. If I had a dollar for all the times she's gotten depressed after a conversation with him, I certainly wouldn't have to be in porn movies to make a living.

"I'd imagine you're pretty tired," she softly whispers when I yawn. "I should let you get some sleep."

"Lo, I'm not tired," I quietly reply, reaching up for her hand. "This is the happiest moment of my day, you sneaking in here to talk to me. Stay…please?"

She gives me a big smile and then pulls back the sheets, which startles me a little because I know I'm still packing some heat and I don't know how she'll react to sitting here with me if she knows I've got a semi hard-on going on. I fidget a little, but she doesn't seem to notice as she climbs under the covers and cuddles up to me.

"I'm cold from the air conditioning, though," she whispers as she presses her firm little body right against my bare chest. "So you have to keep me warm."

Fuck! This is not going to be easy. I can't seduce Lola. I can't even try to seduce Lola. I keep telling myself that, but the part of my brain that controls logic and rational thinking must be taking a night off. Her body just feels so fuckin' good against me!

"Of course I'll keep you warm, Lo," I reply, my voice soft and silky. I'm not sure if she notices, or if she even cares.

I pull her closer to me until we're both on our sides facing each other and my arm is wrapped around her waist. I play with a strand of her long hair as she tangles her legs in mine. I can feel her soft skin and smell her shampoo. I love holding her close like this…but I'd like it even more if we didn't have any clothes on.

"Everything's going to get better, James," she whispers sweetly as she nuzzles under my chin.

I give her a little squeeze in response. I'm definitely feeling better right now, that's for fuckin' sure.

She folds her arm and rests her hand on my chest between our bodies, putting it over my heart. "I hate to see you sad, and it breaks my heart to see what you've had to go through because of your dumbass parents. Everything will be okay, though, and you know I've got your back through anything," she adds.

"I know, Lola," I whisper to her and take her little hand in mine. I bring it up to my mouth and kiss her fingertips before returning it to my chest. It's a little more intimate than our usual thing, but she doesn't seem bothered. "You've been so good to me, and I can't even tell you how much it means to me."

She leans her head up so she can look at me, and she gives me a kind smile. I gaze into her eyes, and I tuck a strand of her hair behind her ear before I rest my hand on the back of her neck. I brush along her jaw with my thumb, and my eyes scan her face. She's so beautiful to me. My little angel. Impulsively, I start tilting her head up so I can kiss her, but I come to my senses before I do it and I plant a little kiss on her cheek instead. Now she seems to notice that I'm feeling kind of romantic, and she gives me a surprised look, though she's still smiling sweetly at me.

I run my nose along hers and then kiss her forehead as my hand moves down her back. She seems very relaxed, and I think she likes it. I know I'm definitely loving it. Her body's so soft and warm, and she's pressed up against me—it feels really fuckin' nice.

I rub her back gently and then move my hand up and down from her shoulders to the top of her perfect, firm little ass. She doesn't stop me; she doesn't push me away or even say anything.

This is what I really needed, something all sweet, intimate—something my sex life is sorely lacking. I fuck a lot, but it's always just for fun or for work. I never share this kind of closeness with those chicks. I want to feel something real, something that goes beyond just fucking and crosses into romantic territory. I've never been a romance kind of guy, but I always kind of wished I was.

The only times I've done anything that could be classified as romantic were with Lola. The picnic, for example, was one of the more romantic things I've ever done with a girl. It was a lot like a date—it even ended with me in her bed, but not in a sexual kind of way. Tonight, I can't stop myself from wanting to flip that around and maybe take it to the next level. I just want to feel something, and I want to feel it with her.

I lightly grab onto her hip and slide my hand down her thigh, guiding her leg up around my side. I roll forward until I'm on top of her with her legs spread underneath me. Her eyes grow wide when she can feel how hard I am as I press against her.

She gasps softly when I start kissing her neck, and I think she's completely taken by surprise, though I feel like she might have seen this coming just a little bit when I started kissing her face and rubbing her back. She doesn't push me away. In fact, I hear her breathing speed up a little bit as I keep kissing up and down the side of her throat.

"James," she objects in a tiny whisper, sounding aroused and out of breath.

"I want you, baby," I breathe against her skin and resume kissing her neck.

There's a spot just below her ear that she seems to like a lot, so I concentrate my efforts there as my hand slides up her ribs and then cups the side of her boob through her shirt. Her nipples perk up almost immediately, and I'm so fuckin' turned on by that response.

I rub my thumb over one nipple, just like I did that time at Keegan's pool party, and I swear, she makes a breathy moaning sound, though it's really quiet. She likes it. She'll like it even more when I get her naked and start sucking on those pretty pink nipples, or when I finger her G-spot, or when I flick my tongue over her clit. She'll really, really like it when I'm inside her.

My hand slides under her shirt and toward her perfect tits, but she reaches up and stops me before I touch her nipple. I head the other direction, taking my hand away and moving it down her body. My fingers slip under her shorts, and I can feel the dampness on her soft little curls as I start getting closer and closer to the Promised Land. She's wet and ready for me, but she reaches down and grabs my wrist, stopping me from going any further.

"James, no," she whispers to me.

"I want you so bad, Lola," I say back. Even I can hear how strained and desperate my voice sounds. "I need you. I need this so bad, baby, you don't even know."

"You don't need it," she softly protests. "This isn't going to solve anything. This isn't going to make anything better."

"It's gonna make me feel good, and I'll make you feel good too," I reply, pushing my pelvis into her a little more so she can feel my hard cock pressing between her legs.

She closes her eyes for a second, like it feels really good, but then she opens them and shakes her head at me.

"I promise you'll really like it. I'll be really gentle, and I'll go slow. It won't hurt at all," I offer.

"You know we can't," she whispers as she looks in my eyes. "Let me just tell you what would happen if we had sex tonight, okay? It would be fun. It would probably be awesome and amazing and mind-blowing." I grin at her prediction. "But we'd both feel like shit about it in the light of day tomorrow."

"I don't think we would," I respond. "I think we'd feel closer than ever, and we'd wanna do it a bunch more times."

She laughs and shakes her head before she reaches up and takes my face in her hands. "You're hurt right now, James, and you think sex is the solution because you've always used sex to feel better when something bad happens. Remember when your mom freaked out because she found out you were failing math? And you went out and had sex with those two girls you and Joey met at the reservoir? Remember when your grandpa died and you had sex with about thirteen girls that week—I don't even know how you pulled that off, honestly."

I snicker. She's got a point.

"Sex is easy for you, and it doesn't mean anything," she says, seeing right to the heart of things. "It's fun and you can do it whenever you want because you're good looking and charming and everybody wants to fuck you." That makes me smile a little bit. "But it doesn't actually solve the deeper problems you're dealing with emotionally. It's a quick fix, that's all."

I'm kind of taken aback by her observation. She's completely right about everything she said.

"Having sex with some girl—or a bunch of girls, or whatever crazy shit you do—it might be fun for a while, but it doesn't actually fix anything. Your parents are still pissed off, and this whole porn fiasco will still be there after you come," she says.

I nod my head slightly. She's totally right.

She reaches up and strokes her fingers through my hair before she looks deep in my eyes. "Can you even imagine the guilt you would feel tomorrow if you fucked me tonight?"

I can't help but smile. Totally right. Impulsively taking Lola's virginity would make me feel like a total dick.

"You've always treated me like such a treasure, James. My whole life, you've made me feel special and precious. You've protected my virtue like you're something out of a fucking fairy tale. I want you to seriously consider how you would feel about changing that on some kind of whim because you were emotionally vulnerable and you didn't know how to deal with it," she softly explains as she tenderly strokes the back of my neck. "You tell me all the time not to have sex until I'm in love, and now you'd fuck me because sex is a little Band-Aid on the gushing artery in your heart? How would you feel if you woke up in bed with me tomorrow morning knowing you'd basically used me for that?"

"Horrible," I admit.

"Exactly!" She laughs quietly, playfully tangling her fingers in my hair.

"Everything you said is totally right." I smile down at her. "You just, like, nailed the truth in five seconds."

"I did get an A in Intro to Psychology," she jokes.

"You're an amateur therapist, and a good one."

"You don't need sex right now anyway," she says, resting both her hands against my chest. "You need to feel loved and appreciated because you're feeling really dejected after the way your parents banished you."

"That's probably true."

"So I'm gonna hold you close and I'll tell you all the reasons why you're special to me and how you're the best guy I know, okay?"

"Okay." I grin widely.

With that, I move off her and lie back on the pillow next to her. She rests on her side with her head on my shoulder and her palm against my chest, just above my heart.

"Okay," she says sweetly, "here are all the reasons you're a wonderful person."

I laugh, and I feel truly touched as she starts listing off all these things she likes about me. She covers everything from the way I always stand up for her when people are mean to her, to the fact that I'm better at driving in the snow than her, to how I make the best basil gnocchi she's ever tasted. By the end of her pep talk, I feel like I could conquer the world.

"See?" She grins when she's all done. "I told you you're the best guy I know."

I pause and look in her eyes. The pain is gone. All those awful feelings in the pit of my stomach from the way that my dad looked at me and the sound of my mom crying, have all kind of melted away. The relief of it is overwhelming, and I grab my chest as I try not to get emotional from this surge of happiness she's just given me.

"Lo," I say sincerely, "you're the best person I know — in fact, I'm pretty sure you're the best person who ever lived. You're my angel, kid, and I want you to know that I love you and I appreciate every second that I get to spend with you — not just now, even back when we were little. I don't think anybody's cared about me as much or made me feel as happy as you do."

"Aw!" She smiles and gives my chest a little reassuring pat. "It's because I adore you, James. I truly, genuinely adore you, and anything I can do to make you happy makes me happy."

I turn to her and caress the side of her face before I give her a sneaky peck on the lips.

"Down, boy!" She giggles and gives me a playful little smack on the shoulder.

"It was just a peck." I laugh innocently.

"I'm not leaving this up to willpower," she says, smiling a little flirtatiously, "because that's a battle nobody's gonna win."

I laugh with surprise. *Ah ha! So she was into it!*

"No kissing, no more touching, just two best friends cuddling like we are now," she says with a grin as she shakes her head a few times like she can Etch-A-Sketch away her attraction to me.

"Then what am I supposed to do about this?" I joke, looking down at my body.

"About what?" she says.

I shift so I'm on my side, and I press my hard-on into her hip.

"Still?" She laughs, her eyes wide with an adorable expression of surprise on her face.

"Huh?"

"You *still* have a boner? I saw you were hard when I came in, but you've really sustained that thing," she teases.

I have to cover my mouth to keep from laughing too hard. I definitely wouldn't want to wake up Theresa right now. I have a feeling she wouldn't be so nice to me if she came into the bedroom to find me in bed with her teenage daughter while sporting a raging hard-on.

"You knew I was hard when you got into bed with me?" I ask with surprise after my laughter subsides.

"Kinda." She shrugs, and her cheeks are just a tiny bit rosy with embarrassment. "I mean, I saw something going on — I'd have to be blind to miss that thing — but I figured it'd just go away after a while."

"It would have, but then I was on top of you and your nipples were all hard…and it got a lot worse," I admit, thinking back to those few hot moments we just shared.

She snickers and rolls her eyes. "You say that like it's an affliction."

"It is, dude." I give her a sly smile. "Maybe you could fix it for me, baby. Maybe it needs mouth-to-mouth resuscitation. Maybe you could nurse it back to health," I joke, cranking the flirtation up to eleven.

"Eeeew!" She giggles wildly, covering her mouth with the blanket to muffle the sounds.

"And then we could swap and I'll do it to you too," I continue to tease. "And then maybe we could both do it at the same time. You ever tried a sixty-nine, Lola? I think you'd like it. You're a good multitasker."

"James!" She flushes pink and keeps laughing as quietly as she can.

"Then you could try putting your ankles behind your head or doing a little reverse cowgirl action," I say, trying to get her all the way to that full blush that I've always thought was the cutest. "By the end of tonight, you could have tried doggy, maybe up against that wall, a little spoon action, and I could get you where we're both sitting up facing each other—you'd definitely like that one 'cause it's more intimate."

She gasps and covers her face as she giggles. I love making her shy like this. She's so innocent, and I really love that about her.

"Or maybe we won't do any of that shit, and I could just cuddle with you and try to concentrate on something not-so-sexy until it goes back down," I say sweetly as I pull her hands away from her face.

"Filthy!" She gives me a pretend glare.

"And that's not even the tip of the iceberg, cupcake!" I tease.

"Cupcake?"

"Yeah, that's right, cupcake," I say with a playfully overconfident grin. "Would you prefer baby doll? Honey pie? Sugar tits?"

Her shoulders are shaking with how hard she's trying to mute her laughter.

"What? I'm just trying them out. I don't get to call girls anything besides 'baby' or porno shit like 'slut' and 'little whore' in movies, so I'm workshopping it." I snicker.

"Testing the waters of terms of endearment," she says, chuckling as she shakes her head.

"Exactly." I nod. "So just go with it…angel pussy."

"James!" she gasps before laughing.

"All right, all right, all right," I playfully concede. "Just Lola, then… and maybe angel pussy on evenings and weekends."

She gives me a smile and then shakes her head like she thinks I'm nuts. I wrap my arm around her and pull her close to me. My sweet, funny, kind, warm, beautiful best friend. She's my treasure. My little angel. This girl means the fuckin' world to me.

We get quiet after that as exhaustion starts to set in. It's been a long-ass day. After a while, I can hear Lola breathing deeply, and I know she's already nodded off. I take a few moments to savor the feel of her skin and the warmth of her body, and I start to feel very calm and content. As much as I want to hold her in my arms tonight, I know Theresa will flip the fuck out if she discovers me in bed with her daughter in the morning.

I gently scoop Lola up and peek out the doorway to check that the coast is clear. It's really late and Theresa's still asleep, so I quietly tiptoe down the hallway to Lola's room. I'm half naked and Lola's exhausted like she's been thoroughly fucked, so getting caught right now would not be good. I deposit her in her bed before pulling up the covers and getting her comfortable.

"James," she says, her voice all soft and sleepy.

"Yeah, Lo?" I whisper.

"Are we in my room?" she drowsily asks.

"Yeah," I quietly reply. "You passed out in my bed and I didn't want your mom to get pissed. Now get some sleep so you're not totally wiped out in the morning."

"Okay, James," she sighs as she lies back on the pillow.

"Goodnight, Lo," I whisper and kiss her forehead.

"Goodnight...cupcake," she says back with her eyes closed and a playful smirk on her lips.

I snicker all the way back to my room. When I get under the covers, I don't feel so cold and frozen inside. Lola's my heart. If I were Popeye, she'd be my spinach. She gives me so much strength by just being there for me and talking things out with me. I love her, and I appreciate her so much. I'm really, really glad she stopped me tonight because I can't imagine how bad I'd feel if I actually did anything to her. She's too perfect, and I'd feel like I was defiling her. It'd be like fucking a sunset or something. I love the way she just sort of laughed it off, too. She's so cool like that, and she never gets weirded out by the nasty shit that I do. I know that, no matter what may happen, me and Lo will be best friends for the rest of our lives because our bond runs a whole lot deeper than anything I've ever felt for anybody else.

Chapter 10

Lola

My final isn't until twelve thirty this afternoon, but I can't sleep, so I wake up around eight thirty, just in time to see my mom leaving for work. The guest bedroom door is still closed as I quietly go to the kitchen to put the coffee on. I fill up the pot with water and turn away from the sink when I gasp. James is standing there in just his boxer briefs with that sweet, shy look on his face.

"Sorry." He smiles bashfully. "Didn't mean to scare you."

"Christ, you're like a ninja!" I laugh at the way he surprised me.

He chuckles and then takes the coffee pot from my hands and pours it in the machine.

There's a slightly awkward pause while we're waiting for it to percolate. I'm thinking about what happened last night, and I'm pretty sure he's feeling just as sheepish as I am. It was no big deal, only a few minutes of action, but there were some lingering emotions there—at least for me. I don't want to admit it, but I liked it. I knew we shouldn't have done it, which was why I put a stop to it, but I can't deny that the way he kissed my neck felt pretty amazing.

"So…I totally tried to feel your tits last night," he says, breaking the ice in that blunt, direct, oh-so-James way I'm so used to.

"Yes. Yes, you did," I laugh.

"Lo, I'm sorry about that. I just—" he starts.

"James, it's okay," I say. "Really, I mean it. Seriously, it's okay. No harm, no foul. It's in the past."

If this turns into a big discussion, I'm worried that I'll reveal how much I liked it and how I'm currently imagining a scenario in which he'd tear off my shorts and take me right here on the kitchen counter.

"I think...I just feel like we should talk about this," he says tentatively.

I swallow hard and nod. Yes, it's true: we probably should talk about it, even though I don't really want to.

"Um, I think it's obvious at this point that I find you very attractive," he says, avoiding eye contact with me. "I kind of...got carried away with that, and...uh...I acted on impulse."

"I understand. It's no big deal," I say before conceding, "I think you're very attractive too. I wasn't all that bothered by what you did; I just knew we shouldn't let it progress any further."

"So...you're not, you know, creeped out about it or anything?" he asks shyly.

"No," I laugh. "God, no, not at all!"

"Really?" He smiles and exhales a big sigh of relief.

"Yeah, man. I'm not going to bullshit you and try to tell you that I didn't like the way it felt. I did, and I'm sure you were very aware that I did—"

"Your nipples are your tell, kid," he teases.

I give him a sarcastic smirk. "Anyway," I say with played-up exasperation, "it's nothing more than what happened at the pool party that time, so it's not really that big of a deal."

As the words leave my lips, I realize that this is the first time I've ever mentioned the incident at Dave Keegan's house that fateful summer. James had this look on his face when we were all alone in that hallway: I call it the James Laird Sex Laser Beam, and I was locked in his sights for those few precious moments.

"Yeah, I don't know what happened to me back then." He chuckles, scratching the back of his neck in an unconscious gesture of embarrassment.

"I didn't have a problem with it, really." I shrug, trying not to give away how much I fucking loved it. "It was very...spontaneous, but it was kind of fun, actually."

"You dug it?" he says with a sly grin.

I nod my head, and I can feel the pink rushing to my cheeks.

"Seriously?" he says in a softer, more sensual tone as he steps closer to me.

I nod again, and he stands right in front of me, hovering over me. I'm practically shaking as I vividly recall the way his lips felt on my neck, both the day of the pool party and last night.

He puts his hands on my hips and looks into my eyes with the diet version of the James Laird Sex Laser Beam. I can feel my heart flutter a little as he moves higher up, gently gripping my ribs before resting his palms on the sides of my breasts. A hint of a smile crosses his lips as he moves his hands forward and softly cups me, not squeezing or making any major motion, just looking in my eyes and subtly caressing my breasts. My lips part, and I can feel my breathing getting deeper as I anticipate his next move.

The coffeemaker shuts off, signaling that the coffee is ready. That seems to break the spell because James drops his hands and shakes his head as he looks away. I take a deep breath and go to the cupboard to get two mugs.

We sit down at the table and take the first few sips in silence, looking everywhere but at each other.

"Lo, I think I should go back to Cali," he finally says.

"What? Why?" I whine. I don't want him to go. I love having him around, even with this strange, sexually charged air between us.

"I'm worried, babe," he says with a new sort of vulnerability.

"About what?"

"I'm just scared that I'm gonna do something…with you."

"Oh," I murmur, looking down at my coffee.

I feel self-conscious. He's afraid of doing *something* with me, but I want a detailed explanation of why he'd feel that way. Of course, my insecurities flare up, and I'm certain that I'm not pretty enough, not wild enough, not sexy or cool or even mildly enticing, and he doesn't want to do something sexual with me because it will be boring and he'll feel like he has to pretend to like it for my sake.

"Why are you doing that?" he says, leaning down on the table to try to get me to make eye contact with him.

"Doing what?"

"Getting all weird. You're, like, paranoid or something," he says, reading my expression like a book.

"I just…" I try to articulate it without sounding like I'm cripplingly insecure about myself when compared with the other girls he's bedded. "I know that I'm not, you know, how most of your girls are. I don't know how to do that stuff, and I'm not freaky like they are. I understand if you don't want to, you know, do anything physical with me because I don't measure up and stuff."

He laughs and then shakes his head. "Babe, are you crazy?"

It puts me at ease a little bit, and I timidly smile.

He gets off his chair and kneels down in front of me, turning me so I'm facing him. He's tall, so even from his spot on the floor, he can be right at eye level with me. He holds my shoulders and gives me a warm smile before taking my face in his hands and looking deep in my eyes.

"I'm not scared because I think you wouldn't be good," he says like I was crazy for even theorizing it. "I'm scared because I'm having a very hard time controlling myself with you lately. I'm finding all sorts of shit about you really sexy, and I can't stop thinking about your legs and your tits and all that stuff."

I giggle. Very direct, as usual.

"Last night, I wanted to rip your pajamas off and fuck the shit out of you," he confesses, which makes my eyebrows shoot up with surprise. "I'm not joking, Lo. I seriously considered it…for, like, several minutes."

I giggle, and he gives me a big smile.

"But then I got my shit together and I realized that'd be fucked up to do. I wanted you so fuckin' bad last night, Lo, you have no idea, but I'm glad you shut it all down," he says.

"So it's not because I won't do some kind of crazy, doggy-style double penetration or something?" I joke.

He laughs heartily. "Nah, babe." He smiles and brushes my hair behind my ear. "If I want wild girls, I can go find wild girls. I really like that you're not like that. Your innocence is beautiful to me, Lola."

He looks right into my eyes when he says it, and my heart swells.

"And that's why I'm scared as hell of being alone with you now. I don't want to…you know…take that away from you."

I feel myself smile at the surprising sweetness of this conversation.

"I just…I don't care about other girls the way that I do about you," he confesses like he's confused by how to explain this. "I don't care about anybody as much as I care about you."

I smile wider now, and I feel warmth spreading through me.

"You're just, like, perfection to me, Lo," he continues with a very earnest expression. "I can't, you know, spoil that. Some things are off limits for a reason, and that reason is because you're precious to me."

I can't stop myself. I throw my arms around him and give him a big hug. He squeezes me tight, and I know that he senses my appreciation.

"And that, young lady, is why I can't be allowed to tear your clothes off and fuck the shit out of you," he jokes when we part from the hug.

I laugh loudly at that and give him a shrug. I can accept that explanation.

"But, um, what if I still want to? Not have sex or anything, but I still want to just be close to you like that—because, James, when you were lying on top of me last night, that was the shit, man!"

He cracks up and shakes his head.

"You've got all this going—" I motion to his abs and his pecs "—and it was pressing against me, and you were so warm and firm with all those muscles. I'm not gonna lie, I dug it."

That makes him laugh harder, and he leans forward and presses his forehead to mine. "You better watch out, 'cause flattery will get you everywhere, little girl."

"It's not flattery. No bullshit, dude. Your body is fucking stunning," I blurt out. "I just really like that proximity we had last night. Isn't there some way you could just…be on me without, you know, being *in* me?"

He practically snorts with laughter, and he seems thoroughly amused by my request.

"Maybe." He grins slyly. "But I don't know if that's gonna satisfy you," he adds as he grabs my hips and slides me forward in my chair so my legs are on either side of him. "You've become quite the seductress. How do I know you won't be hungry for more? You might just take advantage of me."

"If I wanted to take advantage of you, I could have done it a thousand times already, stud," I say in my sexiest whisper, bowing my back so my breasts press into him.

"Fuck me!" he laughs. "You're so fuckin' sexy and you don't even realize it!"

I giggle, and all that exaggerated sensuality disappears as I return to my nerdy self.

"All right, how about this?" he proposes. "I'll still cuddle with you. I'll be all over you if you want, but we have to know that it won't go further than that. Deal?"

I nod my head.

"Because I absolutely, positively cannot fuck you, Lola," he says like it's a formal declaration.

I furrow my brow and salute him, which makes him snicker.

"And you can't freak out if this shit turns me on. No squealing when you feel my hard-on against you—because, baby, being on you like that will, for sure, get me hard."

I laugh, and I feel slightly smug about that. I have the ability to turn James on, which makes me feel like Angelina Jolie or something.

"But...I still do think I should go back to California soon," he adds apologetically.

"Aw!" I whine.

"You're gonna give me a fatal case of blue balls here! My health could literally be at risk!" he bluntly jokes.

I roll my eyes, but I'm blushing at the flattery of that idea.

He pauses for a moment and breathes a big sigh as he looks down at my chest. "Goddamnit, Lola!" he exhales. "I can give you twenty-four hours before this shit just kills me."

I try to hold it in, but my snicker becomes loud laughter.

"Okay." I nod before giving him a flirty glance. "So what should we do with our last twenty-four hours?" I say as I run my hands up his chest and tangle my fingers in his hair.

He tries his hardest not to smile when I slide forward and wrap my leg around him, pressing my pelvis into him.

"I wonder how we could pass the time," I feign innocence as I rock my hips a couple times while I bite my bottom lip flirtatiously.

"Jesus Christ!" He sighs. "How have you never had sex before and yet you can be all seductive like that? You're a fuckin' tease, Lo. You know how to wrap a guy around your little finger."

I laugh loudly, switching off the seduction as quickly as I switched it on.

He closes his eyes and murmurs hilarious, un-sexy things like he's trying really hard to concentrate. "All right, that time Keegan puked in Joey's car, falling off the monkey bars and breaking my arm in third grade and how the bone was poking out, C-SPAN—"

I completely crack up at this list, particularly the last one. "You think of C-SPAN when you're trying not to get a boner?"

"Shut up!" he laughs. "This is all your fuckin' fault in the first place, grinding against me and putting your boobs in my face. You're the fuckin' devil, Lola!"

I throw back my head with laughter, and he snickers. "I'm an evil temptress on a mission to seduce a weary man?"

"Yes!" he teases.

"My apologies to you, sir." I giggle, sitting back on my chair.

"That's better," he pretends to chastise me. "And put a bathrobe on or something. I need there to be another layer between me and your tits."

I burst into laughter and nod my head, crossing my arms over my chest like I feel a sudden rush of modesty. "You cad!" I say like an old time high-society lady. "How dare you gaze upon me like I'm a sex object!"

He snickers and then goes back to his chair, shaking his head.

"*Ha ha!* I totally turned you on," I tease. "You totally think I'm sexy."

"No shit!" he says, blushing just a tiny bit.

I ease off him, not wanting to push this adorable modesty too far. Shy James is so cute, and such a rare occurrence, that I don't want him to think I'm making too much fun of him.

I spend the rest of the morning chitchatting with James instead of studying, which is probably fine because I'm obsessively over-prepared for my test today.

He offers to drive me to school, and I accept. He says to text him when I'm done and he'll come pick me up, which gives me a nostalgic sense of fondness for all the times he did this when we were in school together. One of the best things about my relationship with James is that it can evolve and change over the years, but at the core, it's stronger than a diamond encased in steel.

Chapter 11

James

"This seems a lot like lasagna," Lola remarks as she stirs the meat sauce on the stove.

"It is a lot like it, really," I say, nodding. "Just the Greek version."

Tonight, I'm making moussaka for Lola and Theresa, since this will be my last night here. My grandma on my mom's side, who is Greek, took the traditional recipe and made all these modifications, so it's our family version. It takes a long time to prepare, but it tastes really good.

Lola insisted on helping me, so I gave her the task of peeling the eggplant and then stirring the sauce once I had it simmering. She took these orders very seriously, and I found it incredibly cute. She's a decent cook; actually, she just never even attempts to cook anything when I'm around. That's cool with me. I really dig cooking, and I love to watch her pig out on the stuff I make. The best compliment is seeing her clean her plate and then tell me how she thinks the button is going to pop off her jeans from how full her stomach is.

We've got a little while before Theresa comes home, so we should be okay on time for the meal. It's also nice because it gives me a few hours to spend with just me and Lola. It's fuckin' amazing to me how she can be so sexy and so sweet at the same time. I don't think she has any idea how hot she really is and how much it turns me on when she fucks around with me like she was this morning. I haven't spent all these years keeping guys off her because they *don't* want to sleep with her. If dudes like Joey and Keegan are any representation of my whole generation, a super-hot girl like Lola needs a full security detail.

She's inadvertently flirting with me right now. A few minutes ago, she tasted the sauce and did this thing where she licked the spoon. She had no fuckin' idea how sexy that looked.

I'm not going to lie: I've been flirting with her a little bit too—also by accident. A couple minutes ago, I gave her a little smack on the butt when she bent down to get eggs out of the refrigerator, and it made her giggle in that way that I like. After that, I stood right behind her and guided her hands when I showed her how to cut up the eggplant. I can't help it. I just fuckin' love touching her.

I'm pretty sure she likes touching me too, because she's been putting her arm around me a lot. I like it. It feels really natural. Even though she's tiny, I feel like our bodies click together like LEGO pieces. She just fits right into my side, and my hand can rest right on her hip in a way that's super comfortable and chilled out. I've been looking in her eyes more too—not that I didn't do that before, but now it's like I'm really looking, like I'm sort of gazing deep into them. I can tell she digs it because she always smiles really big when I do it.

Theresa gets home a couple hours later, right when the food's done, and we all sit down at the table to eat.

"So I think I'm going to go ahead and take off tomorrow," I say. "You guys have been so cool to me, letting me stay here and all, but I don't think my parents are gonna budge for a little while, and I don't want to just mooch off your hospitality."

"Don't worry about it." Theresa shrugs. "You're family, James. You're welcome to stay anytime you want for as long as you want."

I wish my mom was like Lola's mom. Although, I'm guessing it's a lot easier to accept your kid's best friend being a porn star than it is to accept your kid being a porn star, so maybe she'd be just as upset as my mom if I was her son.

"You've been so cool to me during this whole thing, Theresa, and I wanted to tell you how much I appreciate it," I say sincerely. "I don't think a lot of moms would just open their doors to someone who did, you know, what I did, and it really means a lot to me that you haven't made me feel like crap about it."

"Of course not, sweetheart." She smiles, putting her hand on mine on the table. "Your choices are your choices. You know the consequences. I mean, obviously it's not the first job I would have picked for you, but I know you wouldn't do anything really, really bad and that your heart's in the right place."

I smile, feeling warmed up inside from how nice that was.

Theresa compliments me on the food, and I make a point to say that Lola helped. She tells her mom how all she did was chop and stir, but I think she likes the compliment because she gets really smiley with me.

I think Theresa thinks something's up with us because she keeps looking back and forth between us like she's trying to figure out why we're so sweet and borderline flirty with each other. She doesn't look outwardly worried, but I'm sure she is. I'm a twenty-year-old porn star, and Lola's still in high school for Christ's sake, so I can see why she'd be a little freaked out at the prospect of us flirting and possibly messing around. I do my best to put her at ease, not checking out Lola's tits as much as I'd like to and not giving her too many flirty little glances.

Around ten o'clock, Theresa goes to bed, and I pack some of my stuff up and get in the shower. I dry off and change into a T-shirt and some boxers to sleep in. I lie down on the bed, but I can't possibly go to sleep. I need to see Lola. This is my last night here, and I need to be around her.

I quietly make my way down the hallway to her room, and I tap really lightly on the door. She opens it, and she's in a bathrobe and nothing more. It's dimly lit with just the small lamp on the nightstand, but the low lighting only makes her look sexier.

"Hey," I whisper, trying my hardest not to scan her whole body in slow motion.

"Hey." She smiles, already on to me.

"Can I stay in here with you for a little while? I wanted to be with you tonight, since I'm leaving tomorrow," I explain.

"I was hoping you'd want to," she says, leading me into her room.

I sit down on the bed and motion for her to come over to me. She stands right in front of me, and I put my hands on her hips. She's looking down at me, and I'm looking up into her eyes.

Just a bathrobe. That's the only thing separating her from me.

I'm staring in her eyes when I slowly pull at the tie. She lets me, and soon it falls loose. The robe is hanging there, just open enough for me to see a sliver of her bare skin, including her cute little bellybutton. I keep looking in her eyes as I slowly slide my fingers inside the robe. I don't push it open too far, don't make any big, sudden movements. I know I shouldn't be doing this, and the last thing I want to do is lose control.

Her stomach tightens up when I make contact with her, gradually moving around so my hand's on her hip inside the robe. I pull her a little closer so she's standing right against the bed in front of me. I'm at eye level with her boobs, and it would be so easy to just push her robe back off her shoulders and get a glimpse of her totally naked.

I can't stop, no matter how much I want to. I look in her eyes for a second before I lean forward and place a little, tender kiss in the middle of her chest. I have to do it again, so I do. Pretty soon, her hand slides up my neck, and she brushes her fingers through my hair. My other hand comes up to grab onto her hip from the other side, and I start kissing onto her stomach and heading down her body.

My hand moves up the inside of her thigh, and my fingers lightly skim between her legs. Her breathing is much faster now, and I can feel her arousal on my fingertips as I start to touch her.

I want more. I want all of her. She smells so sexy, and I want to kiss her and touch her everywhere. I move her to the side a little and start to usher her onto the bed in hopes that I can get her to open up her legs and let me taste her. My lips are right below her bellybutton when we hear a noise from outside the door. I know it's Theresa. *Oh, shit!* She's going to come in here and see Lola with her robe open and me well on my way to letting my lips roam to all sorts of inappropriate locations. We're totally fucked!

We both freeze as the footsteps get closer. *Shit! Shit! Shit!* I just told Theresa how much I appreciate her being so nice to me, and now I'm going to repay her by going down on her daughter? She's going to be fuckin' livid.

I'm holding my breath as we hear the fridge door open and shut. The footsteps get dimmer, and then they fade away entirely.

Lola lets out a sigh. She was holding her breath too. "Oh, thank God!" she whispers. "She was just getting some ice water."

"Jesus Christ," I sigh with relief.

"This is definitely too risky. We're crossing a pretty major line," she says, still a little flustered and turned on.

"All right, we gotta stop," I say, blinking my eyes a few times and pulling her robe closed again.

"Let me get some pajamas on," she says, stepping back a little.

"Not those little short-shorts," I interject.

She giggles and nods before she disappears into the closet.

I flop back on her bed and try my hardest to reset my thoughts about her. This is Lola. Little Lola who used to get scared of *Are You Afraid of the Dark?* and who cried the time Jonathan stepped on a ladybug. She might look very fuckable, but she's not. She's off the table, totally off limits.

"Get in," she says, motioning to the bed when she comes back out in a loose T-shirt and a baggier pair of shorts.

I crawl under the covers and lie back on the pillow as she gets in with me.

"Is this fucked up?" she asks me.

"What?" I say, waiting for my eyes to adjust after she turns off the light.

"The fact that we're fucking around and stuff? I mean, I like it. I like what you're doing to me, and I want you to keep doing it. Is it bad to do this shit if it feels good and it doesn't hurt anybody?"

"I guess it depends on what shit we do." I shrug and try to rationalize it in my mind. "Like you said, it's not hurting anybody and we both like it, so it can't be that bad, right?"

To my surprise, she moves with lightning speed, and in a flash, she's sitting on top of me and looking down at me. I smile up at her, and I kind of like this. I always knew Lola was a tough chick, but I like that's she can be a take-charge kind of girl when it comes to sexual stuff too. She'd be a rad girlfriend because she'd be cool to hang out with and she'd probably just shove you onto the bed and ride you, which is way hot.

"I don't know why I like this so much," she says, smiling. She's not trying to be flirty, but she is. She really, really is.

"I don't know why I like you jumping on me and straddling me with all your clothes on." I grin and let my hands roam up her thighs. "I'd like it so much more if we were both bare-ass naked."

She quietly giggles—since we definitely can't risk a run-in with Theresa while Lola's on top of me.

She looks into my eyes for a second, and I feel so connected to her. I put my hand on her hip, but not in a "let's fuck" kind of way, just to hold onto her, to touch her.

"I just trust you, I guess," she explains. "I feel okay about doing this stuff with you, and I never feel okay about doing this stuff with anyone."

"Really?" I smile.

First, I'm really glad that she likes this and that she doesn't feel weird about it. Second, it's great to hear that she trusts me, because I trust her with my fuckin' life. Third, I'm surprised that she said she doesn't feel okay doing this with anybody else. Anybody? Not a single guy but me?

"I'm really self-conscious around everybody but you," she says, looking down with super-cute shyness. "I get all squirrely when boys touch me or try to hook up with me. I'm, I don't know, high-strung, I guess. I don't feel like that with you, though. I actually like when you touch me. It feels natural, you know?"

Perhaps the best words I've heard in years.

"I feel like that too. I mean, I have no problems touching other girls, or letting them touch me, but I feel totally mellow when I touch you. It's hard to explain. It's like you…you make me all relaxed or something."

"That's how I feel!" she says, giving me a light little smack on the stomach. "Like right now, if you were, say, Mike Bernard or Deshawn Jackson, I'd be shaking like a leaf. When Jeremy Chen felt me up one time, I remember being so nervous that I practically gave myself a migraine. You, on the other hand, touched my boobs in the kitchen a little while ago and I didn't bat an eye."

I chuckle, taking care to be quiet. I love that she feels so comfortable around me. I find that the problem with most girls is that they think guys are judging them all the time. They all hate something about themselves, from their weight to their lips to their hair to the size of their boobs. I like that Lola doesn't get skittish about that stuff when she's with me.

"I bet you'd fuck like a minx, Lo," I joke, resting my hand low on her stomach between us like they want you to do when you shoot those soft-core, late-night cable channel movies so nobody can see the penetration.

She covers her mouth and muffles her laughs. "Why do you say that?"

"I bet you'd be totally uninhibited in the right situation. You'd let loose, babe. The best sex I've had was with girls who just dropped all their insecure bullshit and went for it," I explain. "I mean, look at you right now, getting on top like this. You may be a virgin, but I think you're a wild girl at heart."

She blushes and she looks so pretty. "You think I'd be all aggressive in bed?"

"I do." I nod with a laugh.

I can't help it; I grab her hips and rock her back and forth a little bit to show her how to move. She follows along and pretty soon she's moving all on her own. I can picture it, how she'd look riding me like this. She wouldn't bounce up and down like the chicks in my movies; she'd probably do this slow back and forth thing like she's doing right now. I can just see her throwing her head back and calling out my name.

She puts her hands on my stomach and grinds into me a little. The look on her face is really lustful — and really hot. I can feel myself getting turned on, but before I get too hard, she stops and giggles at me.

"I can't believe I did that," she says, leaning all the way forward against my chest.

"It's no big deal. Just one best friend pretending to ride another best friend's dick," I joke.

She blushes, and she presses her forehead to my chest, hiding her face as she giggles.

I rub her back a few times and let my fingers brush through her hair. It's so long, almost down to her ass, and it's all soft and silky. She hates her hair — like I said, girls hate everything about themselves sometimes — but I think it's really pretty. It's all big and wavy, but she flat irons it a lot because everyone else has flat hair and she says hers looks eighties by comparison. If it was eighties, which it's not, it would be more Kelly LeBrock than Kelly Bundy. Classy hot.

"Will you come visit me next year? I know I'll be all the way across the country and it'll be a pain in the ass, but will you?" she sweetly asks as she rises up, putting one hand on either side of my shoulders.

"Probably." I shrug. "It might be nice to get a change of scenery, get away from our parents and all this shit here."

"I think so too," she says, nodding. "I'll be on my own, which means I'll probably miss you a million times more, and it'll be so fun if you come to campus and hang out with me."

"Okay, then that's what I'll do. I mean, I only work, like, nine days a month, so I've got time."

"Will you do it soon, like, right when I move into the dorms?" she eagerly asks.

I see an opportunity, and I can't let it slip. "I don't know," I say, grinning. "That means I gotta book a flight pretty soon, I'll have to fly for all those hours, and there's check-in and those long-ass security lines. What's in it for me?"

"My company," she says, countering with a sly smile of her own. "And, you know, maybe some more of this," she adds, looking down at her body pressed against me.

I chuckle, and I'm surprised when she sits up again and starts swiveling her hips in that sensual way that's so hot.

"You mean you wouldn't want to fuck around and do shit like this with me anymore?" she says, switching into that sexy Lola that I've only recently discovered below the surface of her sweetheart exterior. "I thought you liked being close to me like this. I like being close to you."

I make an exaggerated growling sound, and I grab her hips and roll her over in one fast motion so I'm on top of her, pinning her to the bed with my pelvis.

"I like being close to you," I say with a smart-ass smile. "Can't you tell?" I rock up against her a few times.

"Jesus! It feels like a fucking tree branch!" she says with wide eyes.

I can't be seductive if I'm laughing, and that totally makes me laugh, so I flop down on her and snicker.

She wraps her arms and legs around me like she's hugging me with her whole body. It doesn't feel sexual anymore; it just feels sweet. She's holding me against her because she likes the feel of me against her, not because she wants to fuck me. In fact, I'm guessing she'd never really fuck me. This is all just a bit of fun for her. She always tells me how she's "totally not sexy" and how she can't be "so seductive like that" with guys, so I think this is her little way to experiment with it. It's her outlet to try being a hot, irresistible siren for a change. She could seduce the fuck out of me any day of the week, but she has no idea that she could have that effect on all men.

"Do you think we should risk you staying in here tonight?" she whispers to me when I push up on my elbows. "I just really don't want you to go. It's your last night here, and I want to stay like this with you."

"What about Theresa?" I ask her.

"I'll set my clock for earlier so we can wake up first," she offers.

She's so cute, and her request is innocent and sweet. I run my nose along hers, and I get that feeling in the pit of my stomach that makes me want to kiss her, even though I know I can't. It's not that I want to shove my tongue down her throat or anything like that. I just want to kiss her lips a few times, just something soft and tender that reflects how I feel about her. She's my little treasure, and she makes me want to be gentle and loving with her.

"Okay." I nod to her after I look in her eyes for a few seconds. "I'll stay here."

"Yay!" She smiles, making sure to keep her happiness quiet.

I scoot down her body so I can lay my head low on her chest. I can hear her heartbeat, and it's a very relaxing sound. She puts her arms around me, and she plays with my hair for a second or two. I have to bend my knees so I can still fit on the bed, but I like being on her like this. It doesn't make me feel horny; it makes me feel warm and loved.

"Lo, you've been the greatest to me during all this bullshit with my parents. I'll never forget that, baby. It means the world to me," I whisper to her.

"I'd do it again a thousand times, James. It makes me feel good to know that I can comfort you and help you out in your time of need," she softly answers. "You're always there for me, always having my back whenever shit goes down, and I was glad I got the chance to do it for you and show you that I feel the same way about you as you do about me."

I wonder if she feels exactly the same as I do. I've thought about fucking her a lot these past few days, and I'm seriously doubting that she feels that way too. Sure, we've fucked around and done little sexy shit with each other, but I've pictured some pretty lewd stuff, and even though she was pretending to be a little vixen just now, I don't think she could even imagine the kind of shit that I've thought about doing with her.

I kiss her stomach at the bottom of her ribcage and roll off her, ushering her to come into my arms. She does, and I stroke her back as she rests her head on my chest.

"We're always gonna have this, aren't we, Lo?" I say, smiling to myself. "We're always gonna be how we are, the way we care about each other so much and stuff."

"Yep." She nods, and I hear her little giggle.

I kiss her forehead, and then it's time for both of us to get some sleep.

Morning comes way too soon for me because I know it means I have to leave. It's early sunrise with that orange light coming in like it was the night after Lola's prom. I'm holding her in my arms, and I never imagined I could like being close to somebody this much.

She's still asleep, and she looks like an angel. Her long eyelashes are resting on her cheeks, and her lips look all full and soft. Her hair is fanned out over the pillow in this way that would take hours to stage if this was a photo shoot.

There are still a few minutes before her alarm goes off, so I decide to wake her up so I can sneak back to the guest room and we can pretend that this whole sleeping-in-bed-together thing never happened once Theresa wakes up. I run my fingers really lightly up and down her arm, just barely touching her. She's warm and smooth. Beautiful. After that, I brush her hair behind her ear and rub my thumb across her lips.

At that point, something comes over me, and I lose control for a second. I roll forward just a little, and I touch my lips to hers, but very, very softly so she won't know I did it if she really is still asleep. This doesn't count as a kiss; it's only a little peck after all, but I can feel my heart flutter in my chest for the brief instant when my lips touch hers. I don't know what it means. I've never had that happen before. Usually my heart only starts pumping when I'm making out with a girl and well on my way to getting in her pants, but I know that's not what I want from Lola right now. These feelings confuse me.

She stirs a little, and I kiss her cheeks and her forehead. She stretches and slowly opens her eyes before giving me a big smile as she reaches up to me and touches her little palm to my cheek. I kiss the inside of her wrist and give her a wink, which makes her giggle.

It's such a heavenly sound—I swear to God, I think an angel just got its wings or something. She's so cute and sweet and pure, and I find her outrageously beautiful right now.

"Good morning, Lo," I whisper to her.

"Good morning, James."

She smiles as she brushes my hair back, and I run my hand down her arm. I swear, I can feel her pulling me closer, and pretty soon, I'm leaning over her with part of my body pressed on top of her and the other half down on the bed.

Somehow—and I don't know how I let it happen—I end up kissing her neck. She smells nice, and her skin is warm and smooth. She extends her neck a little and lets me keep going, which surprises me. This shit is rolling on, and there's nothing I can do about it.

An instant later and I'm on top of her, kissing up and down the side of her throat while she bends her neck back and her legs come up at my sides.

"Mmm," I hear her breathe as she tangles her fingers into my hair in this perfectly aggressive but adorable way.

My hand slides up under her T-shirt, but this time she doesn't stop me. I feel the curve of her boob, and soon my fingertips make a little circle around her nipple. She moans. She fuckin' moans! It's amazingly hot, a really pretty, feminine sound, and I'm beyond psyched that she likes this.

I keep kissing her neck, and I feel her hips rock just a tiny bit, so I decide to move my hand down her body, and I feel her little stomach tremble when I slide it into her shorts. Her eyes are all sleepy, but I don't think it's from being tired. It's that relaxed, super-turned-on look that I love to see on a girl's face.

I just barely graze between her legs when the alarm goes off, turning on the local top-forty radio station.

"Shit," she exhales and flops back on the bed.

"I hate that fuckin' clock!" I sigh, which makes her giggle.

I'm bummed that I have to take my hand out of her shorts when I was so close being able to touch her there, but I know that I should. I sit up on the bed and look down at her on her pillow. She's all hot and bothered. I can tell from the way her nipples are poking into her shirt. Her chest is moving up and down a little faster, too, and her lips are parted as she breathes. If only I had, like, three more minutes, the pleasures I could show this girl!

I swallow hard and stand up from the bed. She giggles when she can see the obvious effect she's had on me.

"Totally your fault," I whisper with a smirk.

"Sorry 'bout it!" she says in a playfully mocking tone.

I give her a wink, and then I slip out the door and back to the guest room, totally undetected by Theresa. The covert operation was a success, and I got to hold my little angel all night without starting some huge shitstorm at her house.

I'm out at my car with my keys in my hand. I have to leave. I have to leave Lola and go back to California, even though it's going to damn near kill me to say goodbye to her.

"I'm sad that you're going," she admits with tender honesty.

"I'm sad too," I reply.

"I miss you all the time, James," she says, her voice trembling just a little bit.

I swallow hard. If she's going to cry, I'm going to have a breakdown. I can't handle it when Lola cries. When we were kids, her gerbil died and she started bawling. I had to be about eleven, but I remember giving her a big hug and crying too. It killed me to see her sad, and it was like I could feel her emotions myself. Jonathan, of course, called me a wuss and said it was just a gerbil and that me and Lola were total babies.

"It's okay, Lo," I whisper to her, holding her in my arms. She's up on the curb, and I'm on the street, which gives her a few more inches, but she still feels tiny against me.

"Please promise me you'll visit," she says through sniffles.

"Of course I will," I say.

I hold her head in my hands and wipe the tears off her cheeks with my thumbs. I can feel my throat tightening. I concentrate really hard on not crying.

"Don't cry, Lo," I whisper to her. "You're gonna make me cry, and then we'll both be a fuckin' mess."

She sniffles and gives me a little smile. There, that's what I wanted. No more tears.

"I'll be out there to see you before there's even snow on the ground. Give me, like, six months and I'll be knocking on the door of your dorm room begging you to let me cuddle with you again," I say optimistically.

"You can always cuddle with me, James," she whispers to me in a way that was intended to be sweet, but instead comes off as super sexy.

"All right, kid—" I smile at her "—I gotta go."

I take a look back at the house to see if Theresa is watching this borderline tearful goodbye, but she's not peeking out the window anymore, so I give Lola a sneaky peck on the lips, and she gives me a naughty smile. This sexual chemistry we've been having is like a little secret just for us. Shit, it was a secret *to* us a few days ago!

I get in the car and head out of my old neighborhood. With my parents hating me and Lola going off to college, I don't know that I'll be around here again anytime soon, so it's kind of surreal to be leaving town for what may very well be the last time. Sure, Keegan and Joey are here, but those dudes are already chomping at the bit to come visit me so they can get onto the set and meet some porn stars. It'll be a rude awakening for them when they see how boring and not-at-all sexy those shoots can be, but I'm guessing Keegan's reactions will be a crack-up.

I hit the highway and concentrate on the future. I've got a shoot with Lexi Jaxxxon in a couple weeks, and she's way sexy, so that should be kind of hot. Rick said he's thinking about hooking me up with a line of sex toys that will be molded from my anatomy. That kind of shit is normally reserved for the very small number of guys who are huge stars, but I've been generating a pretty major buzz and Rick says I'm doing really well with the female market, so it could be a big moneymaker. Then, of course, there's Lola. I'm going to plan a trip out there to visit her as soon as I get back to my apartment. I'm thinking October, after she's started classes and gotten settled into college life.

Thinking about her makes me miss her already. My little angel. My best friend. I have a real bond with that girl, and sometimes I feel like I just need to be around her, like I have to do it to survive. The next six months without her will suck, but it'll only make it sweeter when I see her again.

I crank up the stereo and pull onto the interstate for the long-ass drive back to SoCal.

Chapter 12

Lola

Soft kisses up and down my neck. The weight of his muscular body pins me down against the bed, his excitement very evident from the firmness pressing into me. His hands drift up and down my body, seemingly everywhere at once. My heart races and my pulse jumps when his lips close over mine, claiming my mouth in a passionate kiss. I realize that I'm no longer wearing my pajamas, and my bare skin curves into his. He's warm — more than warm. He's hot to the touch, melting me with overpowering sexuality.

"I want you," he whispers to me as his hand reaches down to tease my nipple.

I only answer with a moan, my neck arching back, allowing him to kiss the side of my throat.

He smiles when he slips his fingers under the covers and between my legs. "You're wet for me," he says with a hooded, lustful gaze. "You want me too."

"James," I breathe as he rubs and teases me.

My body is on fire, burning white hot from just the feel of his fingertips against my sensitive flesh.

His hazel-green eyes sparkle with delight as he gazes down at me. "Do you want me inside you, Lola?" he asks, a devilish grin spreading over his lips.

I close my eyes, not able to come to terms with my answer.

"Tell me, Lola," he softly commands. "Say it out loud."

"I can't," I reply in a nearly inaudible whisper.

"Yes, you can," he assures me. "You can't deny it, not anymore. Just look in my eyes and say it to me. Tell me what you want."

I take a deep breath, forcing myself to look up at him. "You, James," I reply. "I want you."

"See?" His smile grows even warmer. "That wasn't so hard, was it?"

I shake my head, and he gives me a soft kiss, which puts me at ease.

"Be with me, Lo," he says in a half-plea. "Let me show you how good I can make you feel."

I concede with a nod of my head, and then I feel him easing into me. I can barely hear over the beating of my heart as he fills me. God, it feels so good. His hips move slowly at first, but he starts to pick up the pace, and I start to moan his name, which spurs him on.

"You want me this way," he says into my neck. "You want to be mine, and you want me to be yours."

"It's not like that," I reply, trying to fight off the longing I feel for him. "It's only attraction. It'll go away. It's not real."

"I don't think so," he says with a teasing grin.

"I can't let myself get emotionally wrapped up in you this way." I shake my head, wishing I could stop the swirl of feelings that are making me dizzy.

"But you *are* emotionally wrapped up in me." He smiles, continuing his gentle but persistent thrusts. "You know it's more than attraction. You know it's deeper than that. Stop running from it."

"James, we shouldn't—" I gasp in protest, but my objection is cut short when I feel a strong, very pleasurable ache flaring up from low in my core.

"See how good it could be?" he whispers as the sensation builds.

I moan louder, and I know something is about to happen—something I'll thoroughly enjoy. He's going to get me there. I've never been *there*, and I have no idea what *there* feels like, but I know with every fiber of my being that he could take me there. I can feel the sensation building up, and I'm holding my breath as I eagerly await its glorious arrival.

Somewhere in the distance, I hear Christina Aguilera's "Ain't No Other Man" playing. It gets louder and louder like an approaching ambulance.

"Where's that coming from?" I ask James as I look around the room. He doesn't respond, just gives me a little wink.

A second later, I open my eyes to find that I'm alone in my bedroom with a light sheen of sweat on my skin and a surging heartbeat. Christina is belting out her trademark vocal flourishes from my alarm clock, and I'm starting to realize that I just had a vivid sex dream about the very last person I should be fantasizing about.

"What the fuck?" I whisper to myself as I sit up and put my hand to my head. "You have got to be fucking kidding me," I add in a disappointed jab at my own brain. *Stupid neurotransmitters making me think about James that way!*

Needless to say, I am freaked the fuck out. Never in my life have I had a single sex dream about James—Leonardo DiCaprio maybe, but never, ever, ever James. I feel guilty and embarrassed, like Ashton Kutcher will be waiting outside my door to surprise me with news that I've been mentally Punk'd.

Quickly, I get up and rush into the bathroom, trying to shake off the lingering emotion—and horniness—left over from the dream. I brush my teeth with surgical focus and try to clear my mind of James altogether.

What the hell is wrong with me? Why on earth would I even allow myself, subconsciously or not, to let James infiltrate that part of my mind? I wasn't just dreaming about having sex with him; I was dreaming about being with him—in every sense of the word. It's absolutely absurd to even imagine a scenario in which he and I would be some kind of "item" and actually date each other like a regular couple. That seems about as likely as finding Sasquatch riding the Loch Ness Monster in the lost city of Atlantis. Our lives are way too different, so despite how much we care about each other, we could never have *that* kind of relationship.

I'm feeling overwhelmed with confusion, anger at myself, frustration that I can't force the dream out of my memory, and a longing for someone to help me talk this out and figure out how to get over this. Normally, I'd call James and he'd help me sort things out. He's been my sounding board for years, a patient listener who offers me genuinely good advice and always has my best interests at heart. This time, he's the last person I'd want to talk to, since "Hey, how are you? I just had a graphic, ultra-hot sex dream about you" isn't exactly the best way to begin a conversation.

I flip open my phone and try to decide who to call, quickly eliminating half my contacts out of the secretive nature of this conversation. This would be a great time to chat with a girlfriend, but Zoe has had a not-so-secret crush on James for ages and her only advice would be on what position he and I should try first. I need someone sensible, someone who can give me a logical answer and, above all, someone who can keep a secret. Naveen seems to fit the bill quite well, so I call him up and ask him to lunch. He happily agrees, and I pull on some jeans and head out the door.

Naveen greets me with a hug, and we both sit down and place our drink orders.

"How are you, man?" I smile. "All done with finals too?"

"Yep," he says, nodding. "Last one was Thursday. Just getting college stuff together now. How about you? I haven't seen you since prom."

"Yeah, I had a really busy few days." I chuckle at that. *You don't know the half of it!* "James was here, and we hung out, then he had to take off."

"How'd that go?" he says knowingly.

Just then, our waitress comes over and asks us if we're ready to order. Both of us get veggie burgers, and I sip an iced tea before I answer.

"It was good, actually," I continue once she moves out of earshot. "He made my prom night really fun. I had a really great time with him."

"Did you guys hang out at your place or just chill at his place?" he asks, though I still get the impression that this is just a lead-in to the real conversation.

"He planned this little picnic thing for me up in the mountains. It was really sweet." I smile, fondly recalling the evening. "Then we hung out at my house after that. He, um, he slept over."

"Interesting." He grins.

"Oh, please." I snicker. "He used to sleep over at my house all the time. It's no big deal."

"Did you hear about his porn thing?" He's cutting right to the chase.

"How did you know about it?" I say with shock.

"Everybody knows about it," he responds. "I guess somebody found a clip online and then sent it out. Pretty soon everybody was texting me about it asking me if you knew."

Naveen is the editor of our school paper, and he's been my friend since middle school, so people would naturally assume he was in the know about anything in my little James bubble.

"Yeah," I reply in a resigned sigh. "I knew about it."

"How long have you known?"

"Awhile." I shrug. "But I didn't care, and I didn't tell anybody because I knew shit would go down if everyone found out. Man, did it ever."

"What do you mean?"

"His mom and dad found out," I say, my expression grave.

"Oh, shit," Naveen exhales, his eyebrows shooting up.

"Yeah, it was bad. His dad freaked out completely, threw him out of the house, and poor James was a total wreck about it. I wanted to be there for him, so I had him stay with me for a couple days until he was feeling a little better."

"Man, I didn't know all that," Naveen says.

"He was completely devastated. You know how close he was with his mom. He was shaken to the fucking core when she sided with his dad."

"That's so fucked up," he sighs. "I feel bad for him."

"I felt terrible." I hang my head. "That whole night all I wanted to do was hold him and make him feel better."

Naveen looks at me for a moment longer than he should, and I know he's teetering on the edge of saying something, but he's trying to figure out a tactful way to spit it out.

"What?" I ask when I see his hesitation.

"Nothing." He shrugs. "I guess if anybody could comfort him at a time like that, it'd be you."

I narrow my eyes at him, but he starts to smile, and I can't help but smile back.

"You guys have a weird relationship," he says, chuckling. "He's your non-sexual boyfriend."

"Shut up!" I laugh.

"He is!" he continues to tease. "He basically performs all the basic functions of a boyfriend, but without the sex part."

I know I'm blushing, but I try to act nonchalant.

"You guys have this weird love for each other like you're married, but at the same time it's like you're brother and sister."

I crinkle my nose at the comparison, but it's not altogether inaccurate. I'm not entirely certain how to describe my relationship with James — especially now. Just thinking about him at this moment fills my heart with a surge of longing, but it also makes my stomach churn out of fear for what that longing might really mean.

"Something happened," I confess, looking down at the table.

"What?" he eagerly inquires, leaning closer.

"Nothing major, just something," I say, trying to figure out how to tell him about James moderately feeling me up, and how much I loved it.

"You did *not* have sex with James, did you?" he gasps with a big grin on his face. "Don't tell me you succumbed to temptation like every other girl in school."

"No." I shake my head and blush so hard that I must be turning purple. "We just — there was a moment. I feel like something changed for me, and now I'm not really sure what I feel."

"Oh, shit, Lo," he says, leaning back in his chair. "You have a crush on James."

"I do not have a crush on James!" I vehemently insist. "But," I begin a little more timidly, "I have started thinking about him a little differently."

"So are you saying you have feelings for him now — feelings beyond friendship?"

"No," I say, not even sure if it's the truth. "I think I just missed him a lot, and then, after what happened, I started to realize that there's an attraction element at work too."

"What happened?" Naveen asks, narrowing his eyes.

"Hm?" I ask, trying not to acknowledge my new lust for James.

"You said you had a moment, then you said 'after what happened', and I want to know *what* happened. Clearly something went down if you're suddenly finding yourself all jumbled up like this," he continues, his journalistic instincts telling him to pursue the answer.

"There was just a little incident — nothing significant. He came on to me a little bit," I shyly confess. "At the time, I pulled the plug on the whole endeavor, but I'm wondering if that was the right decision."

If Naveen were James, I'd be spilling all the dirty details. James always wants to know every single aspect of any of my sexual encounters—which have been few and far between. I think it's because he shares detailed histories of all his sexual conquests with me, and he likes when I can throw a story or two in there too, despite his utter distaste for any of my ventures into the sexual wilderness. If James had been the one I was confiding in right now, I would have spilled it all—the kisses on the neck, the touching, the way my heart fluttered in my chest when he moved his big body on top of me, the way my body kept telling me to let him roll with it, even as my brain told me to shut it all down.

"So you had a window, you closed it, and now you're wondering if you should have?" Naveen smiles, and I can see him trying to analyze this in his head.

"Yeah, kind of," I say, shrugging one shoulder. "I've just never really thought about him like that, so my first impulse was to steer him away from that direction, but then I started to wonder if maybe *I* wanted to go down that path with him."

Our waitress brings our burgers, and we both take a bite before he replies.

"I've always thought James was a good dude," he says, "and he's always treated you better than any of the girls he hangs out with, but I think you really need to weigh whether that's what you want. No disrespect to him—because you know I like him a lot—but he has a rep. With the porn thing, that rep has increased to supermarket tabloid level. Just from a PR standpoint, I'd tell you not to even attempt it."

I laugh lightly at his sudden turn from buddy to publicist.

"You're not tarnished by rumors and gossip, but he is. Let's say you guys do hook up and that he really does become your boyfriend, then all that shit would reflect back on you. There are girls right now who are denying they ever slept with him—girls people literally watched him have sex with—and they're trying to act like they never touched him because they know he's a porn star now. It's different from when he was just the school's reigning manwhore—"

I laugh loudly, and Naveen gives me a smile. It really is the perfect way to describe James; I'm not going to lie. If he was a woman, they'd call him a skank, a slut, a whore, a nympho, but because he's a guy everyone applauds him for his hypersexual behavior.

"The whole point is, when he used to sleep with all those girls before, it was a behind-closed-doors kind of thing, even when it was out in the open at parties and stuff. It was a smaller circle, and only people who were there saw it firsthand. Now he's all over the Internet doing videos with all these different girls, everyone's seen it, and he's gone from *rumored* slut to *legit* slut."

I breathe a resigned sigh. "You have a point."

"Personally, I think you should try to put a little distance between you and him. A lot of rumors are going to be swirling, and you don't want this to somehow follow you all the way to college. What if you meet really cool people there and they're freaked out that you're best buddies with a porn star? And imagine how much worse that would be if you were dating him!"

"I'm not that bothered by what people might say. Nobody's opinion will threaten my friendship with him...but I see your point."

"Honestly, Lola," Naveen says, "think about everything you have ahead of you. Do you even know what percentage of kids who apply to that school even get in? Hardly any!"

I feel a little surge of pride and nod my head as he continues.

"Your life hasn't even really taken off yet, and you'd want to get tied down with a guy you've known since elementary school?" he asks. "Think about the cool people you're going to meet — smart people who will graduate and get killer jobs doing amazing things instead of making Internet porn."

"You're right," I quietly answer, feeling a little dismayed. "I think I just got hung up on him because he was here and the whole flirtation thing was new for us. It messed with my usual flow. I *should* be focusing on college and moving forward with my life — but I absolutely will not leave him behind. He's a part of my life, no matter what capacity that may be, and I'm not going to cut him out just because people might judge me for his career."

"I think that's very admirable of you." He smiles and gives me an approving nod. "That's one of your best qualities, Lo: your loyalty. If you care about someone, you have their back, and that's not something that can be said about a lot of people our age. You're a good friend — to everyone, not just to James."

"Thanks," I proudly reply.

"So be his friend, be proud of him and all that, but don't try to turn him into your boyfriend. We've both seen that he doesn't do particularly well in that role, and there's no reason to try to change him when you already like him the way he is."

It's true. James has never been very good at playing the part of the doting boyfriend. He's "dated" lots of girls, but that usually just means he slept with them, wanting nothing beyond sexual companionship. I've watched several of them try to *transform* him into a faithful boyfriend, but it always ends in disaster. Once, during spring break, he had sex with a random girl in his pseudo-girlfriend's hotel room when she suddenly walked in and caught them in the act. According to legend, he told her to join in. The whole time, she thought she was a big shot for taming *The* James Laird, ultimate player. It was only when she saw them going at it that she realized her definition of boyfriend was a lot different from his.

"You've got a point," I concede. "He's awesome as a friend. He means the world to me, and he's like family. I know he sucks at relationships because he can't keep his dick in his pants, so I definitely need to drop this whole thing and focus on what's ahead of me."

"Exactly!" he says. "You guys are always going to be close, that's a given with all your history together, but you can be close as *friends*."

"True," I say, smiling.

"See? Problem solved." He chuckles and tips his glass to me before taking a sip.

We chat about school and summer plans as we chow down on our meals. Naveen's whole family is going on a lengthy trip through Europe to celebrate his graduation and acceptance to NYU, and he's completely psyched about it. I can't blame him. It sounds amazing. My summer will be a lot more low-key. I'll be here, probably working some kind of summer job to save up a little cash, then packing up and starting life anew across the country. Of course, there's always the possibility of a visit from James once I'm all settled in, but I don't want to think about that because it conjures up images of us cuddling in a dorm bed and me surrendering to the immense temptation of having him pressed against my body.

I feel a lot better about the situation by the time Naveen and I part ways. I need to let go of all this James stuff and focus on the potentially bright future in front of me. I assure myself that I will do just that as I get back into my car and pull out of the parking lot.

Chapter 13

James

"How could you?"

"You're a fuckup; you always have been."

"I just can't believe you'd do something like this."

"As far as we're concerned, our youngest son is dead."

I gasp for air as I jolt awake, those hurtful words still echoing in my brain. I've probably only slept about five hours in the past three days. Every time I close my eyes, I see my mom's disappointed face, the vein in my dad's forehead bulging with rage, the pattern on the kitchen floor tile blurred through my tears, the ornate metal on the screen door as I stood on the porch feeling the impact of my parents' rejection. I'd hoped it would stop hurting by now, but that dull ache is always there in my heart. I fucked up big time, but there's nothing I can do about it. We're way past the point of reconciliation, and I'm trying to get used to knowing that my parents will never talk to me again.

As if that wasn't depressing enough, I miss Lola. I miss her a lot. I didn't feel this bad when I was with her—when I listened to her breathing after she fell asleep next to me, when she held my face in her hands and whispered comforting words to me…when her nipples firmed up as I kissed the side of her neck. She smelled so good. Her skin was so smooth. Her ass was so firm. She was panting a little bit through those full, pouty, kissable lips. She wanted me. Her body couldn't lie. No matter what she said, there was no denying that she wanted me in that moment. *Fuck!* I wanted her too — so fuckin' bad! If just her words made me feel so much better, imagine what her body could do.

I get that restless, antsy, agitated feeling again, the one that makes me feel like I need to burn off some of this nervous energy. I hate being jittery, and I need to mellow out, but my options are limited. Last night I tried jerking off, but that wasn't cutting it. I need more. Aside from a lengthy, emotional conversation with Lola, there's only one thing that can cure this condition.

I reach over the photo of Lola that I moved from the dresser because I wanted her closer to me and pick up my phone from the nightstand. I scroll through my contacts until I find the one I'm looking for.

Tara Morgan has been flirting with me pretty hard since we did our shoot a few weeks ago. Sometimes she'll leave me dirty voice mails or text me naked pictures of herself, but most of the time it's just a little sexting. She wants it bad. I know she's down for a non-work, recreational fuck — she told me almost exactly that after the shoot — so she's looking like a pretty good option right about now. I type out to her:

Hey, you up?

A few seconds later, my phone chimes.

I could be...

Wanna come over?

Is this a booty call?

Maybe ;)

I'll be there in 20.

I get up out of bed and stretch, not even bothering to get dressed, aside from a pair of boxer briefs. No point in putting clothes on if I'm just going to be taking them off when she gets here. I can feel myself start swelling with anticipation as I go into the living room to wait for her.

It's really quiet in here, and I don't like it. The last thing I need right now is to be alone with my thoughts, but my mind keeps splicing together this unsettling montage of everything that happened. I hear my dad calling me a failure, but that's accompanied by a visual of Lola's long legs. *I'm a disgrace*—the little beauty marks on her back that I got to look at when I zipped up her prom dress. *I'm a disappointment*—the feel of her thighs pressed up against my body when I was kissing her neck. *I'm an embarrassment*—the dampness between her legs when I was so close to fingering her. This whole mash-up is really freaking me out. I'm so disgusted with myself over how bad I hurt my family, but it makes me feel even worse to be thinking of Lola as a sexual object. She's not. She's special. She's not just some girl you screw. She's a girl you fall in love with. *Ugh, love.* That opens up a whole new can of worms, and I'm definitely not ready to deal with that shit right now.

I'm grateful when there's finally a knock on the door, and I open it to see Tara in one of those pink tracksuits with *Juicy* written across the butt. She's got on flip-flops with it, but her blond hair is curled and she's got a lot of makeup on, so clearly she got dolled up before she came here, even though she's trying to act like this is how she looks when she hops out of bed. Her beauty isn't of the natural variety, like Lola's, but I don't really give a shit about that right now. She's a girl and she's here. That's about all that matters to me at the moment. Any port in a storm, as they say.

She grabs me and kisses me, her mouth crushing mine. I wrap my arms around her and kiss her back, lifting her up and carrying her into the apartment. We're just inside the living room when she pulls back from the kiss and unzips her jacket. She's got nothing on underneath, and she pushes her silicone-enhanced boobs together and licks her lips at me.

In response, I lean down and take her nipple in my mouth. Her moan is a little exaggerated—*we're not on the goddamn set, Tara*—but I know it feels good, so I move on to the other one, teasing and nipping at it.

"I wanna suck your cock," she exhales in a horny, husky whisper.

I move back and lean against the couch, my hands resting against it near my hips. She steps over to me and drops to her knees, sliding my underwear down and focusing her eyes on my cock. She pumps me with her fist a few times, then closes her mouth around the head of my dick and starts slurping me down her throat. Tara is known for her blowjobs—she's got awards and everything—and the girl can deep throat like a champ. Because of my size, a lot of girls can't really do this with me, so they'll fake it on camera by using their hands as they suck me, but Tara's one of the rare ones that can take me all the way until her forehead bumps into my stomach. She keeps me there until she has to pull back and draw in a gasp of air. There's always this level of desperate enthusiasm to her blowjobs, and it makes them feel fuckin' unreal, like she's trying to defuse a bomb and the only way to do it is to make me come as quickly as possible.

"I'm gonna come in your mouth," I breathe as I push her hair into a ponytail and use it to direct her back and forth.

"Mmm, give it to me!" she says, her eyes flashing up to me before she takes me deep again.

My hips start pumping back and forth, driving my cock in and out of her mouth faster with each stroke. She moans and the vibration from her voice pushes me over the edge. I come hard, my pent up frustration making me spurt down her throat in thick bursts. She greedily swallows down every drop like she can't bear to see it go to waste. That's the kind of cock-hungry shit that made her famous. The girl acts like she'll go crazy if she doesn't get a dick inside her, and it makes for some pretty fuckin' wild shoots.

"Go to the bedroom," I exhale, my voice coming out gravely and rough.

She happily stands up and slides her pants down her legs before walking toward the bedroom. Like most porn stars, she has no tan lines, and she's purposely swaying her hips a little to make me focus on the wiggle of her ass as I walk in behind her.

"On the bed," I instruct, "on your back with your legs spread."

I'm not that bossy with girls usually—they always seem to do what I want without me having to ask them to—but I can get a little domineering in scenes and that carries over into my off-the-clock sex with co-stars. Tara's into this too, so I know I can run with it tonight.

"Touch yourself," I softly order when she lies down with her head on the pillow.

She happily complies, one hand teasing her nipples while the other rubs down below.

"Put your fingers inside," I say, directing her like I'm behind the camera on one of our shoots. "Now lick them off. How does it taste, baby?"

"Mmm, it tastes like I need to get fucked," she replies, sliding her tongue up and down her fingers. "I want you, James. I want to feel that big cock in my tight little pussy."

This is so porno. If there were a few lighting dudes and some cameras, you could just assume this was a line from one of our movies. Tara likes talking dirty in her scenes, and I'll admit that it's a turn-on. She gets really lewd and starts moaning all these filthy things. It kind of makes you feel like you're fucking the modesty right out of her.

I start stroking myself as I watch her moaning and writhing on the bed, her fingers working faster and her legs spreading even wider than before. She's putting on a show for me, and I'm into it. Now this is definitely the kind of distraction I was looking for.

"Please," she whines, opening her eyes to look at me. "I want your cock so bad, James. Please give it to me."

I step over to her and grab her hips, flipping her over onto her stomach. She pushes up until she's on her hands and knees, and I move behind her. The noise she makes when I thrust inside her is like a combination of a moan and a gasp—but if those two things were performed by an overacting soap opera star. I grab her hips and really fuckin' give her the business. Sweat is starting to drip down my forehead as I pant, and the sound of skin slapping against skin fills the room, drowned out only by her loud moaning.

"Yes!" she practically screams. "Fuck me hard! Oh, God! I want it! Give it to me!"

I keep going, tuning out her whole production when I glance over at Lola's picture on the nightstand and feel a huge wave of shame.

"This isn't going to solve anything," I hear her voice say.

Be quiet, Lola. I'm trying to concentrate.

"This isn't going to make anything better."

Shut up! You shouldn't even be in my head right now!

"You think sex is the solution because you always use sex to feel better when something bad happens."

You're right, okay? Now zip it and let me fuck this girl!

I manage to mute my Lola-voiced conscience and refocus on the moment. Tara is panting and gasping, and I can tell she's about to come, so I reach around her and rub her clit. She goes off immediately, and I can feel her squeezing me from the inside.

I grab her ass and kick it into high gear, driving into her hard and fast. Sliding my hand inward, my thumb traces a circle around her rear entrance before I push inside just a little bit, shallowly pumping in and out. That does the trick again, and she screams a loud string of obscenities that sounds like "oh-fuck-that-feels-so-fucking-good-fuck-me-harder-oh-fuck-yes!" as I continue.

I'm used to video shoots, and I can hold off coming for hours on the set, but I feel like I should start to wrap this up. With this kind of emotionless sex, it's more about concentrating *on* coming than concentrating on *not* coming, so I close my eyes and focus on how it feels when Tara squeezes and milks me from the inside. For a brief instant, Lola pops into my mind, but I quickly shut her out and open my eyes again, deciding to watch the way Tara's ass moves as I fuck her.

"Come in me, James!" Tara nearly wails. "Fill that pussy up with come! I want it so bad! I want to feel your hot come dripping out of me!"

Classic Tara Morgan dirty talk. But it's effective. The filthier she gets, the more it makes me feel far away from the sweetness of being around Lola and all the emotional confusion that goes with it. It's not such a bad thing, really. Lola's too good for me anyway. A girl like Tara is more my style, and maybe doing this will help me prove it to myself.

I shut my eyes tight and let loose, giving her just what she asked for. As soon as I've stopped coming, I pull out and give her a little smack on the butt, which makes her giggle. It's cute, but not as cute as the way Lola giggles when she's being shy and adorable.

"Come on," I say, nodding to the bathroom, "let's get cleaned up."

"Can I stay over?" she says, rising from the bed and throwing her arms up over my shoulders. "I might wake up in the middle of the night in the mood to suck your cock."

"Well, in that case…" I chuckle.

She laughs and then follows me into the bathroom. After a quickie in the shower, we're both cleaned up, and she crawls into my bed. I try to cuddle with her in the hopes that it'll make me feel calm and relaxed the way cuddling with Lola did, but something about it feels off. My annoying conscience chooses this moment to creep up and tell me that I've made a huge mistake, that I'm repeating the same bad choices I always make, that I'm using Tara to make myself feel better, that I'm running from my problems instead of facing them—all the painfully true stuff I try to keep out of my mind.

I don't wake up until nearly noon the next day, mostly because Tara woke me up twice during the night to blow me and ride my dick. I'm still feeling tired as I shuffle into the kitchen and start making some food. Even though it's late, I decide to cook us breakfast. The girl let me come in virtually every orifice, so the least I could do is make her some fuckin' eggs.

Everything is almost done, so I go back into the bedroom to wake her up and tell her to grab a plate. I stand in the doorway and look at her sleeping in my bed for a moment or two. She's pretty, but her skin is too orange, her hair is too blond, her tits are too big and they stick up on her chest as she lies on her back. They're not like Lola's tits, which were soft and pliable in my hands. Unfortunately, this comparison makes me feel like a total dick. I shouldn't be dissing Tara for not being Lola. Nobody is Lola. Nobody is even in the same galaxy as Lola. Tara's hot, she likes to fuck, she spent hours fucking me, and I should be psyched about that. A guy like Joey would cut off his own foot *Saw*-style just to be me right now.

I sigh with lingering regret as I go over to her and gently wake her up, brushing my fingers over her shoulder. She greets me with a too-white smile and eyes smudged from old makeup. She's not ugly; she's just not the girl I wish I was waking up to in the morning. I tell her breakfast is ready, and she throws on one of my T-shirts and follows me to the table.

"Wow! This is delicious," she says with surprise when takes a bite of her scrambled eggs—which I mostly made because they're easy and fast. *Kind of like her.*

"Thanks," I reply. "I like to make them with Swiss cheese from that gourmet market nearby and then add some basil, this assorted pepper that they have there, and a few veggies if I have them."

"I didn't know you could cook," she says, enjoying another bite.

"It's just something I like to do." I shrug. "I don't really study it or anything, just kind of a hobby, I guess."

"I can't cook for shit," she says, chuckling. "Boiling water is a lot to ask from me."

I laugh lightly and stand to get more coffee.

"So did you ever do that trip to see your parents and stuff?" she asks. "I wanted to book you for something the other day, but they said you were out of town."

"Yeah," I respond in a low, more somber voice, "I went out there, but it didn't go well. They found out about the movies, and they completely flipped out. My dad went fuckin' ape shit, my mom cried; it was a fuckin' disaster."

"That sucks," she says with an exaggerated pout. "I don't know why they'd get all pissed off about it."

"I don't think this was high on the list of careers they'd want their son to have." I chuckle, but thinking about all this is eating away at me inside.

"Who cares?" She shrugs. "My mom said I was a whore when I first started, and I was just like, 'Yeah, Mom, I am a whore! Fuck you!'"

I really have no response to that, so I just take a sip of coffee.

"People want to hate on us, but it's just because they're jealous," she continues. "We're hot, we make a lot of money, and we party. Everyone wishes they could be us."

Sure, Joey and Keegan might act like they wish they had my job sometimes, but I seriously doubt they'd *actually* be into all the stigma that comes with being a porn star. Keegan's a fuckin' country club kid, for fuck's sake, so his family would probably be even more embarrassed than mine. That's the part you don't really think about when you're just starting out in this business. You know it's inevitable that someone from your past will find out eventually, but you just assume it'll be way down the road and you won't care by then.

"The whole thing was really fucked up," I sigh. "At first, it was awesome. I got to hang out with my friends. I got to spend time with Lola—I'd fuckin' missed her like crazy. Then it all sort of went up in flames."

"Lola's that high school girl, right?" she says just a little bit flippantly.

"She's graduating tomorrow," I say, incredibly regretful that I won't be in the stands watching her in her cap and gown.

"She's the one who was your neighbor or whatever?"

"Yeah, she lived next door. We hung out pretty much every day of our lives from elementary school through high school," I explain, feeling kind of happy to be talking about Lola and not my parents.

I don't think Tara really has the capacity to understand how fuckin' hurt I am by what went down with my mom and dad.

"So she's like your girlfriend or something?" She rolls her eyes.

"No." I shake my head. "Best friend."

"Hmm," Tara says, looking at me suspiciously.

"What?" I chuckle.

"Are you guys fuck buddies, friends with benefits?" she pushes.

"No, it's never been like that."

"Is she a lesbian?"

I laugh loudly at that. "You're saying that she'd have to be a lesbian to not fuck me?"

"Yes," she says, and I'm not sure if she's joking.

"Well, she's not a lesbian. She's just one of the rare women who's not susceptible to all this," I joke, flexing my bicep.

"Mmm." Tara smiles seductively. "That just means there's more for me."

A few seconds later, she's on her knees under the kitchen table sucking me off. I let my mind go blank, focusing only on the sensation. It's harder this time because I can't stop thinking about what happened and about how much I wish Lola was with me instead of Tara. Not wishing that she was blowing me or anything, just sitting on my couch talking to me and making me feel like I'm not worthless.

I fuck Tara twice before she says she has to go get her nails done. The second I close the door, I feel like shit. Lola was right. That little foray didn't make me feel any better, and I'll still be stuck in this shitstorm regardless of how many times I come. The worst part is, I know I'll totally do it again.

Chapter 14

Lola

The sun is beating down on me as I sit on the football field listening to our principal address my fellow graduates. The cap shields me a little, but this black gown makes me feel like I'm baking in an oven bag. My classmates surround me, equally hot but all very enthused about this culmination of our high school years.

I take a glance into the stands at the proud faces of friends and family members. Naveen's parents are sitting together with his older brother, who is getting an engineering degree at the university. Zoe's mom and dad are there in hippie attire, complete with dreadlocks, tie-dye clothing, and Birkenstocks. My friend Jacob's parents are sitting there with his grandpa and grandma, his aunt, and his younger cousin. My eyes finally reach my family, and I see my mom's wide smile as she looks over at me. She's seated next to her brother, Pauly Coletti, and his wife, Diana. Beside them are my two younger cousins, Frankie and Mike, a.k.a. Little Mikey. To my mom's other side is my Nana Lucia. One row down from them, seated alone and looking down at his BlackBerry is my father, the eternally indifferent Kevin Caraway. I was a little surprised he even showed up, considering he's missed pretty much every other significant moment in my life. Notably missing from the picture are my stepmom, Nikki, and my half-brother, Zach.

My mom is forcing me to have a meal with my dad after graduation, likely in an effort to make us spend time together even though we're not exactly buddies. I'm completely dreading it. Last time I had dinner with my dad, he kept taking phone calls and making fun of me for my opposition to pork—a belief I've held since I saw *Babe* as a kid. He also managed to get in a few jabs about my appearance, criticizing my general disinterest in fashion and designer labels. I left feeling like I was an ugly, poor, overly sensitive nerd. James came over, and I started crying when I told him about it, but he joked around with me until I was feeling lighter.

That memory makes my heart sink very slightly. James isn't here. He's not out in the stands, not here to cheer me up when my dad tears me down, not here to give me a big hug or applaud for me when they hand me my diploma. The thought makes me miserable. I really miss him—sexual tension or not. He's family to me, and there's a palpable void in his absence.

I zone out through most of the speeches, though I cheer loudly for Naveen when he gives his valedictorian address. Finally, they move on to calling names and handing out diplomas. I'm thankful that my last name comes early in the alphabet because I can go up there and get it over with. I'm not sure why I'm so soured on this whole thing. I love my friends and my family, but I feel very impatient and agitated by everything right now. Maybe I'm mentally preparing myself for the drastic change that will come when I depart for college, trying to get some emotional distance from this part of my life so it won't hurt so much to leave it behind; or maybe I'm just tired of sweating in this gown.

After we're proudly presented as the class of 2006, we toss our caps into the air, and I breathe a sigh of relief. This part is over. Immediately, I unzip my synthetic, non-breathable gown and make my way over to the parents currently swarming onto the field. Many of my friends' parents give me congratulatory hugs and wish me well before I finally get to my family.

Uncle Pauly scoops me up and gives me a huge hug. Aunt Diana is equally enthusiastic as she shamelessly praises me. Even my vaguely obnoxious cousins seem proud, and it makes me feel good. My Nana is crying and not-so-quietly whispering to me that I'm the smartest person in the family, which cracks me up.

"I took so many pictures I think I filled the memory card," my mom says, laughing as she looks down at her camera.

Just then, my dad moseys over a bit sheepishly, probably because everyone here knows he's an asshole, and gives me a very forced hug. I notice that everyone takes a step back, leaving just me and dear old Dad.

"Congratulations, honey. You've got a bright future ahead of you," he says. But it doesn't sound genuine. Instead it's like the trite, clichéd sentence you'd see on the inside of a generic graduation greeting card.

"Thanks, Dad," I say, trying my best not to let my annoyance show. "Where's Nikki?"

"She and Zachy are at home. I didn't want to buy three tickets just for this."

There we go. There's that selfish asshole I'm used to.

"Just for my graduation?" I roll my eyes and can't hold back a scoff.

"Look, I'm here, all right? I think I should get a little credit for that."

"Really? Credit for attending your firstborn child's high school graduation? Someone should get you a medal," I snap.

"Lola, I'm not going to start with you," he sternly replies, effectively cutting off any further discussion.

My mom must see the tense exchange because she comes over and puts her arm around me. "Want to head back to the house and get changed before your dinner with your dad?"

"Yes." I nod, breathing an annoyed sigh as I struggle to let go of my urge to lay into my dad about his many faults.

We part, and my dad asks me to meet him at the restaurant, since I think he can tell Uncle Pauly is about five seconds away from exchanging some heated words with him. My whole family knows what an absentee father he was during my childhood, as if divorce meant severing all ties with that part of his life, and they're all shooting him some serious stink eye. It makes me feel strangely loved and supported.

"You can't just fight with him when you guys go to dinner," my mom says the second we get into the house. "You just have to grin and bear it, sweetheart."

"I wish he hadn't shown up at all," I grumble. "I don't even know why he's here. He hasn't given a shit about me since I was three years old, and now, all of a sudden, he wants to pretend to be a dad."

"He feels like he's supposed to be here." She shrugs, stepping back out onto the porch to grab a cardboard box I didn't notice when I was angrily stomping inside.

She hands it to me, and I see my name in black Sharpie. I recognize the handwriting as James's mom's, and I purse my lips as I decide what to do. I'm so angry at the Lairds right now that I want to smash it to bits, but this isn't my war to fight and Brenda and Jon have always been very kind to me, so it seems wrong to get dramatic.

I open it up to find an Apple box inside with a brand new iPod Nano. There's a note from Brenda inside that says they're proud of me, they wish me the best, a "bright future," a quote from *Oh, the Places You'll Go*, they've always considered me like a daughter to them, blah, blah, blah. As much as I want to be angry, this is really nice of them, and I know they're in a weird spot right now which they're trying to handle as cordially as possible. If they'd given me this gift a few weeks ago, I would have been overjoyed and endlessly grateful. Hell, I'd be on my way over there right now to thank them profusely. I have to put my beef with them aside and accept that they still love me, even if they choose to no longer love James.

"Oh, a nano!" My mom smiles as she peeks into the box. "That'll be great if you're in the library or your dorm."

"Yeah," I say, swallowing my last bit of anger. "It's really cool of them to get me something."

She looks at me knowingly. "I get it, honey," she says, smiling, "but you've got no dog in this fight, and you have to just let it slide."

"I do have a dog in this fight, though," I refute. "They treated him like shit, Mom. They broke him. It wasn't fair, and they never should have reacted that way."

"Lola, you know I love James like he's my son, but you have to understand how they must feel about this," she says quietly as Uncle Pauly slips past her to grab a seat on the couch in the living room.

I feel my brow furrowing with anger, but I don't respond.

"Really, honey, think about it," she continues. "They feel deceived, and nobody likes feeling that way. They think of it as a betrayal, something that will reflect badly on them as parents, like they failed to instill morals in him. Something like this is huge enough for them to overlook all the good qualities he has and write him off. But I'll bet you a hundred bucks they mellow out on it after they cool down. Once everything settles, they'll see that their reaction was a bit extreme."

"I hope so," I reply, though my voice is tinged with skepticism.

The doorbell rings, and I'm praying it's not Jon or Brenda. I'll send them a nice thank-you note, but I don't want to speak to them in person for fear that I'll unleash a tirade about how much they wounded my best friend. I can be very defensive when it comes to people I love, and James falls firmly into that category—perhaps even more so with this attraction weirdness. But all that is too confusing to dwell on.

I walk over to the door to see a FedEx guy standing on the porch. He asks me to sign for a box, and I curiously take it. I've already received graduation gifts from most of my family, and I'm not expecting anything else.

A big smile spreads across my face when I see that it's from James. I literally sigh with longing as I run my fingers over the address.

"Who's that from?" my mom asks, coming up behind me.

"James," I say, beaming.

"Well, what are you waiting for? Open it." She chuckles and motions excitedly to the package.

My jaw drops when I pop the box open. There's a white Apple box inside with a picture of a sleek, white MacBook on the front.

"Shut the fuck up!" I whisper to myself as I take it out. "He got me a Mac!"

"Wow!" my mom gasps.

"It's the new MacBook!" I gleefully continue. "He knows I was going to use my old iBook for school, and he got me a brand new Mac! This is insane!"

"What's with all the shrieking?" Uncle Pauly says as he comes in.

"Lola's best friend bought her a laptop for graduation," my mother fills him in as I stand with my mouth agape with surprise.

"Wow! Which friend got her this?" he asks.

"James," she clarifies.

"Oh, yeah, the neighbor kid," he says. He's met James a few times when his family would visit us, but it's been several years.

"What?" Aunt Diana asks, coming into the room too, followed shortly by my cousins.

"That neighbor boy gave Lola a laptop for graduation," Pauly says.

"I wish I had neighbors like that!" Diana chuckles.

"Your boyfriend bought you a laptop?" Mikey asks with disbelief.

"He's not my boyfriend." I shake my head.

"Lola, guys don't just randomly buy girls laptops," Frankie chimes in. "For my girlfriend's birthday, I bought her a necklace—and we've been going out for over a year."

"Well, he's just a very generous person," I retort.

Mikey nudges Frankie, and the two exchange looks that clearly translate to "Lola must be giving it up to that guy on the regular if he'd spend over a grand on her."

I give them a momentary glare before I roll my eyes.

Nana shuffles in to see what all the fuss is about, and she looks at the box with bemusement. "Am I interrupting the meeting?"

"Look, Nana," I say with a smile, holding it up for her. "James gave it to me for graduation."

"What is it?" she says, squinting as she looks at the picture on the front.

"It's a laptop," I reply.

"A what?" she asks again, messing with her hearing aid.

"A laptop."

"A laptop computer?" she says, her eyebrows shooting up. I nod. "Oh! He's a big spender, huh?"

I laugh and nod again. "I can't believe it. It's so thoughtful and cool of him."

"What a good kid." She smiles with approval. "He's always been such a sweet boy."

She likes James, always has. Sometimes when Pauly would bring her for a visit, James would sit down and talk to her for hours. She's got a razor sharp wit, and I think he found it fascinating and amusing. She thought he was a crack-up, and she even passed along some of her most prized recipes—something hugely symbolic for her.

"Why wasn't he at your graduation this morning?" she says, asking the question I was sort of hoping to avoid.

"He had a big audition in LA," I lie. "He's trying out for a spot on a TV pilot," I fictitiously clarify.

"We'll see his name in lights someday?" She chuckles. "Tell him I want an autograph next time I see him. What's that website where they bid on things, Pauly?"

"It's eBay, Mama," he laughs.

"I can put it on the eBay and make a fortune. There was an article in the paper the other day about it. The guy sold a baseball for two thousand dollars," she muses.

"I'll have him send you an eight-by-ten." I snicker.

"Better be a picture with his shirt off, since that boy loves to show off his muscles. That'll get the girls bidding," she jokes, which makes everyone erupt into laughter.

"I'll be sure to pass that request along," I say when I've recovered.

We all retreat to the living room, and I try to pretend I'm not worrying about this dinner with my dad. I'm supposed to be going to a few graduation parties tonight, and I try to focus on that, but the dread is creeping up in my stomach, and I feel kind of sick. I need to calm the hell down, but I don't want to go off on a rant about my dad to my family because they'll agree with me and it will supercharge my hatred, which will not be good if I have to sit across from him and pretend to be chipper.

Thankfully, now I have an excuse to call James and take my mind off the whole thing. I go into the front room and away from the prying ears of Mikey and Frankie as I dial his number.

"Hey, babe!" he answers.

"You're the best ever!"

"So I take it you got it?" He laughs.

"I got it, and it's the best gift anyone's ever given me. Thank you so much, James," I say. "You're out of your mind for spending that much money on a graduation present, but I fucking love you for doing it!"

He laughs loudly. "Your iBook is old as shit, and you were due for an upgrade," he responds with predictable modesty.

"It's just a huge gift, not even just because they're expensive. It means a lot to me. You picked something so perfect for me. You want to know what my dad got me? A fucking Coach bag. He spent, like, three hundred bucks on a fucking purse—and it's not even big enough to fit a book in!" I rant.

James knows I'm not a designer handbag kind of girl, so he scoffs and replies, "Probably came recommended by Nikki."

"It's probably one of her old ones." I shrug. "She's not even here. He said he didn't want to buy tickets for her and Zach. Apparently this would interrupt her busy schedule of mani-pedis and Pilates."

"She's not even fuckin' there?"

"Nope. Not worth the trip, I guess. And it was only about five minutes into our conversation before he got snippy."

"Aw, that sucks, babe," he says. "I can't believe your dad's being a dick like that."

"Eh, what else is new? He was bound to fuck my day up somehow. I have to go to dinner with him tonight, and I'm—"

I hear a distinctly female laugh in the background before James whispers, "Hang on, I'm talking to my friend."

"Are you busy?" I say, feeling just a little irritated.

"No, just giving my girl Lexi a ride home from the shoot," he replies nonchalantly.

Lexi Jaxxxon, clearly. When he was out here he mentioned that he had an upcoming shoot with her. I guess it went pretty fucking well if he's "giving her a ride" home. I can read between the goddamn lines. He's going to fuck her. Again. He's taking her home right now, and he'll surely head right to her bedroom and have wild, freaky, porno sex with her. For some reason, that infuriates me so much I want to throw the phone against the wall.

"I should let you go," I say, now feeling overwhelmingly dismayed about what I'm currently imagining will take place once they arrive at their destination.

"Nah, babe, I'm good," he says.

"It's not a big deal. You're busy, and I can just talk to you later," I say with a sigh.

When James is focused on getting laid, it's very difficult to derail his train of thought. That's his goal right now, and despite how polite he's being, I know I'm only getting a fraction of his attention. It makes me feel weirdly jealous. It's stupid, of course, because he's not doing anything wrong. He's just being James. He's on a mission to fuck, and I've never been one to stand in his way.

"Listen, I should start getting ready for this dinner with my dad." I try to sound upbeat, but I'm guessing he can see through it—or rather *hear* through it.

"Lola, baby, I can talk. I'm not busy. It's fine. I can talk and drive at the same time. Tell me about what happened with your dad," he insists.

"Really, it's nothing. Just me freaking out, as usual," I say with a fake chuckle. "I'll call you tonight to tell you how it goes. You go do your thing with your lady there."

"You sure?" he asks, probably making that face he makes when he can tell I'm lying.

"Yeah, it's cool. I'll have more to vent about later," I reply.

"All right," he says, finally accepting that I'm done, "but I want to hear all about it, okay?"

"Uh-huh. Thanks again for the laptop. You made my day."

"You're welcome, babe," he says warmly. "Definitely call me tonight."

"Yep. Will do."

"Okay, well, congrats on graduation, and I hope everything goes well with your dad," he says to wrap up. "Talk to you later, kid."

"Bye, James," I say before hanging up.

I sit there for a couple minutes, trying to figure out why I'm so damn angry right now. Whatever he's doing or planning to do with Lexi is none of my business. He can do what he wants. He's been doing what he wants with every girl under the goddamn sun for years, so I shouldn't suddenly start giving a shit now. I did what I needed to do, thanked him for the Mac, and I didn't need to have a big conversation about my dad with him right away. I'll have more to talk about after dinner and that's probably when I'll really need him. By then, he'll be sex-sated and ready to listen.

Deep breath, Lola. Shake it off. I get up and sit with my family for a while before I go to my room to pick out what to wear to this inevitably awkward dinner.

Chapter 15

James

As soon as I hang up the phone with Lola, Lexi reaches out from the passenger seat and starts rubbing my crotch.

Today's shoot was hot as fuck, and she was turning me on big time. The rumors were true, and she is, in fact, very flexible and wild. She dug it so much she said she's going to request me for a few more shoots this month. I'm psyched because she's really famous in the business and her shoots pay more than the ones I've done in the past. This could be a great opportunity for me to take that next step to bigger movies. I've been keeping a low profile because I was worried my parents would find out about my job, but now I don't give a fuck, and I want to shoot for the fuckin' moon.

"You know what I want?" Lexi smiles as she unzips my fly.

Oh, I've got a pretty good idea what she wants.

She starts stroking me, and I concentrate as hard as I can on the road. She leans forward and takes me in her mouth just as we pull up in front of her place. It's way nicer than mine, a duplex instead of a shitty apartment building, and I'm a little nervous about getting head in the driveway like this.

"Come on, let's go inside." I smile at her when she looks up at me. "I want a repeat performance of the shoot today."

She giggles and nods, quickly hopping out of the car while I tuck myself back into my jeans and step out. She leads me to her door, and we practically fall in as she starts kissing me.

We go into her bedroom and start fooling around, but I'm having a slightly hard time concentrating. I keep thinking about my conversation with Lola and everything surrounding her graduation.

I wish I could have been there for her today. I needed to just man up and stick around for her, even if it meant being in the same town as my parents. I would have loved seeing her get her diploma and taking lots of pictures of her. I'm really proud of her, and it sucks that I wasn't there to show her that.

She was there for me at my graduation, hooting and hollering when they called my name and giving me a huge hug afterward. She even made a couple sassy jabs at Jonathan when he tried to act snobby about how he got way better grades than me when he was in high school. I loved having her there at my side, being supportive and proud and all that. I should have done that for her. If things weren't so fucked up, I totally would have.

I'm a little distracted when Lexi starts blowing me again, and I try really hard to live in the moment. It feels good, and that's what I should be focusing on right now. I have to stop this constant stream of Lola thoughts.

I go down on Lexi, she blows me, then we run through the playbook from missionary to doggy to all sorts of advanced positions that are mostly just reserved for people in our profession, and I feel slightly calmer by the time I get back in my car.

Still, I have a weight in my stomach. I don't know why I keep feeling so fuckin' guilty after sex, but it sucks. I've never felt this way before, and I can't stand it. I need someone to talk to, and I'm sure the fuck not going to call Lola and tell her how my intense attraction to her has left me so conflicted that I'm having trouble enjoying the one thing I really love doing.

I find myself on the doorstep of a small but well-kept bungalow, knocking on the door and keeping my fingers crossed that someone's home.

A vato-looking dude with a full sleeve of Day of the Dead tattoos, dressed in a wifebeater and gray sweatpants opens up the door and gives me a hug.

"James, what's up, man?" he says.

"Hey, Alejandro. You got a minute? I just need to talk to somebody," I say.

"Of course, come on in." He smiles as he ushers me inside. "Everything okay?"

"Eh, kind of." I shrug.

"Who was that?" a lean, lanky, blond-haired, blue-eyed guy in a navy T-shirt and jeans says, stepping out from the kitchen to take a look.

"It's James, baby," Alejandro says.

"How funny! I was literally just talking to Alejandro about inviting you to dinner tonight," Chad says, giving me a warm hug.

Chad and Alejandro are my best California friends. They're both well-known stars in the gay porn world, and we met at the very first Sin Cinema party I ever attended. We were instant friends, and they've been like my caring, understanding big brothers through my whole journey in the biz. When I have a problem that I can't bring to Lola, these dudes are always there for me to turn to.

"You look bummed out," Chad says, leading me into the kitchen.

"I just...I feel like shit," I say, immediately realizing that I might be more bummed out than I originally let myself believe.

"What's going on?" Alejandro asks sympathetically.

"A Lola problem," I reply, a little ashamed to admit it.

The guys exchange looks, and Chad walks over to the fridge and grabs three beers, motioning for us to go out onto their sundeck and take a seat. He's prepared for this to be a lengthy conversation.

I open up my bottle and take a long sip before setting it down and trying to figure out how to broach this subject. "I didn't tell you guys the whole story of what happened when I went back home," I finally begin.

Both of them look very interested in what I'm about to say.

"I told you about my parents and a little bit about the whole prom situation, but there was more...Lola stuff."

Chad leans forward, resting his chin on his hand as he eagerly awaits the rest of the story. Both of the guys know about Lola—since I talk about her all the time—and I get carried away, so I tend to reveal more than I probably should. They're always shooting each other little glances when I start going on about her, and I'm sure they have their own suspicions and assumptions about my relationship with her.

"While I was staying at her house, I sort of hit on her a little bit," I say, trying to downplay the incident. "She flirted with me too, so she was into it. At one point, I tried to…sort of…do something with her."

Chad gasps, and a grin spreads across Alejandro's lips.

"You finally had sex with her?" Chad excitedly asks.

"No, no, nothing like that. It didn't go that far." I note his use of *finally*, and I smile to myself with embarrassment.

Of course these guys would think that I've been waiting to hit it for years. I haven't exactly kept quiet on the subject of Lola's beauty, and I actually remember saying something about how I used to try to convince her to play doctor with me so I could look at her body.

"Well?" Alejandro grins. "Go on!"

"I kissed her neck, and I kind of felt her up a little bit," I murmur. "She stopped me the first time—"

"There was more than one time?" He chuckles.

"Yeah," I shyly admit. "The first time was right after the blowout with my parents, and I figured I was just feeling emotionally vulnerable and looking for a pick-me-up—at least that's what she said."

Again, they exchange sneaky little looks.

"The second time, though, it felt different," I say, looking down at my beer and not wanting to make eye contact for fear that they'll spot some kind of tell that would blow my cover. "It was early morning, and we were in her bed. Something just came over me, and I was on her and feeling her up. She was letting me, she was even moaning and stuff, and I was just about to finger her, but her alarm went off and it sort of jolted me back to reality."

"Very interesting," Chad says with a smart-ass smile.

"I could have probably…you know…I mean, if there had been a little more time. She was really receptive to the idea all of a sudden, and I felt a whole wave of emotions that freaked me out."

"You were conflicted," Alejandro correctly summarizes.

"Yeah, I wanted to do it, but part of me was yelling that it was totally wrong. And now it's just gotten worse," I confess. "I keep feeling guilty after sex. I fucked Lexi today and it was awesome, but the second I left I felt like a piece of shit for thoughtlessly fucking her. I felt like I took advantage of her. And it was even worse with Tara—"

"Oh, shit," Alejandro says under his breath.

"What?" I ask, turning to him.

"Tell me you're not fucking Tara, James," he says with exasperation. "You don't need to get tangled up in that shit."

"Just a couple times," I confess, feeling like a child who's about to be grounded.

"James!" Chad reprimands me. "You know that's stupid. You know how Tara is. She gets very attached, and she's not going to let go easily. If you keep fucking her outside of work, she's going to assume you want a relationship with her—and she's been dying to get her skanky hooks into you since you guys did your first scene."

I laugh, despite his condemning tone. Chad and Alejandro do not care for Tara Morgan. They've been in the industry for longer than me, and they've seen her rapid rise to fame. According to them, she can be ruthless and vindictive. And they've been very clear that I absolutely should not fuck with all that.

"She's just always there. She's always available whenever I want. It's so convenient, and I don't have to put any fuckin' effort into it."

"Like you had to put a lot of effort into it before!" Chad teases.

"Yeah, but this is seriously zero effort. I literally text her, and five minutes later she's on her knees with my dick all the way to her tonsils," I explain.

Both guys make gross-out noises, and I laugh.

"When I need it, she's there. When I feel like I absolutely have to fuck, she's down." I shrug.

"Okay, but why do you think you need it in the first place?" Alejandro wisely asks.

"It's funny, Lola kind of asked me the same thing," I say after a brief pause. "She was giving me shit for always wanting to get laid when things bother me."

"I believe they call that self-medicating," Chad says, raising an eyebrow.

"It's not that bad." I chuckle, shaking my head. "I'm not fuckin' addicted; I just like getting laid. It makes me feel good, and I like to do it regardless of how emotionally fucked up I am at the time—and you two can both stop doing those little glances like you guys are diagnosing me behind my back!" I add with a laugh.

Both of them snicker, totally caught in the act.

"I don't *need* to fuck all the time. Most of the time when I'm really bummed out or mad, all I *need* to do is talk to Lola. So see? If I was a sex addict, that wouldn't work. I'd be constantly trying to get my next fix, not wishing I was cuddling with Lola while she talked me through it."

"You realize what you just said, right?" Chad smirks. "Do you hear yourself? You've just equated cuddling with your best friend to sex. You're admitting that you like it as much as sex. Sounds like a deep emotional connection to me."

"Shut up," I say, knowing I'm blushing.

"Oh, my God, look at him!" Alejandro laughs, hitting my arm.

"Both of you can fuck off." I chuckle, unable to contain my embarrassed smile.

"That's where all your guilt is coming from," Chad says. "You're *in* it, my friend. You're emotionally invested. You need to take a look at what's going on inside and come to terms with what you're feeling."

"I don't need to take a look anywhere," I reply, still feeling like I've been busted. "She's my friend, and I like being around her. So what? You guys are my friends, and I like being around you. It doesn't mean there's more to it than that."

"But neither of us is a beautiful girl you've known since childhood who you suddenly want to sleep with," Alejandro teases.

"I don't want to sleep with her!" I roll my eyes, though I'm not certain if that's the truth. *Fuck! Now I'm more confused than when I started!*

"Okay," Chad says with a hint of snarky sarcasm.

"I don't!" I attempt to refute.

"Sure, of course you don't," he continues.

Alejandro laughs his ass off at this whole thing, and I give them both fake glares.

"Fuck you guys!" I laugh. "You've just never seen how it is with us. You're assuming that just because she's really beautiful and sweet and I care about her a lot, it means I want to fuck her. I don't want to fuck her; I just *like* her. I want to spend every day with her. I want to sleep in her bed and watch movies with her and cook her dinner and stuff, not plow her."

Chad gives me the cockiest smirk. "It sounds like you're in lo—"

"Don't even fuckin' say it!" I chuckle, pinching the bridge of my nose between my eyes like this whole thing is giving me a migraine.

Alejandro nearly falls out of his chair laughing.

"I hate you guys so much right now." I snicker, which only makes them laugh harder.

When they give me shit like this, it totally feels like they're my older brothers, but they're always supportive, unlike Jonathan.

"Maybe you guys should just talk this out," Chad says once he gets over how fuckin' hilarious all this apparently is.

"It's too weird," I say. "It was weird enough to even admit that I thought she was hot. I can't get into any of this deeper shit with her. What if it freaks her out? I don't want her to know."

"I'm just saying," Chad replies. "It's better to get it out there so it doesn't get really weird later."

There's a long pause as I think about what would happen if I really did spill all this to her. *"Hi, Lo. I'm completely obsessed with you, and I want to fuck you so bad that it's ruining my sex life with other girls."* Yeah, that definitely wouldn't freak her out.

"I was kind of rude to her today." I sigh, feeling guilty again. "She called to thank me for her graduation present, but I was in the car with Lexi and I kind of cut her off. She was telling me all this stuff about graduation and her dad, and I was thinking about how bad I wanted to fuck Lexi. I am such a dick!" I throw my head back as the impact of it hits me. "What the fuck is happening to me? I'm being an asshole to her on the phone, but all I want to do is hug her and kiss her, yet I keep doing shit that will push her away."

"There's just a plethora of issues at work here." Chad shakes his head.

"The first thing you need to do is stop being a dick to her," Alejandro advises. "It's not her fault that you're feeling this way about her, and you definitely shouldn't take it out on her. The next thing you need to do is get your shit together and figure out if you really do like her. If you actually feel that way about her, you need to man the fuck up and let her know."

"The gayest dude I know telling me to man the fuck up," I tease.

Chad bursts into laughter, and Alejandro pauses to snicker before retorting, "Yes, but am I wrong, James?"

"No, you're totally right," I admit.

"If you decide you don't want to go down that path with her, you need to commit to that idea and move on. You're getting mixed up with girls like Tara Morgan, and you should be focusing on something simple, like work. Channel all this emotion into motivation."

Chad smiles broadly at Alejandro before turning to me. "He's so smart," he proudly remarks as he brushes his fingers down the back of Alejandro's neck.

I shrug and nod because he's kind of right. Alejandro is really observant, and he's a good listener, so he always has some kind of insightful advice.

"Well, in the meantime, do you want to stay for dinner?" Chad snickers.

"Sure," I reply. It's good to have somebody to talk to when your emotions are all scrambled like mine have been, and I can always be myself with these dudes so I don't have to hide anything.

I'm feeling better, though still a bit mixed up about the Lola situation. I definitely agree with the guys about Tara, though. She's a very persistent chick, and I shouldn't blur that line between work sex and real-life sex. Using all this to get motivated for work seems like a good idea. It'll give me something to focus on, something with clear-cut goals and accomplishments. *How many scenes can I shoot in a month? How many times can I make my co-stars come in a single shoot? How many different girls can I work with?* These things are easy to keep track of, and they'll provide a measurable goal. So that's what I decide to do. Climb the ladder, focus on my career, and go the friendship route with Lola until I decide what the fuck I actually want to happen there.

Chapter 16
Lola

Five times. My dad has checked his BlackBerry five times since we sat down, and we don't even have our salads yet. The first was right after our waitress took our drink orders. The second was when I started talking about college and he made a snippy comment about how much it was going to cost him—because apparently he doesn't understand that he and my mom are splitting the miniscule percentage that isn't covered by scholarships and loans. The next BlackBerry offense came after he told me that Nikki wanted to get me some new school clothes so I'd fit in with the wealthy students at my *egregiously* expensive school. After that it was BlackBerry time again before a comment about how my hair looks more professional when it's straight and that I should wear it that way in class so my professors won't think I'm some kind of hippie. This last glance down at the screen has been going on for several minutes, and I'm just thankful that he's not finding yet another thing to make me feel insecure about. It's not like he's even texting or emailing anyone. His phone hasn't beeped or chimed at all. I'm guessing he's just using it as an escape because he doesn't want to have dinner with me—and the feeling is *very* mutual.

"So what did you think of graduation?" I say, attempting to break the growing silence between us.

"Hm?"

"Graduation. What did you think?" I repeat when he finally looks up.

"Oh, it was nice," he says dismissively. "You should have seen Nikki's nephew's graduation. They had a general come to speak to them. Very inspiring."

I manage to unclench my jaw. "But Tyler goes to a private school, so I'm sure they had more money to court speakers," I say, inexplicably defending the local news anchor who gave our public-school-budget commencement address.

"Best school in Virginia," my father agrees, completely missing my point. "He's a straight A student, too."

So am I, Dad, but you would only know that if you paid attention to me for the past fifteen years since the divorce.

"They had their prom in an old mansion, really beautiful space," he smugly adds.

"I'm sure it was fabulous," I say, trying rather unsuccessfully to mute my sarcasm.

"Your mom said you didn't even want to go to your prom," he says, taking a sip of the exorbitantly expensive wine he ordered for himself.

"I'm not a dress-up kind of girl." I shrug in the most noncommittal way possible.

"Come on," he says with a snicker, "all you girls live for your prom and your wedding. Those are the two biggest days in a girl's life."

I strain to avoid rolling my eyes as I sigh. "Not for me."

"You didn't want to get all dolled up with your prom date and be like Cinderella?" He smirks like he's certain I'm bullshitting.

"Nope." I shake my head. "I went with a friend, so it wasn't like he was officially my date. I only stuck around for a little while. James was in town, so I had a good excuse to bail."

"James was in town?" he scoffs. "What was he doing here?"

"He came to visit me," I reply, already feeling myself starting to get defensive and defiant.

My dad and James have met several times, but neither seemed to take a particular shine to the other. James knows my dad can be quite cold to me, and I'm sure my dad thinks something must be wrong with James if he wants to hang out with a snippy, nerdy, homely, social outcast like me, so they're not exactly buddies.

"So you went to prom with James, then?" he snickers.

"No, he was here visiting, and I hung out with him after prom," I clarify.

Because my father never listens to me, he continues with, "I just don't see why a twenty-year-old guy would fly all the way here to go to prom with you."

"He *didn't* go to prom with me!" That seems to go in one ear and out the other.

"Didn't he have anything better to do than go to a high school prom?"

"Dad," I say, angry, "if you'd listened to me for the past few minutes, you'd have heard me saying that I *did not* go to prom with James."

He scoffs and shakes his head like I'm the asshole, and he sits back in the booth and takes another sip of wine.

"What's the prom king up to out in LA these days?" he says with a judgmental, snarky smirk.

"He's doing very well, actually," I snap. "He's had a lot of auditions, done some commercials, and a few big modeling jobs. He's earning good money, and he really enjoys his work."

"Christ, I'm surprised that kid can even read a script let alone memorize one," my father scoffs.

Okay, that does it, now I'm pissed. "Why do you always do that?" I scowl as I cross my arms. "Why do you have to say things like that about him? Every time I bring him up, you have some nasty, cutting thing to say about him, and it's grossly inappropriate considering you barely know him."

"I know enough," he grumbles.

"You obviously don't!" I fire back. "If you knew him at all, you'd know that he's wonderful. He's sweet and caring. He's funny. He's been there for me through every bad thing that's happened in my life — including all the times you've made me feel like crap — so maybe you should reconsider the way you speak about him."

"You need to reconsider the way you're speaking to me, young lady," he sternly replies, trying to assert some unearned parental authority.

"Not when you're going to make snide remarks about my best friend," I retort with a glare.

"I'll say whatever I want about that kid." He shrugs as he dismissively waves his hand in the air.

The waitress brings out our entrées, and I'm seething with such rage that I can barely chew a single bite. He doesn't notice — or more likely, he doesn't care—and he makes a crack about how I came to a steak house and ordered salmon instead of steak. He ordered veal, something he knows I find morally questionable, and he even gets in a few jabs about how my distaste for the flesh of baby cows apparently makes me some kind of tree hugger.

"So your mom said you're going to some graduation parties tonight," he says, attempting to segue.

"Yes," I tersely reply.

"Are you excited for those?"

"Thrilled," I continue with another monosyllabic answer.

"Lola, I don't need this attitude. I took time off work to come here to watch your little graduation, and you owe me some respect. I'm your damn father!"

"I'll show you some respect when you *earn* some respect. I'll respect you when you start respecting me—and my friends!"

He puts down his fork and glares at me, but I return his glare in spades.

"And how is everything tasting?" our waitress asks as she stops back by.

"Great," I answer. "Can I get a box, please? I don't think I can finish all this."

"Of course." She nods with a smile and darts off toward the kitchen.

The angry glares continue as she returns with a box, and I scoop food inside. My salmon is largely untouched, but it might be good later when I'm not so pissed off. I close the box and take out my keys.

"Dad, it's been a joy, as usual," I say, standing from the table.

"You're just going to get up and walk away?" he asks with outrage.

"I can leave you some money if you'd like, but I'm such a pauper that I'll have to sell my Coach bag to do it," I spit.

"That's enough!" he growls.

"See you in four years at the next graduation, if you decide it's worth your time," I flippantly reply as I make my way to the door.

I'm sure that he's livid, and for a second I wonder if he'll follow me outside and really lay into me about being snippy with him. Of course, he's all about appearances and he would never do anything to cause a scene—that kind of behavior is only for poor, unattractive, socially awkward teenage girls with unintelligent best friends, I guess.

I slam my car door and whip out of the parking space on my way back to my house. I'm so overwhelmed with anger that I feel like I should take a shower to scrub it off. I want to hang out with my friends tonight, and I won't let this cloud linger over me.

As I wash off, I think about how much I jumped down my dad's throat for dissing James. I can't even begin to imagine how awful his comments will be if he ever finds out about James's career. He already thinks of him as a fuckup, a slacker, and a criminal. If he learns that James is essentially having sex for money, there will be no end to the amount of assholery I'd have to endure. I'm sure that he'd jump to the conclusion that I'm a slut by association and treat me like I was Satan incarnate.

Maybe Naveen had a point about the potential consequences this might have on my reputation, even within my family. Surely Uncle Pauly wouldn't exactly be ecstatic that I was so close with a porn star. Nana would probably have a goddamn heart attack if she found that sweet James from next door was actually a professional cocksman. Frankie and Mikey would be merciless, and it would only justify their idiotic assumptions about why James got me such a generous graduation gift.

Ugh! Why can't people just understand this the way I do? James is my best friend, and I love him to death. He's a beautiful person, inside and out, and he treats me right. He's generous, caring, compassionate, loyal, and we share the same sense of humor. I'd rather spend time with him than with anyone else on the planet, and I could really use one of his big hugs right now. I'd feel a lot better if we were snuggling in my bed, and he was kissing my forehead and telling me to take a water-off-a-duck's-back approach to all this ugliness with my dad. *"Don't let him get to you, kid. He doesn't matter."* I wish he were here right now. I know I'd find a lot of comfort from looking in his eyes. He could make me feel better. He could hold me and kiss me — *shit! How did that creep in there?*

"Fuck!" I sigh to my reflection as I step out of the shower to dry off. "Get your shit together, Lola! Do not even fucking go there! You will not develop some kind of stupid crush on James. Turn this shit off right now!"

I nod, agreeing with my stern solo pep talk, and I squeeze my hair in a towel. My rational side is completely correct. I will turn this shit off immediately and nip it in the bud before I make myself crazy.

Chapter 17

James

"You didn't call me back yesterday," I say when Lola answers the phone.

"I know. I'm sorry. I was really tired, and I just needed some sleep," she replies.

I tried calling her last night so she could tell me about dinner with her dad, but it went to voice mail. I tried again this morning and still couldn't get through, which made me start to feel really bad for cutting her off in the first place. I was worried that she was pissed off at me, but from her tone right now, I can tell we're all good.

"So how'd it go?" I ask her as I plug in the blender on the kitchen counter.

There's a long pause, and she sighs heavily. "Shitty. Horrendous. The term 'train-wreck' just about covers it."

I can't help but chuckle, and I'm glad when I hear her laugh too.

"He was really rude, kept checking his phone, completely disregarded anything I had to say to the point where I was repeating myself constantly. He was ripping on graduation and saying how Nikki's nephew's graduation was so much better. He even made a snippy comment about you when I told him about prom."

"No shit?" I ask.

"I was ready to put two feet up his ass when he said it," she replies. "I wanted to flip over the fucking table and start screaming at him. He can rip on me, he can tear me down, but how dare he go after you!"

I smile broadly. I love that she feels protective of me — even after a scandal of such epic proportions that I'm probably a legend, a cautionary tale for everyone in the whole fuckin' town. Lola's loyalty means more to me than anything I could ever imagine. I can't even put a value on it, especially now after she witnessed all that shit with my family.

"He doesn't know about the porn thing, does he?" I ask, knowing the answer is probably no. If Kevin did know, he definitely would have used it against Lola, and she'd probably be calling me from jail right now because she stabbed him with a fork or something.

"He doesn't know," she confirms. "And it's not like he gives a shit about any aspect of my life anyway."

"Then it's his loss, babe," I reply. "You're awesome, and he's missing out."

"Thanks, James," she sighs, and I can hear her smile.

"Hang on one sec," I say.

I turn on the blender, and the sound fills up the room.

"What are you making?" she asks when I turn it off again.

"Protein shake," I reply.

"Seriously?" She chuckles at the very idea.

"I'm getting buff, Lo," I say, grinning. "Next time you see me, I'm gonna be totally ripped."

"You're already totally ripped," she says, her voice taking on a flirty quality I've never noticed before.

"Listen, I know I'm already super sexy, but I want to take the sexiness to the next level," I joke. "I've got this whole new workout plan going on now. Muscle mass, dude. I'm totally cultivating muscle mass."

She laughs really hard, and I smile at the sound. I missed her laugh, and I wish she was here so I didn't have to hear it through the phone.

"But forget about how sexy I'm going to get, and let's talk about your dad some more," I say, which only makes her laugh harder.

She tells me a little more about what went down and how it made her feel, and I listen attentively and give her my two cents when she needs it. Very few of her friends know just how deep her emotional scars go with her dad — hell, even she won't admit it sometimes—but I know her well enough to see when there's a crack in the façade. I take my role as amateur therapist very seriously when it comes to this topic.

"Do you really think people will look down on me at school?" she says meekly when she finishes her initial rant. "Now he's planted this seed that people are judging me and that I don't fit in with that echelon. Do you think they really will reject me?"

"Absolutely not, Lo," I reply. "You're there. You got in, which puts you at the exact same starting point as all of them. Besides, nobody could talk to you for even five seconds and judge you for anything besides being beautiful, smart, and totally fun to hang out with."

"Thanks, James," she softly replies, and I can practically see her bashfully looking up at me through those long eyelashes.

"You're amazing, Lola. You've always been cool, but you've grown into this awesome woman who fuckin' destroys any girl you compare her to."

"Well, now you're just trying to flatter me." She giggles, and the cheerful sound makes me smile.

"I'm trying to tell you how great you are, how I see you. I wish you could get in my head and take a look at yourself from my perspective because you'd see how rad you are, and you'd never let anyone shake you up again. Next time you come out here, *I'm* gonna hold *you* close and tell you all the reasons why *you're* special, huh?"

She giggles again, and I can tell she's probably blushing. "You have a deal, Mr. Laird," she replies. "So what's with the workout plan?"

"I'm trying to channel my energy," I answer. "I've been feeling kind of scattered, and I wanted to try to focus on something, have a measurable goal." *Translation: I've been fucking just about any girl with a pulse and it's completely unfulfilling, so I'm trying to engage in more productive physical activities.*

"Wow, good for you," she says, and I think she's genuinely impressed.

"I was thinking about what you said, um, that night when I first… uh…when we had our long talk," I explain, trying to tap dance over the landmine of my growing attraction to her. "When you said I fuck to feel better after something bad happens. I think that's kinda true. I decided last night that I was going to refocus the energy I'd put into getting pussy into doing something better, like getting buff and booking lots of work."

She pauses for a moment, and I know she's debating whether to call me on the fact that work is sex and that I'm technically still using sex to feel better, just doing it for a paycheck instead of personal gratification. Thankfully, she doesn't make a beeline for that topic, and instead she says, "It sounds like you've done some reflecting in the past twenty-four hours."

"I have, indeed." I smile. "And I have another brilliant little plan too."

"Yes?"

"I want you to come visit me," I say. "I want to show you around. You can meet some of my friends, see my apartment. My bed is big enough for two, so…you know, if you felt like it, maybe you could let me cuddle with you again."

"Oh, shut up," she says. "You already know that I totally want that, so don't even pretend like you're being coy!"

I laugh hard, and I appreciate that she can see through me so easily.

"I'm down," she says. "I really want to see your place."

"End of summer? Maybe Labor Day?" I propose.

"Yes!" she gleefully replies.

"Good," I sigh. "Because I can't wait all the way until Thanksgiving or Christmas break to see you. I'll go fuckin' crazy by then."

That gets another adorable giggle, and I can feel my lips pulling into a proud smile. I've always liked making her laugh, and this particular cute, sexy, playful little giggle is my favorite variety of Lola laughter.

We talk about school, and she tells me she's excited for college, but that she'll hate being so far away. I assure her that a plane ride is a plane ride, and no matter how many hours, I will make sure we still see each other regularly.

I'm feeling better about our situation by the time we hang up. The good thing about talking to her on the phone is that I don't get distracted by her beauty. I can focus on the aspects of Lola that I love the most: the humor, the sweetness, the sass, the total openness and honesty we share. If I can just block out how hot she is and keep all those amazing personality traits at the forefront of my mind, I think I can move back into that "just friends" space and stop seeing her as a girl I really, really want to have sex with. It's not going to be easy, but I'm up for the challenge.

Chapter 18

Lola

I'm on hour three of my shift at Garth Fitness Center, our local gym, and I wish the computer behind the check-in desk allowed access to Tumblr, because I'd much rather be doing that than sitting here hoping no more sketchy dudes come up to me. I only took this job because I needed to earn a little income this summer — hopefully at least a thousand bucks — so I'll have some money for living expenses once I get to college. I applied at the gym, and they hired me on the spot. That was about a month ago, and I learned the (incredibly boring) ropes very quickly. A lot of our older male patrons seem keen on shamelessly flirting with me while not-so-subtly flexing their biceps as they chat me up.

Brad, who is one of the trainers, comes up to me with his usual high-energy greeting. He's sweet, but he's also one of those meathead guys who will talk about reps and super-sets until he's blue in the face.

"How you doing, Lola?" He's got that hyped-up bounce to him, like his blood is made of Red Bull.

"Great. How about you?" I reply.

"Really great," he says, nodding. "Waiting for a client. She's been really happy with her plan. She was telling me how she wants to focus on her glutes now that she and her husband are separated. She's already rockin' a nice bikini bod, and she just wants to firm up some more."

"Oh...well, that's good." I smile, not really having a response.

"You been hitting the StairMaster? Your glutes are looking great," he comments, giving my butt a once-over.

"Thanks." I laugh and shake my head. Brad isn't doing this to hit on me; he's doing this to assess the muscle groups I need to build up to have an official Body By Brad — his personal slogan.

For some reason, big, buff dudes take a shine to me. Brad has been stopping by the counter to talk to me quite regularly since I started here about a month ago, and he's even offered me a referral bonus for anyone I convince to try out his personal training services. I can deal with guys like this, guys who don't have ulterior motives and who are just generally psyched about their bodies and their jobs. It reminds me a lot of another strapping young man I know.

I've been thinking about James a lot lately, and I've come to the conclusion that "just friends" is the best place for us to be. I still talk to him on the phone every day, and we've even planned out the dates for my visit, but time has helped me become less smitten with him and more able to see the big picture. James is lovely, a truly wonderful person, but a romantic relationship is out of the question. It would fuck things up between us, and I know monogamy would put an enormous strain on him, so why put either of us through that?

Brad's client arrives, and she looks ready and raring to go. He enthusiastically leads her into the gym after I check her in, and I'm left back at the desk with a wandering mind and no fucking Tumblr.

The door opens, and a familiar face greets me with a smile. Dave Keegan approaches me in cargo shorts and a polo shirt and nervously drums his fingers on the desk when he reaches me.

"Something I can help you with, Keegan?" I smile back at him.

"I want to get a membership," he says.

"Dude, your family has a country club membership. Why don't you just work out there?" I smirk.

"Do you get a commission if you sign me up?"

"Yeah."

"Then sign me up."

"Keegan, what are you doing?" I chuckle and shake my head. *I'm on to you, dude.*

"I'm interested in a gym membership, and I've heard this place is really great." He grins and leans over the counter flirtatiously.

"If you're doing this because you think it will make me go out with you, you're sorely mistaken," I tease.

"I know," he laughs. "You think I'd want to unleash James's fury? He'd rip my fucking arms off if I even touched you."

I snicker, but I nod my head.

"I just want to make sure I keep an eye on you, and this gives me an excuse to do it."

"Keep an eye on me?" I raise an eyebrow.

"Yeah." He nods. "Just see how you were doing, how your summer is going, stuff like that."

"Is this some kind of directive from headquarters? Is he enlisting you to do this?" I ask, putting my hands on my hips.

"No, no." He smiles and blushes a little. "Just something I wanted to do."

"What are you hoping to get out of this, Keegan?" I narrow my eyes at him.

He laughs at my suspicion. "I just thought this would be a good way to hang out with you. It must be boring, and if I have a membership, I could hang out up here like I'm asking you questions."

"And you're fully aware that this will not make me suddenly drop my panties for you?"

"Do you even have panties on under those tight shorts?" he jokes.

I reach over the counter and give him a playful smack on the shoulder as he laughs.

"Oh! Hitting the customers, are we?" He grins, grabbing his arm and pretending to wince like it's a major injury.

As I'm giving him a playful I-want-to-kick-your-ass look, the door opens again and another one of my regular, seedy "admirers" walks in.

His name is Keith, and he's in his late forties with poorly dyed hair that looks like a toupee. I've nicknamed him Uncle Rico after the character in *Napoleon Dynamite*, though this guy is far creepier. I think he knows what days I work because nobody else has seen him as frequently as I seem to. He's made a point to tell me that he's divorced and that he's "young at heart" and enjoys doing "youthful" things—which, apparently includes youthful girls. It's very mid-life-crisis, and I want to inform him that I was in high school up until about a month ago.

Keegan observes as Keith strolls over to the desk and checks me out. His lingering eyes make me start to question our uniform choices of tight T-shirts or running tank tops paired with volleyball shorts. To be fair, the guys dress in equally form-fitting attire, all in an effort to show off their fit bodies. I'm not fit. Aside from yoga, I hardly ever work out, and with the exception of my annoyingly large boobs, I'm naturally scrawny. But James has inspired me, and I've been forcing myself to hit the treadmill after work on occasion. Unfortunately this is the kind of attention I was hoping *not* to attract with my new physique.

"Hey there, sweetheart." Keith grins salaciously. "You look lovely today."

"Thanks, Keith," I say with a strained smile.

"I like that tank top," he says, using this as an excuse to stare directly at my tits.

"It's new," I reply, trying to contain the urge to tell him to go fuck himself. Don't think that would score me points with the boss.

Keegan narrows his eyes at Keith just like James would do, and I have to admit that I appreciate it.

"So, gorgeous, how have you been today?" he asks me.

"I've been okay." I smile falsely. "It's been a long day, but good."

"Well, you're off work in an hour, right?" he says, confirming my suspicion that he's way too familiar with my schedule. "I'd love to get you a nice meal, get you off your feet for a while."

"Yeah, but I, um, I have some stuff to do and—"

"Baby, I thought we were going to that movie tonight," Keegan interrupts, giving me a wink.

"Yeah, yes, uh-huh." I nod, smiling in appreciation of his save.

Of course, I start wanting to smack him again when he comes around the desk and puts his arms around me, kissing the side of my head as he lowers his hands onto my ass.

"I've got a nice dinner planned for us, and after the movie we can go back to my place," he says in the most ridiculously overplayed seductive tone I've ever heard.

"That'll be nice," I say, looking up into his eyes and trying to subtly signal that I will kick his ass if he attempts to take this any further.

"Well, I'm all checked in then," Keith says, realizing his presence is no longer wanted.

"Enjoy your workout." I smile and give him a little wave.

Keegan, that sneaky little shit, pulls me into him and kisses me. I close my eyes to hide how hard I'm rolling them, but I dig my nails into his arm as hard as I can.

Keith walks off to the locker room, and Keegan lets me go.

"You little fucker!" I say, playfully punching him in the chest.

He's cracking up and trying to block my swats.

"Don't you ever pull shit like that again!" I blush and giggle.

"Hey, it worked, didn't it?" His stupid grin says he's still incredibly amused.

I furrow my brow and give him a bunch of tiny punches in the arm as he holds his stomach with laughter.

"That was my one opportunity to do that, so don't hate," he says still chuckling. "I seized the moment and went for it. I'm committing it to memory as we speak."

"Get me out of your fap file, Keegan!" I tease. "I heard all about your nasty fantasies of me, and I would like to be removed from the cast list right now!"

That only makes him laugh harder, which only makes me want to smack him more.

"The next time you attempt to kiss me, I will slap the shit out of you," I warn, though my giggles make it a lot less stern than I'd hoped for.

"I was looking out for you, that's all," he says. "I was being protective. I was doing it in James's honor. He's my friend, and he would have wanted me to play bouncer for you with that dude."

"James wouldn't want you to fucking kiss me!"

"I committed to the role, Lola," Keegan jokes.

"Fucker!" I shake my head at him as I blush.

"So can we actually go to a movie tonight?" he says with a smart-ass grin.

"Keegan, I will slice your dick off with the yoga sign-up clipboard!" I declare.

He laughs hysterically again and then raises his hands in surrender. "Will you still sell me a membership, though?"

I pause, take a deep breath and reach into the drawer for the blank cards. "Fine," I reply with exasperation.

He cracks up again, probably reveling in his small achievement as I prepare his registration.

While I might want to kick him in the balls for this little stunt, I know that Keegan is a good guy and his intentions really are to keep an eye on me—even if that also includes keeping an eye on my boobs or my ass. I think that, with James out of town and me nearly on my way to college, he feels some sort of responsibility to take on the role of protector James used to have. The last fucking thing I need is *two* guys putting up a border fence around me, but I can't say that I don't owe him one for deterring Keith just now. Keegan knows he will forever be in the friend zone with me, so I doubt he'll take this all in a creepy direction.

I sign him up for a membership, and he gives me a sweet smile.

"Thanks for earlier, I guess," I reluctantly mutter.

"My pleasure," he says, grinning.

I sigh and shake my head as he walks out the door.

Chapter 19

James

I'm still out of breath as I put on a bathrobe and grab a bottle of water from the snack table. I've just finished my last shot in *Naughty Nymphos* — literally *just* finished — and I'm still sweaty and coated in the sweet smell of Natalie Monroe, a gorgeous, voluptuous blond starlet.

Work has been a blast these past couple months. I've managed to check my whole Lola thing, and I've set my sights on raising my game. It's completely paid off, too, because I've had about eight shoots this month alone, and my bank account would be considered morbidly obese if it was a person. Yesterday I made three grand for four hours' work.

I'm just getting ready to go clean off when Rick comes up to me. He's short, stocky, and has dyed black hair that he wears slicked back like a mobster, but he's got a big smile on his face and an envelope in his hand.

"Kid! You were great in there today," he says in his raspy smoker's voice as he pats my shoulder. "I got your check right here," he adds, handing it to me.

"Thanks," I reply, returning his smile.

"I've never seen a performer last that long," he continues, "and definitely not with a girl like Natalie sucking your dick."

I chuckle. That kind of compliment would sound so weird to someone outside of our business.

"Shit like that it exactly what will make you a superstar." He smiles, and I can see the dollar signs in his eyes. "And on that note, I wanted to talk to you."

"Okay." I nod, urging him to go on.

"We're building up a new division, a different genre, you might say," he begins. "It's gonna be very lucrative."

"And what 'genre' is that?" I ask suspiciously.

"It's a little less glossy than what you've been doing," he says, cautiously approaching the topic.

"Come on, spit it out," I say, laughing.

"We're looking to expand our S&M selection," he replies, finally getting to the point. "People want BDSM now, and they're willing to pay for it. I've seen how you are with these girls: you're an alpha dog in there, kid. I think you'd be great."

I nod, recalling some of the bondage videos Sin Cinema has produced in the past.

"You okay with getting rough with the girls?" he inquires, clearly hoping I'll respond with a resounding yes.

"How rough?" I ask with uncertainty.

"You know, manhandling them a little bit, spanking them, tying them up, shit like that," he says.

I think back to Becky Callahan, one of the girls I was with in high school. She loved it rough, and she was into being tied up and spanked. Hell, I remember one time when she asked me to write "filthy whore" in Sharpie across her ass before I took her through the backdoor. She was wild, and not just for a normal girl. I know industry girls who would blush at some of the shit that girl asked me to do to her.

"Am I going to know how rough to be?" I ask Rick. "I definitely don't want to hurt anybody."

"Of course, kid." He smiles, putting his hand on my shoulder reassuringly. "Everybody will go over their limits first, you'll have a list of things that are okay to do, and if anything gets too intense, there's always a safeword that will stop the scene."

Becky and I had a safeword, though she never used it. I remember thinking she was going to once when I spanked her with a hairbrush, but she moaned for me to do it harder, and I had to tell her that I was worried it would leave a big welt. That was something that always freaked me out a little bit, seeing her ass turn bright red when I spanked her. One time she had a bruise on her right butt cheek, and I refused to spank her again for a week because I was terrified that I had really hurt her.

"Seriously, Rick, I want to make sure I don't actually hurt anybody," I say, recalling the momentary pit in my stomach when I saw the bruise on Becky's ass. "I'm cool with going all dominant on these girls, but injuries and rape fantasies are definitely not my thing."

"Understood," he replies. "I respect your concern for their wellbeing, kid. That's the kind of shit that's made you so in-demand. Our female subscribership has tripled since you started with us. You're a fuckin' legend on the Internet because they say you always make your co-stars come."

"That's true." My resulting smirk is just a little bit cocky.

"Get outta here!" He gives me a look that says I must be exaggerating.

"No, seriously," I say. "To me, the scene isn't over unless they've come at least once."

He steps back and looks at me, not saying a word. A huge grin spreads across his face, and he shakes his head as he chuckles. "Jesus Christ, I'm gonna make you a fuckin' superstar," he says.

I laugh, and I'm practically beaming. Rick's worked with some pretty big-time dudes in the industry, and for him to say that I'll be a star—a superstar even!—means I really do have what it takes. I might have sucked at school, I might be terrible with relationships, I might not be smart like Lola or rich like Keegan, but there's one thing I can do better than anybody else and that's fuck.

Now I'm inspired. Fuck all my other goals. I'm going for the fuckin' gold now. I won't stop until I'm the most famous male porn star in the world.

Chapter 20
Lola

"Fuck," I whisper to myself as I navigate my way through the giant textbook room at our campus bookstore. Why the fuck would the psychology section be so hard to find? I have my syllabus and my required reading list, so now I just need to purchase the books and my focus can shift from looking like an idiot in the bookstore to panicking about doing well in the class.

"Need some help?" a smooth, deep voice says from off to my right.

I look up to see an extremely handsome upperclassman giving me a big smile. I can tell that he's part of the whole "helping pathetic freshman like me to feel that we're not completely drowning during our first week of college" crew, and his warm demeanor is very welcome right about now.

"I, um, I'm looking for the psych area," I timidly reply.

"Let me help you out," he says. "It's right over here."

I follow him and try not to drool. He's so hot. He stands at about six-foot two, and he's got broad shoulders and a lean build like a basketball player. I'm totally captivated by his beautiful, large, deep brown eyes. His hair is dark brown and short, his smile wide, and his clothes probably cost more than I earned all summer. Good God, man! This boy is handsome like he should be on the cover of *GQ*. He reminds me of a preppy, clean-cut Josh Hartnett. And I'm digging that.

"I'm Nathan." He smiles as he reaches out his hand once we reach our destination.

"Lola," I reply, and I know I'm blushing and batting my eyes.

"Let's see if we can find you what you need, Lola," he says warmly.

Oh, Nathan, I'm guessing you could find me all kinds of what I need.

"Which ones were you looking for?" he asks, reaching out for my reading list.

"Unfortunately there are, like, fifteen on here." I blush as I hand it over.

I take a brief glance at the prices on the books, and I cringe. $175, $89, $210 — this is outrageous! *Ugh, fucking educational scam! As if it doesn't already cost enough to attend this school!*

"These are the first two," he says, motioning to a shelf with gigantic, heavy books. I don't even want to look at the price tags on these. "Looks like you've got this one — " he hands me a smaller book " — and this one here." He smiles, handing me another one.

"Wow," I sigh to myself. "This is going to cost me."

"They're pretty pricey," he says, overhearing my comment.

"Are there used ones?" I shyly ask. *Help me, Nathan, I'm poor!*

"Yeah, you have to look for the ones with the orange sticker," he sweetly replies, scanning the shelf.

He patiently assists me in grabbing as many discounted books as possible and even carries them up to the cash register for me. *Cute and a gentleman, very nice.*

"Do you need any help carrying them back to your dorm?" he volunteers with a hint of flirtation.

"Sure," I reply with a sexy smile — at least I'm attempting a sexy smile.

We walk through campus, and he asks me about my classes and my suitemates. He's really warm, and he seems like he's really listening to me when I talk. I can't even describe how nice it is to flirt with a guy who can't be intimidated by James. Nathan doesn't even know that James exists, so he can't be influenced by his caveman posturing and territorial behavior. Plus, I learn that Nathan wants to be a lawyer, and his conversation is deep and intelligent—not that I've never had deep, intelligent conversations with James. It's just that Nathan is an Ivy League man, the kind of guy who will get a job based on brains instead of looks.

My heart pounds in my chest when he asks me if I'm on Facebook. He says he'll friend me and then tells me he and his housemates are having a party this weekend and he'd love for me to come.

I'm practically giddy, though I play it cool when I reply that maybe I'll check it out. *A cute guy flirted with me, and I can act on it without James-related consequences!* College might turn out to be completely awesome! Maybe I'll find a boyfriend—a real boyfriend who isn't my childhood best friend. This could be exactly what I need to finally break me of the James spell.

Chapter 21

James

I've barely put the car in park outside my apartment building when Lexi and Tara hop out. We just wrapped a threesome shoot, and we're all still horny, so I invited them back to my place. In the back of my mind, I know it's kind of fucked up, since Chad specifically warned me about recreationally fucking Tara, but I figure having another girl there will show her that I have no intentions of making any type of commitment to her. If I fuck Lexi too, she won't think that she's got any kind of privilege with me.

We head in the apartment, and I decide this would be a good time for tequila, though I know the girls don't need anything extra to get them loosened up. I pour us all some shots, and the girls take theirs. Tara proposes a toast to my cock, which makes me laugh really hard, and we all down the first of many shots of the evening.

Today's shoot wrapped late because we were shooting outside at night, but I'm guessing I'm in for an all-nighter with these two. They are the epitome of wild girls. They're fuckin' insatiable, and they like going at it with each other as much as they like going at it with me, so I know I'll get to take a breather every now and then while I sit back and watch the show.

By about shot number five, we go into the living room, and Lexi shoves me down onto the couch. She starts making out with me while Tara unzips my jeans and starts stroking my cock. It's not long before my dick's boxing with her uvula and her loud slurping sounds are turning me on big time. As all this is happening, Lexi's boobs are in my face and she's moaning when I pinch and suck on her nipples.

None of us showered after the shoot and something about that is really hot to me. It's like we can't stop fucking, like we're animals during mating season or something.

Lexi drifts down my body, and soon she and Tara are alternating on my dick. I've had double blowjobs before, and they're sexy as fuck. One time back in high school, we were all playing truth or dare in Angie Gutierrez's basement when two girls from our rival high school got dared to simultaneously blow me. I barely knew their names, but they enthusiastically agreed. Everybody was watching as they both got to it, and I think the exhibitionism aspect of it was kind of thrilling for me because I remember looking around the room and really digging the fact that all eyes were on us. Maybe that's how this whole porn thing started.

Both Lexi and Tara are now curled up on the couch leaning over my lap as they work me with their hands, lips, tongues, and throats. I take the opportunity to slide my hands down their backs and palm their asses. Tara's a little bonier than Lexi, but both of them are arching their backs to push their butts up more, and the visual is fuckin' outrageous. *Shit, this might be even hotter than the shoot.* They're both in the same position, like a mirror image of each other, but Tara's skin is a gold-orange fake tan, and Lexi's is like a fuckin' Godiva you just can't wait to get a taste of. They're both so hot, and they're both so into this right now. Irresistible.

They start making out with each other as they lean over me, and then the three of us all exchange one sloppy, frenzied kiss before I nod to the bedroom.

The girls are giggling as they strip in front of the bed. I stand back and slowly undress as I watch them. *Let the games begin.*

They know I'm watching, they dig that I'm watching, and I can tell they're really performing for me. Lexi gets on her back on the bed and opens her legs really wide as Tara comes over to her. After some making out and a little nipple action, Tara moves between Lexi's legs and starts going down on her. I defy anyone to find a guy who doesn't think this shit is hot, and I love hearing Lexi moan about how good it feels. A lot of normal girls don't get this vocal—but then again, a lot of normal girls don't put on spontaneous girl/girl shows for their boyfriends. *Ah, the benefits of fucking other porn stars.*

They move into a sixty-nine for a little while, but it's too hot and I can't sit back and watch any longer. I come over to them, and they switch it up so I'm taking Lexi doggy-style while she goes down on Tara. This is almost exactly what we did in the scene—life imitating art—but I did Tara first on the shoot today.

It's only after we've been going at it for about an hour and Lexi sits on my face while Tara rides me that my mind starts wandering. I realize how weird it is to think about Lola at a time like this, but she's always kind of on my mind, I guess. She'll be here next week, and I'm really excited for her visit. It's been over three months, and I can't wait to see her. She said school is going well and she's made some new friends, which makes me happy. She's in her element with those smart kids, and she's exactly where she should be.

The girls switch positions, and Tara comes almost instantly when I start licking her. She tells me all the time that she loves my tongue, and I lick her into her fifth and sixth orgasm of the evening. Meantime, Lexi's writhing and panting as she rides me reverse-cowgirl. Both of them are getting really loud and shouting all kinds of porno shit. "I love the way that big cock stretches my tight little pussy!" "Rub your tongue on my clit, baby!" "Harder! Harder! Fuck me!" It's all very performance-ish, but sexy in this context.

Shit like this is fun. I'm officially out of my guilt funk, and I'm enjoying every second of fucking these two. Wild girls, that's my thing. Not innocent, sweet, delicate little flowers like Lola. Maybe intimacy is overrated. After all, sex is really just biology, so why weigh it down with all kinds of emotional baggage? Making love is a myth. It's just fucking with more eye contact. I don't need that shit. I need this—crazy, cock-hungry girls who scream obscenities and live for having my cock inside them. Lola would never do that, and I wouldn't want her to, which just goes to show that she's not the one for me.

"Wait," Tara pants as she moves off me.

"Uh-huh?" I ask, wiping my mouth with my hand.

"Lube," she says.

"Top drawer," I say, pointing to the nightstand.

"I want it in my ass." She smiles as she reaches into the nightstand and grabs the lube.

I watch them make out with each other for a while before I get behind Tara and start taking her via the backdoor. Lexi gets underneath her and rubs her clit, and I'm kind of ashamed to admit that I zone out for a little bit in the middle of things. I'm thinking about totally mundane shit, too. *Remember to tidy things up next week before Lola gets here so she'll think it's nice and not a fuckin' pigsty. Fill up the tank in case I have to circle the airport when I pick her up. Groceries. And turkey bacon—she's got that whole thing with pork. What should I cook for her? Will she sleep in my bed with me when she's here? I hope I get to cuddle with her. That's my favorite thing to do.*

All these random thoughts are running through my head, and I'm kind of disconnected to Lexi and Tara, but not necessarily in a bad way. I'm still an active participant in this whole thing; I just don't have to be emotionally invested in it. "Going through the motions" isn't exactly the right way to put it, but this is almost like muscle memory for me at this point. I know how to shift my pelvis when I'm deep inside them. I know how to work them with my fingers and my tongue. I know how to pull their hair or talk dirty to them, so it's not even something I have to consciously think about.

The three of us are sweating buckets, and I can feel my muscles starting to burn from just how long we've been carrying on with this. Thankfully, they seem even more worn out than me, and I can tell they're ready for me to finish, probably so we can all just crash in my bed. That idea is sounding progressively better as I pound into Tara over and over.

"Oh, fuck!" she wails, her voice raspy from all the moaning. "I'm coming! Oh, God! Fuck meeee!"

Sweat drips off my forehead and lands on her back as I grab her hips and fuck her hard, fast and deep. It starts building up for me, and I close my eyes and let myself really feel everything.

"Does that tight little ass feel good, James?" Lexi purrs as she moves to kiss me.

"Fuck yeah," I pant.

"Mmm, are you gonna come, baby?"

"Uh-huh," I exhale as another bead of sweat drips off my brow.

"Pull out and come on my titties, sexy," she whispers to me as she nudges Tara.

Both girls turn and flop onto their backs, opening their legs and playing with themselves while I stroke myself to completion. They moan louder than I do when I finally pop, and they start making out with each other as I try to get my heart rate somewhat back to normal. This feels so porno, and it's almost an exact reenactment of what we did at the shoot today.

That night, I go to sleep with two hot chicks tangled up with me, and I feel like such a fuckin' pimp.

See? My life is rad, even when Lola's not around me.

Chapter 22

Lola

It's funny how everything seems to move in slow-mo when you're in a hurry. As I stand here waiting to get off the plane at LAX, everything and everyone around me is annoying the crap out of me because they seem to be taking their sweet time. Take the guy un-wedging his bag from the overhead compartment right now, for example. He smushed it in there so hard that I'm not surprised he's grunting and yanking at it to try to free it. They really should have made him check it—then he'd be hurrying to get to baggage claim just like I am. I wish this guy with the bag and the mom with her two little kids would get a move on. James is waiting for me at baggage claim right now, and I wish I could harness the power of teleportation so I could jump into his arms and give him a huge hug.

It's not like it's been ages since I've seen him, but still, I missed him terribly. I've successfully completed my first two weeks in college, and I feel like a different person, a more mature person, the kind of person who's rational enough to not get sidetracked by her best friend's spectacular good looks and charm. I can handle it this time. I can look at James and appreciate his gorgeousness while still keeping him firmly in the friend zone in my mind.

Finally this dumbass gets his bag down and the flow of traffic off the plane can continue. The flight attendant greets everyone with "buh-bye," and I nearly run down the jetway to get to baggage claim. I'm clipping along in my espadrilles, which were just a bit too summery to wear back in New England but are perfect for Southern California, and I hike my carry-on bag up on my shoulder. *Move it, people! My best friend's waiting!*

Finally, I get to baggage claim, and I spot him immediately. *Sweet Jesus!* James has always had an athletic body, but his recent fitness kick has taken him from buff-guy-in-your-hometown to buff-guy-who-should-be-in-an-action-movie. He's built like fucking Conan the Barbarian now! I can see a hint of his chiseled pecs peeking out from his V-neck, his biceps are stretching the fabric of his T-shirt, his shoulders look broader than before, and his chocolate brown hair seems wavier and wilder than before. He's like a walking romance novel cover: the muscles, the long hair, the swagger that says he could rip your bodice and ravish you...or maybe that's my stubborn attraction trying to break out of the mental cage where I've locked it.

He scans the space, searching for me. A huge, perfect, bright white smile spreads across his face the second his eyes meet mine, and he runs over and throws his arms around me, scooping me up and twirling me around while he kisses my cheek over and over.

"I missed you so much, kid!" He grins and kisses the top of my head as he puts me down.

"Same." I smile. "I was, like, ready to kill people if they didn't get the fuck out of my way so I could race down here to get to you."

"That would have been an interesting news story," he says, laughing. "KTLA reporting live from the scene where a tiny girl has just murdered six people because she wanted to hurry to see her best friend."

"That's basically what it would have been." I chuckle.

"Come on," he says, patting my butt, "let's get your shit, and you can see my apartment."

As we wait at the carousel for my bag, he puts his arm around me, resting his big, strong hand on my hip. I always feel so small when I'm up against him like this, but I love it. It's very symbolic of our relationship. He's big and strong, I'm little and scrawny, but we just click together like we were designed as a pair.

"It's that one, the red one," I say, pointing to my bag as it slides down the chute.

He grabs it one-handed and pops out the handle, rolling it along as we walk out to his car. He's parked right outside, and I don't know how he got away with that. They're normally so strict about letting unattended vehicles park within so many yards of an airport. I soon realize that the guard at this section of the curb is a woman, and she eyes James like he's filet mignon. This dude has lived in a hotness bubble his whole life, and he can get away with murder as long as a woman is involved. He's such a charmer, and a flash of his smile opens doors that would be closed to us mortal human beings. The guy's a fucking sex superhero, and the old, reliable James Laird Sex Laser Beam seems to immobilize the rational mind of nearly every girl he sees.

We hop in Pansy, and it's nice to be riding in this car again, even if it has nearly two hundred thousand miles on it. We buckle up, and we're on our way to his apartment. I like seeing palm trees and sunlight. It's a nice change of pace from the colonial, Founding Fathers era, stuffy educational institution I've recently moved into.

We arrive at his apartment complex, which looks like it was built in the late seventies or early eighties. It's three stories with outdoor staircases and hallways. The doors are all painted turquoise, and the railings are all a Pepto-Bismol pink—very eighties colors. I know these places aren't particularly expensive, since James knows how to be thrifty, but they're really not too bad. Even cheap apartments out here are probably twice what they would cost in our hometown, and even though he's making pretty good money now, I'm glad he didn't try to splurge on some extravagant place. He's smart like that, knowing that he should save up for the day when he can no longer fuck for a living.

We get to his door, and he unlocks it and ushers me inside. His place is surprisingly roomy, and aside from the low ceilings, it doesn't look all that dated inside. The floor plan is pretty open with the living room to the right and the kitchen straight ahead. There's a breakfast bar looking over a small table by the window. On the other side of the room is a small area with a desk and his MacBook Pro closed beside a stack of what appear to be porn photos—probably stills from his movies. The bedroom is down the hall, and the bathroom is next to that.

I recognize a painting his mom did several years ago hanging on the wall between the kitchen and the bedroom, and it makes me feel a little sad. It's sweet that he still has this memento of his mom in his place, even though it's probably a hurtful reminder of the happy family life he once had.

"You hungry?" he calls out as he puts my bag down in his bedroom.

"Yeah," I reply. "I had a bagel this morning, but I was too psyched to eat lunch."

That makes him grin proudly, and he comes over to give me a hug. I can tell that he missed me from the way he completely envelops me, blanketing me with his adoration. It makes me feel warm inside to know that he cares about me so much because I cherish his friendship and the deep bond that we have.

"There's a sushi place I want to take you to. It's one of those trendy places that the cool people go to—which is lame, I know—but they have really good unagi, so you'll like it," he offers.

"Sweet," I say, nodding. "Can I change into something more trendy and fashionable, you know, since I'm gonna hang with the cool kids and all?"

"Sure." He chuckles. "But you look beautiful already."

It makes me smile, and his words melt into me like marshmallows in hot cocoa.

I go into the bedroom and put on a cute, casual, sleeveless dress. It's got a green, floral pattern that distracts from my enormous boobs and makes my body look less top-heavy. I run a brush through my long hair, dab on a little lip gloss, and I think I look decent enough to hang with the in-crowd.

"Gorgeous," James says when I emerge. "When did you get this?"

"I bought it right before I moved because it was really hot and muggy, but then it got colder and I only got the chance to wear it once," I reply.

"See, think about what it'd be like if you lived out here," he says with a grin. "You could wear sexy stuff like this all the time."

"Wouldn't that give you heart palpitations?" I snicker. "You're already paranoid enough as it is about guys checking me out. I'm sure you'd be a nervous wreck if I walked around showing skin."

"Yeah, but *I'd* get to look at all your skin," he says flirtatiously. "And I'd just stare down anybody else who tried to do it."

I roll my eyes with a laugh and reach for my purse.

We get to the sushi place, and he's right: it is trendy. Everybody here looks like they're an actor or a model, and I feel a little self-conscious. All their looks are very put together, but in that I-just-threw-these-clothes-on-because-I-don't-care kind of way. Very calculated, but trying to look like it's totally effortless.

We sit down at our table, and the waitress comes by to get our drink orders. She's pretty, probably early twenties with flat-ironed, blond hair, and a totally SoCal tan. She flashes her bleached white smile at James, and he returns it with a sexy smile of his own. *Such a flirt!* She likes what she sees, and she barely even looks at me, which I pretty much expect at this point. It happens whenever I go out somewhere with him. The ladies are just hypnotized by his square jaw, hazel eyes, high cheekbones, and pouty lips. Can't say I blame them. He's got the face of a male model and the body of Greek god.

"So how's business?" I smile at him. "Last I heard you had another shoot with that Lexi Jaxxxon girl," I say, referencing the pretty porn starlet who looks like a combination of Aaliyah and Gabrielle Union.

He nods. "It was a fun one. She gets wild, dude. She's all flexible, too, so we were doing some crazy positions—shit that wasn't even on the lineup for that day."

I laugh and shake my head. "You got her to bend the rules for you?"

"Hey, she was the one who suggested it. You should have seen this blowjob she gave me. Epic, dude! She does this thing with her tongue that's just—"

"I don't need all the details." I put up my hand as I chuckle.

"Sorry." He snickers with that smart-ass grin. "Don't want to offend my pristine little princess."

I give him a pretend scowl and blush.

"I just don't need the play-by-play on a blowjob," I say. "So the gist of it is that things are good for you. The shoot went well, and you're out here dishing out dick like it's going out of style."

"Pretty much," he says through hearty laughter.

"Well, good. I'm happy for you." I chuckle. At least he's channeling that hyperactive sex drive into work and not just plowing random floozies.

"You'll meet Lexi tomorrow," he adds. "She'll be at Rick's party."

Rick is the guy who owns Sin Cinema, the production company where James does the majority of his movies. It's Labor Day weekend, and Rick's having a barbecue at his house. James invited me to come as his date, since I was dying to come out to California and visit him anyway, and I happily accepted. There are going to be a lot of industry people there, and I'm a little nervous because I've never been to a porn party and I have no idea what to expect.

"Are there gonna be, like, people fucking everywhere? Is it going to be like the Playboy Mansion or something?" I meekly inquire. "I mean, is this going to turn into some kind of orgy?"

"Yeah, Lola, I'm *so* sure I'd bring you to an orgy," he says dryly. "I don't want any guys to fuckin' touch you, so the first place I'd bring you is to a big, giant fuck fest."

"Well, how am I supposed to know?" I laugh. "I don't know what you guys do. These are all people who have sex for a living the way other people would send a fax or fill out a spreadsheet. How do I know I won't end up plugged in both ends by two guys in a grotto or something?"

"Rick doesn't have a grotto." He grins mischievously, leaving out anything about the whole double-stuff scenario.

I shoot him a smirk.

"Besides, you know I'd never let you lose it at some porn guy's party," he adds with a smile. "You deserve, like, a candlelit, romantic, passionate situation — like maybe in front of a fireplace or some romancey stuff like that."

I burst into laughter, and he looks amused. I think James has envisioned my perfect first time more than I have.

"So you'll be my bodyguard for any guys who want to introduce me to anal?" I joke.

"I will defend your virtue and your ass to the death," he says in a knightly vow.

"Good." I giggle. "Glad to see I have such an honorable, upstanding gentleman for a best friend."

The waitress brings out a giant plate of sushi that probably cost a fortune. James has insisted on paying for everything — including my plane ticket — and whenever I object, he tells me how he's making up to four grand per scene and sometimes shoots four scenes a week. I like that he's saving up by keeping his expenses low. It's smart and mature, and I'm proud to see him exhibiting those qualities.

The food is delicious! The tuna, salmon, shrimp, and eel are all amazing. We chat about being able to use chopsticks and how we're way too cool to ask for forks. Our fifth grade teacher lived in Japan for a while, and we used to have field trips to a sushi place in town so we could all experience the cuisine as part of an effort to provide cultural enrichment. Our school was cool like that.

James gives me shit when I ask him to let me pay my half of the check, and I eventually give up and let him treat me. It's cute when he tries to be a gentleman like this. Hard to believe that he's chivalrous and respectful when you think about all the kinky stuff he's done and the gargantuan number of women he's bedded.

We get back to his apartment, and I'm wiped out from the long day. The boring flight and the time difference kicked my ass, plus I'm sleepy from being so stuffed with food. He lets me take the first shower, and I change into some pajama shorts and a tank top. Last time I wore these skimpy pajamas, he got all hot and bothered, and we ended up having a little romp in the guest bedroom at my house. I can't say it wasn't in the back of my mind when I packed this ensemble. It's not that I want it to happen again — well, maybe I do a little bit — but I like the idea of him finding me sexy. He's sampled every girl, every type, every shape, every height and race, and it's cool to think that I would score a high rank on his hotness list.

His eyes get wide when he sees me, and I know that he's on to my little game. He gives me a flirty grin as he passes me to go into the bathroom. He knows what I'm up to, and I wonder if he'll act on it.

He gets out of the shower and he walks into the living room in just a towel. Clearly he's going to combat me with a little display of his own. As I sit on the couch, I try not to be too conspicuous as I quickly steal a glance at his washboard abs and broad, toned shoulders. *Yep, his hours at the gym have certainly paid off.*

"Get up." He grins, motioning for me to stand.

"Hmm?" I reply.

"You're sleeping with me," he says like it's totally obvious.

I try to suppress it, but that puts a big smile on my face. He takes my hand and leads me into his bedroom, and I'm beaming. I didn't want to be presumptuous, but I was practically praying I'd get to sleep all cuddled up to him tonight.

I get under the covers in his bed, and he gives me a flirty grin as he unwraps his towel and reaches for a pair of boxers from his dresser. My eyes are wide as I try not to gasp. He's got a perfect ass, and I blush as I catch a little glimpse between his legs. *Yeah, that definitely lives up to the legend.* I've seen it a few times before, but not in the past several years, so it hasn't entirely lost its scandalous allure.

When he turns around, he smirks the second he sees my expression. He knows I was surprised, and he totally digs that he ruffled me. He crawls over me on the bed, briefly pausing above me and giving me a sexy smile before he gets under the covers with me.

"Come on," he says, "get over here and let me hold you."

I can't help it. I'm beaming from how sweet that sounds. Not come over here and let me fuck you, come over here and let me rip your clothes off, but come over here and let me *hold* you. He was just subtly flashing me his dick, but all he really wants to do is snuggle. I love it!

He kisses my forehead as I rest my cheek on his light sprinkling of chest hair. A wave of relaxation and contentment comes over me as he lightly strokes his fingers up and down my back and plays with a lock of my hair. He can be so tender when it comes to me. I smile myself to sleep feeling completely adored.

Chapter 23

James

"Stop messing with it. It looks really good," I say to Lola as she looks in the visor mirror and brushes her fingers through her hair for the zillionth time on the drive to Rick's house.

"I just want it to look right," she says, biting her bottom lip in concentration. I love when she does that. It's sort of sexy in an innocent way.

"It does look right, so quit fucking with it," I say with a laugh.

She looks great. I don't know what she's worried about. Her petite, little body's looking toned and firm in all the right places. She's got on a red sundress that gives off kind of a hippie vibe, and her legs are looking mad long in her heeled sandals. Her hair is loose and wavy in that natural way that I've always thought was pretty, and she's always thought looked too messy. She's got on a little necklace with a small, silver hummingbird that I got her for her fifteenth birthday, which is really sweet and sentimental to me, and it hangs off her neck just above her cleavage — which is lookin' mighty fine, if I do say so myself. She looks hot, as always, but she's being all girly and getting self-conscious.

We pull up in Rick's driveway, and Lola looks impressed. It's one of those Spanish villa types of places, and he's got a fountain in front of the circle drive and gold everything like he's Donald Trump. Rick's got money, for sure. He's been in the business since the late eighties, and he's worked with some of the biggest porn stars in history—household names that even regular people would recognize. I started out working with him when I was nineteen and he put me in my first porn flick with Shawnna Hendrix, who was one of the biggest stars in porn at the time. She was ten years older than me and on her way to retirement, but that woman rocked my fuckin' world, and I was hooked on the business after that.

Rick's got waiters running around dishing out drinks, and one of them leads us to the backyard, where Rick's grilling food and everybody's hanging out around the pool. The whole Sin Cinema gang is here, and I like that Lola's going to meet my work friends.

"Come on, let me introduce you to some people," I say, taking her hand and leading her into the sprawling yard.

First, I want to introduce her to Rick, since he always makes fun of how much I talk about her. He gives me a giant smile, and his eyes get all big when he sees the gorgeous girl on my arm. *That's right. I told you she was a stunner.*

"Lola, this is Rick, the owner of the company," I say to her before turning to him. "Rick, this is my best friend, Lola."

"Very nice to meet you, sweetheart." Rick smiles at her as he shakes her hand.

She grins, and I know what she's thinking. He looks like a walking stereotype of a porn producer. In real life, he's a nice dude, but he wants to look like something out of *Goodfellas*. Eh, to each his own, right?

"I've heard so much about you. This kid won't shut up about how gorgeous you are. Glad to see he wasn't bullshitting me. You're a knockout, honey," Rick says to her.

"Jeez, thanks," she says, blushing. "I've heard a lot about you too. James loves working for you."

"That's good to hear, since I love working with him," Rick politely replies. "He's gonna be huge. I keep tellin' him he's got the makings of a superstar."

I smile proudly when Lola nods in agreement.

We leave Rick so I can take her around and introduce her to people. She meets Rick's assistant, Christie, who's in her early forties and sweet as can be. She got into the business decades ago trying to be a star—she's blond and pretty so it made sense—but she got married and had a son, so she decided fucking onscreen wasn't for her. Now she's Rick's right-hand woman, and she's basically the one who keeps the whole production office together. She loves Lola—*natch*—and they have a friendly conversation for a little while. Lola's easy to like, so I'm not surprised that everyone she meets thinks she's great.

"I thought I saw you over here," someone says as they grab my shoulders from the back. I turn around and see Chad giving me a big smile.

"Hey!" I grin at him. "I didn't see you. I wanted to introduce you to—"

"Oh, my God, you're Lola!" He nearly gasps as he takes her hand and plants a playful kiss on her knuckles.

"Quite the greeting," she says.

"Lola, this is my friend, Chad," I say to her.

She looks very cheerful as they exchange hellos.

Chad and Alejandro are basically the nicest dudes you could ever meet, so I'm certain that Lola will get along great with them.

"Is Alejandro here?" I ask him. "I want her to meet him."

"We're over by the waterfall," he says, motioning for us to follow him.

Lola gives me a big smile as we walk over to the little waterfall Rick's got by the man-made pond in the back yard. She's heard a lot about these guys, and I know she's excited to hang out with them. She knows that they were the first people to really befriend me when I moved out here, and even though they knew I could make bank in porn, they never tried to pressure me into it. They were great because they showed me the best routes to get places, where the gourmet markets were—since I love to cook—and even which DMV always has the shortest lines for when I had to get my California license.

"Honey, look who's here!" Chad says when we see Alejandro.

"Is this her?" he gasps.

"Just as stunning as he said, right?" Chad smiles, and Lola blushes.

"Lola, it's such a pleasure to meet you," Alejandro says to her as he shakes her hand. "You know what, I'm gonna give you a hug because I feel like we're friends already," he sweetly adds as he pulls her in.

She likes it; I can tell from her big smile.

"Now, you're out here visiting during your break from school, right?" Chad says as he ushers her to sit down in a chair with them. I follow and sit next to her.

"Right." She nods. "I had time with Labor Day weekend and all, so I figured it would be nice to come out here, get some sunshine, and see my dude." She giggles on that last word, and I feel really flattered all of a sudden.

Her dude. I like the sound of that.

"I'm so glad you could come out here!" Chad says. "You would not believe how much we've heard about you. We could practically write a biography on you from how much he gushes about you."

Gushes. It makes me get all shy because it's totally true, even though I don't want her to know it.

"When he first moved here, it was 'oh, Lola would love that' and 'oh, I wish Lola was here so we could do this.' He built you up like you were Beyoncé."

She laughs hard and gives me a cute smile like she knows it's true and she's barely biting her tongue on making fun of me for it. I give her a playful smirk, and she doesn't call me on it.

"I hope I live up to the hype," she jokes.

"Well, you're even prettier than he said, so you've already beat that expectation." Alejandro smiles at her.

"Jeez, you guys are too kind," she says, giggling. "I figured no one would even give me a second look at a party full of super-hot porn stars."

"You're fresh meat," Chad teases. "Everybody here has had sex with everybody else here, so we're all bored of each other." Alejandro nods. "You're new blood, and everybody's probably eyeing you."

She laughs hard, and I can see her cheeks start to turn pink.

We're both hungry, so we grab a couple of the burgers Rick's been grilling—veggie for her and regular for me—and we sit down with the guys. They keep revealing how much I talk about her and how I always tell them that my best friend is the coolest, the prettiest, the smartest—all that stuff. I'm so embarrassed because it's all totally true. I do *gush* about her. I can't help it. She's my little angel, and I feel honored that she's even friends with me, let alone best friends with me.

After a little while, we decide to walk around so she can meet some more people. I introduce her to a few of the girls I've worked with, including Amber Blaze, the super-hot redhead whose website gets more hits than any other girl in the biz. Amber's really cool, a very free spirit kind of girl, and way more mature than her nineteen years. I like her a lot, and since I did a shoot with her a couple months ago, we've hung out and had lunch several times. She's super nice to Lola — probably because she's heard me go on and on about her too — and they seem to get on pretty well.

Lola's getting a raspberry lemonade from the bar when we're approached by Lexi and Tara Morgan. Frankly, I'm a little nervous about how this is going to go down.

"Hey, baby," Tara says, grabbing me and kissing me on the mouth. "It's good to see you."

"We saw you over here lookin' sexy and wondered why you hadn't come over to say hello to us," Lexi adds with a sultry purr.

Lola's a little bit behind me, so I can't get a read on her reaction.

They both don't even say hello to her, which is kind of rude, so I make a point to introduce her. I can tell from her expression that she's not exactly thrilled to meet them. They act just a little bit arrogant, and I know she doesn't dig their attitude.

"You're the high school girl, right?" Tara says in a vaguely condescending tone.

"College, actually. A university." Lola smiles defiantly. *Such a tough cookie, my girl.*

"Oh," Tara says like she's a little surprised that Lola checked her. "And you're the one that's known him since you were kids?" she asks her in a way that seems kind of like she's talking down to her.

I want to step in, but Lola's got this. I've seen her deal with this kind of girl rivalry bullshit before, and she's no delicate flower when it comes to this stuff.

"Yes." She nods. "James and I have been best friends since childhood. We grew up together. We're practically family."

"Closer than family." I smile at her as I put my arm around her and give her a wink to acknowledge that I see how the girls are a little bit bitchy.

"I see," Tara says, looking her over.

"That's cute," Lexi chimes in condescendingly.

"James has made lots of new friends out here." Tara grins smugly. "Lots of very tight friends," she says, thinking she's making some kind of clever play on words.

Lola can't hold back an eye roll, and Tara looks none too pleased to see it.

"Have you ever seen any of his work?" Lexi asks.

Lola shakes her head. "No, just heard his stories about it."

"Well, he's very good at what he does. Personally, he's my favorite guy to work with. In fact, I'm planning to do another shoot with him very soon," Tara says with a conceited smile. "He and I always have a lot of fun."

"I'm sure you do," Lola replies with the vaguest hint of a scoff.

"All of us just love James around here," Lexi says, flashing me a flirty smile.

Lola nods, and she's got the most perfect fake smile on her face. "I'm not surprised," she says. "He's easy to love."

I can tell these girls are annoying her, but she doesn't need me to step in. She's tough as shit, even though she's tiny and adorable, and chicks like this aren't going to ruffle her feathers. Still, I put my hand on her shoulder, just to make that physical contact and show her that she's the winner here. No matter how weirdly arrogant and possessive Tara or Lexi might be about me, I'd ditch both of them in an instant to hang out with Lola.

They exchange those fake pleasantries that girls give to each other when they secretly don't like each other. I've never understood why girls don't just say what they mean. Lola doesn't like them. They have some kind of weird mean-girl cockiness toward her, and I don't know why they're even standing here trying to pretend to be polite to each other, but this is some kind of weird chick code where they'll be nice to each other's faces and then stab each other in the back the first chance they get. For as much experience as I have with girls, I will never understand some of the shit they do.

I make up some excuse about wanting to ask Rick something, and I take Lola's hand as we walk away from them.

"Okay, what's up with those two?" she asks when we get somewhere more private. "What's their deal? They're all bitchy and combative."

"Who knows." I shrug. "Maybe they're jealous." I don't really want to get into *why* they're jealous, since I know that's a little bit my fault.

"Jealous of what?" she scoffs with a laugh.

"Because you're prettier," I say, kissing her forehead. "And sweeter," I add as I kiss her right cheek. "And smarter." I kiss her left. "And all-around cooler than they'll ever be," I conclude with a kiss on the tip of her nose.

"You're such a charmer," she says with a flattered giggle.

"But I'm also honest." I grin at her.

As we're walking back toward Chad and Alejandro, I see Ethan Dane—my rival, my nemesis, the Newman to my Jerry Seinfeld—walking toward us. He's scoping Lola pretty hard, and I can feel my jaw clench as I step a little in front of her. It's one of those possessive displays of canine dominance à la Cesar Millan, but it's instinct for me at this point.

"Hey, man. How's it going?" Ethan smiles at me.

I give him a nod. "Great, dude, and you?"

"Really great," he says, cutting the greetings and looking at Lola. "Hi." He smiles flirtatiously as he reaches out and shakes her hand. "I'm Ethan."

"I'm Lola," she says. "Nice to meet you, Ethan."

I've told Lola about Ethan Dane, but not a ton about him. He and I are both the passion guys, the ones that have a growing female following. He's only about five-foot nine, but he's really buff and he's got a tattoo on his shoulder of the lyrics from a Bob Dylan song, which somehow makes him deep, I guess. We're always in the running for the same movies, and we've had this professional rivalry since my second or third movie. We started out around the same time and both of us are getting pretty big, so we're kind of competitive. Right now, it looks like he wants to compete over Lola. Little does he know, that shit ain't gonna happen.

"Ethan works for Rick too," I say, putting my arm around her waist and pulling her into my side.

"That's right! I've heard of you." She smiles at him and curls into me a little more. I can tell she's cool with playing things up because she knows I'm annoyed and I want to tell Ethan to back off of her.

"Oh, yeah?" He grins, practically licking his chops at her. "Have you seen any of my movies?"

"I haven't seen any porn movies," she says, giggling. "Not even his."

It's true. She's seen a couple of pics, but it was mostly me blurry in the background while the camera focused on the girl I was plowing. She told me she's too scared to see my movies — which is too adorable!

"You should check them out." Ethan smiles. "You might like what you see."

"Maybe she'll watch a couple of mine this weekend," I say, unconsciously amping up the sex appeal. "She could see how a pro does it."

She giggles and looks into my eyes with this really sultry look that takes me by surprise. Lola can be so seductive without even realizing it.

"How long are you in town?" Ethan asks her, licking his lips.

Dude licks his lips while he's making eyes at my girl! What the fuck, man?

"Just the weekend," she replies. "Just a little visit out here to be with him," she says, putting her hand on my stomach in a flirty gesture of her own.

"Nice. Are you going to come down to a shoot?"

"I don't know if I could handle that." She blushes, probably imagining something totally lewd and nasty.

"It's not so bad. In fact, I hear it can be a very memorable experience," he replies, sneaking a glance at her cleavage.

"I don't doubt that!" she says through a big laugh.

"I have a shoot tomorrow," he says flirtatiously. "You should swing by."

"I'm taking her out tomorrow," I interrupt with a little more bass in my voice. "She's visiting me, and I'm planning to spend every waking minute with her."

The expression on Lola's face is a cross between a blush, a flattered smile, and a very amused smirk. But she rolls with it, and she doesn't even flinch when I slide my hand down to her hip and tug her closer to me.

Ethan seems to take the hint, and he keeps the flirtation to an acceptable level for the rest of the brief conversation.

"So that's the infamous Ethan Dane?" she says with a chuckle once he's out of earshot. "The rival. The great adversary."

"Yep." I nod. "The challenger to the throne."

She snickers loudly and rolls her eyes. "Not much of a challenge, babe."

I pause and smile broadly at her before I reply, "You are the coolest girl in the world, I swear."

"Hey, just like you, I'm honest." She winks, referencing my comment from earlier.

I grab her face and kiss her forehead as she laughs.

We go back over to Chad and Alejandro, and we hang with them for a while and talk shit. Lola and Chad both love shitty reality shows, and they compare notes about the best bad movies or the worst music videos. They're pop culture heads, and they're practically best friends by the end of the day. I knew she'd get along great with these guys. They're good dudes.

When we leave the party, we decide to go see a movie and then go back home to chill out. I want to take Lola to the beach tomorrow—and not just because I want to see her in a bikini. I think she'll like relaxing in the sun, and I'll like relaxing with her while she's in a bikini. It's more of an added bonus than a straight-up goal.

She seems to be getting less self-conscious by the minute, and she comes out in just a towel after her shower. There are still little beads of water on her shoulders, and I love that she's all wet and sexy. I'm in the room when she goes over to her suitcase to get pajamas. I pretend to look away, but I totally check out her ass as she pulls off the towel and changes into some boy-shorts and a jersey knit nightie. *Hot.*

We crawl under the covers together, and I rest my arm over her waist as she lies on her back. She turns her head to look at me and gives me a sweet, shy smile.

"James," she says, "thanks for sticking by me at the party...you know, especially with those girls and stuff. I think I would have been a lot more nervous if you weren't right by my side the whole time like that."

"I'll always stick by you, Lo. I got your back." I give her a little squeeze.

She doesn't reply. She just brushes her fingers down my shoulder and then leans in to kiss my cheek. It's gentle and loving, that kind of sweet kiss that makes your heart flutter like some shit out of a cartoon. I close my eyes and absorb the feeling as she plants little, soft kisses across my cheeks, up the bridge of my nose, across my forehead, and along my jaw. The tenderness of it is what gets me, and I feel all warm and cozy.

"Goodnight, James," she whispers, kissing my cheek one more time and then curling into me.

"Goodnight, babe," I softly reply.

What an awesome way to fall asleep.

Chapter 24
Lola

James holds my hand as we shuffle toward the marina. He's arranged something today, and the only thing he would tell me was that it involved a boat — or yacht, I guess. I know absolutely nothing about boats, but most of these look pretty expensive. We head down a dock to a large yacht with dark wood paneling and gold railings. The writing sprawled across the back in gold cursive says "Dirty Oar."

"Seriously?" I smirk at James.

"It's dumb, but come on." He smiles broadly as he leads me up some stairs and onto the deck.

A handsome older gentleman who looks a little like Sean Connery steps out and introduces himself as Captain Scott. "The others are already here," he says, motioning for us to go inside.

We step into the cabin, and it's tacky opulence everywhere. It looks like Louis XIV threw up in here, gold everything, white leather sofas, marbled wood paneling on the walls. I instantly know who the yacht belongs to, and I give James a look.

"Rick said I could use it." He grins mischievously, nearly laughing at the way I'm holding back from commenting on the decor.

"Chad, honey, they're here!" Alejandro says, emerging from an outside door.

"They are?" I hear Chad's voice call from the main deck.

Alejandro gives James a hug before moving on to hug me. He's so cut, and I can feel his bulging biceps around me. He looks totally hot in shorts and a black wifebeater that shows off his sleeve of beautiful sugar skulls and other Day of the Dead emblems. Chad comes in soon after in shorter shorts and no shirt, showing off his golden tan and making his blue eyes really pop. He walks his tall, lean frame over to me and gives me a big hug, kissing my cheek and telling me that the orange, cotton sundress I have on over my bikini looks gorgeous. With compliments flying like this, I could really get used to hanging out with these guys.

It seems that James and the boys called in a favor from Rick to take me out on his yacht today for some fun in the sun. I feel sappy for admitting it, but I find it so touching that the three of them put this together. James does nice stuff for me all the time, but it's so sweet of Chad and Alejandro to come along too. I had so much fun with them at the barbecue, and it's really cool to spend this time getting to know them better.

I want to put my purse down and change, so I start off to find the bedrooms — turns out there are three, including a master suite with a king bed. James follows on my heels and closes the door a little bit behind him when we arrive in a large room with a mirrored wall and black wood everything. It looks like every eighties shopping mall crammed into one room. I'm guessing Rick bought this boat quite some time ago, probably late eighties or early nineties, which would coincide with when Sin Cinema first took off, according to what James told me.

I turn to him and snicker when I hit a switch that reveals recessed lighting around a big octagonal mirror on the ceiling.

"If the boat's a rockin'…" he jokes.

"Yuck!" I laugh.

"I hope this is cool," he whispers as he pulls his T-shirt shirt off and starts unbuttoning his jeans. "Chad sent me a text that said how much they loved meeting you, and I wanted to take you out here with me anyway, so I thought they could come too."

"I'm psyched," I reply. "I think this was a great idea."

"Really?" He grins with pride.

"Really." I nod and put my hands on his shoulders as I lean up to kiss his cheek. It makes him look adorably bashful, and I love it.

He slides his jeans down, and I blush a little bit, assuming I shouldn't stand there and stare while he changes into his trunks. I turn away from him and pull my dress over my head, leaving me in a bikini and flip-flops. I take the hair tie from my wrist and start gathering my hair into a ponytail when I catch a quick glimpse of James in the reflection from one of the many mirrored surfaces. He's totally naked, chiseled to absolute perfection, and he's looking up and down my body as I attempt to tame my hair. He's just so…sexy. It gives me a little shiver to think that such a beautiful guy is checking me out, but I shrug inwardly when I remember that the beautiful guy in question is my best friend, not some hottie boyfriend.

James and I emerge from the bedroom to find Chad and Alejandro on the back deck, Chad soaking up the sun at the patio table and Alejandro preparing the grill.

"Damn, girl!" Alejandro grins when he sees me. "You've got a body by Gucci!"

I laugh loudly and curve forward a little in an attempt to hide my huge boobs, which must be what he's referring to. They're way too big for my body, and I've been self-conscious about them for years, but Alejandro's being playful, and it's cute.

"Come over here, Hottie Boombalottie," Chad says, patting the chair beside him. "Come sit next to me."

I happily oblige, squeezing out a dab of sunscreen from the bottle on the floor and lathering it on.

Captain Scott fires up the motor, and we start heading out into the water. Once we're sufficiently far from the shore, we park — probably not the proper nautical term, but whatever. Alejandro tells us to leave the grilling to him and go enjoy the sun on the main deck, so the three of us head up to the big deck on the front, which Chad refers to as the foredeck. I blush a little and smile to myself. I'm so not a boat girl, and James laughs whenever I joke about starboard sides and going aft.

"Here, we have mats and towels if you want to lie out and tan," Chad says, handing me a towel and motioning to the cushion next to him.

I unroll it and recline back, letting the sun soak into me. James grabs a towel and lies on the mat next to me so I'm between him and Chad, the focal point for our conversation.

"So," Chad asks, "how did you like the party? Did you meet any sex-crazed porn stars?"

I laugh and shake my head. "Only some regular, normal ones. I was half expecting orgies and a giant fuck fest to break out, but everybody was so sweet and nice."

"Well, orgy night was last week." James smirks.

Chad laughs and smiles at James with genuine appreciation. I can tell that he and Alejandro really love James and that they think of him like family.

"You'll have to fly out again for gangbang night," James teases.

I giggle, and I notice him giving me a big, pearly white smile. He doesn't think he's being obvious, but his eyes are making quick little darting movements over my body like he's trying to be as discrete as possible, but not exactly pulling it off. He's checking me out. James is checking me out again. It's both funny and flattering. He's seen me in underwear and stuff—hell, he's seen my boobs before—but he seems extra captivated today.

"Everybody there was nice, except for those two girls," I add.

"Who?" Chad excitedly asks. "I have to know!"

I laugh loudly and bite my bottom lip before revealing, "Lexi and Tara. They were sort of catty, just that girl tone where they talk down to you. It was weird because I don't know them, I've never met them, and they were acting bitchy to me. It felt like high school bullshit."

"They're jealous," Chad says without even pausing to think about it. "Porn's most eligible bachelor walks into a party with a really pretty girl on his arm, and they go ape shit. They have a crush on him, you know." He points to James.

"They do not." James chuckles and shakes his head.

"They do and you know it!" Chad teases with a knowing little grin.

"Very interesting." I smirk at James. "So not one but two porn stars are crushing on you, eh?"

"Shut up, the both of you," he says, his smile sweet and embarrassed.

"Tara's been in love with him ever since their first scene together," Chad mercilessly continues, much to my delight. "She's literally been telling everyone that he's the best fucker in the biz. And Lexi, I heard she yelled at a girl she was doing a scene with and told her to get pussy licking lessons from James."

"No way!" I gasp with loud laughter.

"That is so not true!" James protests.

"It so is true," Chad retorts. "It's him; he's a heartbreaker. Every girl who's done a scene with him falls in love with him. Apparently he's just that good."

"So you got that going for you." I poke at James, and Chad laughs.

"Don't believe a word of it." James smiles at me. "He's a smart-ass, and he's bullshitting."

"Oh, am I?" Chad grins with an exaggeratedly raised eyebrow.

I laugh loudly and roll onto my stomach so I can prop myself up on my elbows and look at both of them.

"Who to believe…" I smirk. "Such a tough call."

"Is it?" James grins in his classic, beautiful, enticing, trouble-maker style.

In a flash, he's up and sitting on me, immobilizing me with his weight as he tickles at my ribs. I'm flat on my stomach, and there's nothing I can do but laugh hysterically.

"Okay!" I gasp between bouts of laughter. "Okay! You win!"

"Good," he says.

Chad's laughing when I turn my head to look at him and give him a this-kind-of-thing-happens-all-the-time shrug.

"Did you put sunscreen on your back, young lady?" James says.

"I was lying on my back, your highness," I reply.

"Chad, will you hand me that bottle?" James says.

Chad does it, and with no preamble, James starts rubbing sunscreen onto the hot skin of my back. His touch is soft, but there's a slight aggression to it, like he wants to assert his possession of me, pinning me to the deck beneath him.

I lower down until I'm flat on the towel and absorb the strong, soothing feel of his hands. This is no mere sunscreen application; this is becoming a full-on massage. His hands are large and so strong that my muscles feel thoroughly relaxed. I love it.

"Can I untie this?" James asks, tugging on the string of my bikini top where it joins across my back.

"Okay," I say before I realize what I've agreed to. The idea of James taking my clothes off should make me a lot more nervous than it does.

His long fingers deftly unfasten my top, and he smoothly brushes the strings off my back, affectionately rubbing sunscreen across my bra line. His touch is reverent and soft, like I can feel adoration coming through his hands.

Once he's done, he moves off of me and back onto his towel, leaning over to kiss my shoulder sweetly before he lies down.

I look at him with a big smile, and he gives me a wink as he crosses his fingers behind his head and stretches back, allowing me the chance to watch those amazing abs flex as he breathes. I almost hate myself for how attractive I find him right now. He's my friend, and I shouldn't feel this way about him at all, but I have eyes and I can't deny what I see.

The three of us chat for a little while longer when James volunteers to see how Alejandro is doing with the food. He gives me a little smack on the butt as he gets up and then disappears off to the rear deck where Alejandro is grilling.

"He's such a sweetheart, isn't he?" Chad smiles at me.

"Definitely." I grin and nod in agreement. "He looks big and tough, but he's so adorable sometimes — of course, he can be a smart-ass too, but I like that."

"You two get along so great," he says. "I'm surprised you haven't dated. When James used to tell us about you, I always kinda thought you were his girlfriend. He just went on and on about how you were beautiful and how he used to stop other guys from hitting on you."

"He told you that?" I laugh loudly. "I'm glad he's taking owner-ship of it now. He's been building a brick wall around me for ages, and he always used to act like I was crazy when I'd call him on it."

Chad laughs and smiles warmly. "He cares about you. He wants to protect you. It's so sweet."

"It is pretty sweet." I shrug. "Even when it annoys me, I know his intentions are good. His heart's in the right place, even if he's making sure I don't ever go on a date with anybody."

"Maybe you should go on a date with him," Chad says, grinning.

"Are you trying to orchestrate a little maneuver here?" I giggle with a sly smile.

"I'm just saying I think you'd be cute together. Christ, you already adore each other, and it's obvious that he's into you."

"Is it now?" I say through a big laugh.

"You didn't see him when he first moved here." He smirks. "Every five minutes we had to hear about how he missed you and how he hoped you weren't hooking up with some guys back at your school. Every girl was compared to you, and he used to go on and on about how he would kick somebody's ass if they didn't treat you right."

"Bullshit!" I reply.

"It's so true," Chad says. "How do you think me and Alejandro know that you almost got felt up at a school dance but James intervened? How would we know that he once punched a guy in middle school for making a remark about your boobs? How would we know that he says the happiest moments of his life are when he sleeps in bed with you?"

"He says all that stuff to you?" I say, my eyes wide with amazement.

"All that and then some." Chad nods. "See? Told you he's into you. Can you guys just please hook up already? Me and Alejandro need to pick out what we're gonna wear to your wedding."

That cracks me up, and I roll onto my back as I laugh.

"You've never thought about it? You've never considered going out with him?" he asks me.

"Well, I mean, not seriously. Obviously he's gorgeous, that's clear as day, but I don't think he's the dating type. James has always been a casual-hook-ups-and-fuck-buddies dude. He's never really had a girlfriend, in the traditional sense," I explain.

"But people can change." Chad shrugs. "People can do crazy things when they love someone. Who knows? Maybe everything would be different if you two went for it."

"I don't know," I reply. "He's amazing, beautiful, funny, and sweet. He cares about me a lot, and I totally adore him, but I just don't see that being a thing. I mean, he's a porn star — no offense."

"None taken."

"I just think we're on such wildly different pages when it comes to our views of intimacy and sexuality. I don't see how those two paths could meet. I mean, you and Alejandro are both in the industry, so you both know exactly what it's like to have this unique job. I'm just some girl in college all the way across the country, and James is here doing three-ways and double anal penetrations."

Chad throws his head back and laughs loudly. "Those can be fun, you never know," he jokes.

I giggle. "Yeah, I think I'm about ten thousand years away from that. I mean, if this was the scale of sexual evolution, I'm the fish that just grew legs, meanwhile James has opposable thumbs and he's constructing the microchip."

"You mean you've never…?" He raises an eyebrow.

I shake my head, and my cheeks turn red.

"Never?" he says again, his mouth agape with surprise.

"No, never…you know…done the deed," I reply.

He sits up and leans back like he's really taking me in. "I should get my camera," he jokes. "Working in this business, I don't even remember the last time I met a real life, bona fide virgin."

I roll my eyes and laugh. "If you have a Sharpie, I'll give you an autograph."

"It makes sense, though," he says, nodding like he's come up with a brilliant theory. "James is protective of you because you're probably the only virgin he knows—and you're really pretty, which must make him a nervous wreck." I blush at that. "He's afraid of guys flirting with you because he doesn't want anybody to deflower you, so he pulls a Rapunzel and locks you away in a tower so nobody can get to you."

"That's shockingly accurate," I reply with a chuckle.

"It's sweet." Chad smiles and cocks his head to the side as he looks at me. "He's protecting your innocence. It's a romantic notion, really."

"Romantic?" I smirk in response.

"Yes!" He grins broadly. "Think about it. He doesn't want any-body to get to you because he doesn't think anybody deserves you. Nobody's worthy of you in his book, so he takes it upon himself to save you from horny guys who only have one thing on their minds."

"What about if they don't just have one thing on their minds? What if some of them actually like me and want to get to know me but he blocks them?"

"Sweetheart, all guys have one thing on their minds," he says, lowering his sunglasses to give me a devilish grin.

"All right, fair point." I laugh.

"I think it's adorable." He smiles. "James loves you so much that he'll do anything to protect you from all the horny men of the world who can't wait to get into a pretty young thang's pants."

I snicker and shake my head. "It's kind of sweet," I concede. "It's neurotic, but sweet."

"I still think you guys would make a cute couple, though." He grins, sitting up and reaching for his flip-flops. He offers me his hand and helps me up before adding, "I think you'd be an adorable, sexy pair that would make other couples jealous."

"Yeah, right!" I follow him toward the back deck for lunch.

Everyone chats casually as we eat. James has clearly had a hand in the menu—since he's a tremendous cook—because we're having turkey burgers made with feta, sun-dried tomatoes and basil on some really delicious whole wheat buns that I love. He learned to make these a few years ago, and I practically lived at his house that summer so I could eat them whenever he decided to light the grill.

We lounge around the deck for a while before we decide to take out the Jet Skis. Rick has two on the yacht, and they're both covered in Louis Vuitton print, but with Rick's initials instead of the classic "LV" pattern. *Keepin' it classy.*

James makes me put on a life vest, despite my avid protests, and he ushers me to hop on behind him.

"Feel free to wrap your legs around me, baby," he says with amped up sexuality when he gives me a flirty glance over his shoulder.

"Shut up." I giggle and squeeze him tightly when he hits the gas.

Chad's in front on the other Jet Ski with Alejandro behind him. A spontaneous race breaks out, and I'm clinging to James as we glide over the water neck and neck with the guys. It's kind of scary because I know I could totally wipe out, but it's also really fun, because I know James will be careful with me. We finish the race, our team emerging victorious, and cruise around for a little while before heading back to the boat.

"You good, babe?" James says as he turns back to look at me.

"Better than good," I reply, leaning my chin up and kissing his cheek, which earns me an ear-to-ear smile from him.

The sun starts to set, and everyone's pretty exhausted, so we say our goodbyes, and James and I hop into his old Honda Civic and head back to his apartment.

When we get to the parking lot, he darts around the car and opens the door for me, making me laugh at his surprise sweetness. He reaches down and holds my hand as we walk up the flight of stairs and down the hallway to his door. I feel close to him right now. It's far greater than proximity alone. We're connected. That surge of warmth flows through me, and I put my arm around him and curl into him as he fishes for his keys and eventually unlocks the door.

We're both too tired to do anything, so we microwave some popcorn and opt to watch a movie. I go over to his massive shelf of DVDs—he and I are movie buffs, so we've both amassed a pretty sizable collection—and I browse the titles. I'm narrowing it down and trying to decide between *Young Frankenstein* and *The Princess Bride* when an obnoxiously busy yellow and blue DVD cover catches my eye. *Horny Housewives IV MILF Madness* is the title. In the center is a naked, silicone-enhanced blond woman on her knees deep throating a guy. All around the main image are smaller photos of "housewives" spread open or bent over doggy-style while being penetrated by a hardbodied guy whose head is cut off from the shot. I guess disembodied torsos are okay because guys in porn are really only there to be props for the girls, at least according to what I've heard from James. It dawns on me, of course, that the abs and pecs of the man in the center photo look remarkably familiar. I swallow hard, and I know it's James. *Should I keep looking at it or put it away as fast as I can?* I can't decide what to do.

"You picked one out yet?" James says, approaching fast.

I fumble with the DVD, and he totally catches me.

"Or is there something else you'd like to watch?" He grins as he cranks up the sex appeal.

"Is it weird that your face isn't on the cover? The whole focal point is your dick," I reply.

"Is it weird that you could instantly identify me by seeing just my dick?" he teases. "How'd you know that was me, Lola? How could you immediately tell I was on that cover, huh?"

"Shut up!" I whine as I blush.

"Wanna watch it?" he says with that mischievous smile.

"No!" I laugh loudly. "I couldn't handle that!"

"Wanna watch another one?" he continues, reaching over me and grabbing another video.

This one's even more outrageous. A pretty redhead whom I recognize from the party stands in the middle with her back facing the camera and her hands on her ass, spreading her cheeks as she peeks over her shoulder. *Amber's Anal Adventures.* Seriously?

"Dude!" I gasp, averting my eyes.

"Or maybe this one," he says, tossing another box at me.

Co-ed Initiation: Sorority Orgy Volume 7. Because apparently six just wasn't enough.

"How many of these things do you fucking have, James? You've got, like, the porn Criterion Collection in here!"

He snickers and then kneels down next to me, getting on my level and picking up the DVDs I've dropped like they were hot lava.

My eyes scan the shelf again, and I see that there are more. Lots more. They're mixed in with regular movies, which is what really makes me laugh. *Eternal Sunshine of the Spotless Mind* on the same shelf as *Cockhungry Sluts XII*, and hilariously enough, *The Girl Next Door*, a mainstream film about a teenage boy who lives next door to a hot porn star whom he eventually falls in love with.

"Let me show you one," James says, giving me a smile that's decidedly sexier than before. "Come on. You've never seen one of my movies, and you should check it out, see how I roll."

"I can't watch porn with you, let alone *your* porn with you," I say, giggling. "How am I gonna look you in the eye after I see…what's this one…*Tittyfuck Teens? Tittyfuck Teens*, James? Really?"

He laughs hard, nodding his head like he concedes I have a point.

"This is just…wow." I snicker.

"How about if we just watch, like, five minutes of one? Just enough for you to get a feel for it?" he presses.

"You have got to be fucking kidding me!" I cackle. "You'd actually want me to see you fuck on film?"

"Yeah, dude." He shrugs like there is absolutely nothing insane about this picture. "You might see somethin' you like," he adds with a wink.

I don't know why — I really, truly have no idea what comes over me — but I say yes.

He jumps up and offers me his hand, hiking me up from my seat and motioning for me to sit on the couch. He puts the DVD in and turns on the TV, joining me and resting his arm on the back of the couch around me.

"This isn't an anal one, is it?" I meekly ask, already preparing to cover my eyes. "I definitely can't watch you do that."

"No," he says with a chuckle. "This is *Naughty Nymphos*. This one's pretty soft, not a lot of close-ups, and all pretty normal positions."

"So the nymphos aren't really that naughty, are they?" I joke.

"We'll see who's cracking jokes in five minutes." He grins at me and hits play on the remote.

I take a deep breath and mentally prepare myself for what I'm about to see. It's not like I've never seen porn at all—anyone with a broadband connection is bound to stumble upon some kinky photos at some point—I've just never seen my best friend's porn. I've heard detailed accounts from James of all his sexual escapades, but I've never witnessed them firsthand. *Okay, here we go.*

The scene opens with James and a voluptuous blond walking into a bedroom decorated in all white. She wears a white nightie, eerily similar to the more modest one I packed to sleep in this weekend. He's in a white wifebeater and white drawstring pants. His skin looks smooth and tan, a deep olive shade like his Greek relatives on his mom's side of the family. His hair is back in a ponytail, and his expression, his posture, even the way he breathes just radiates sex. He came to fuck; nothing's ever been more obvious. This is the James Laird Sex Laser Beam set to nuclear level.

There's no dialogue, and he starts kissing the girl passionately, claiming her mouth with his in a way that's both aggressive and sensual. It's a hot kiss, I'm not going to lie. There's a teeny tiny part of me—I mean subatomic small—that wishes he'd grab me and kiss me like that. To know that kind of passion...what a thrill!

He takes her top off and starts feeling her up, and she's closing her eyes and moaning—that whole production. His hand slides into her white cotton panties, which were probably chosen to convey some type of innocence, and her moans get louder. When he slides the panties off and lodges his face firmly between her legs, she starts bucking her hips and throwing her head back. It looks so...real.

I can see him out of the corner of my eye. He's looking right at me with a big smile on his face, and it's like he's trying to read me for even the slightest micro-expression. I purposely keep my face completely impassive, revealing nothing.

The girl tugs his pants down, letting his massive erection spring free. *Jesus!* Certainly a lot bigger than I remembered it—of course, I've never seen it so...turgid. She starts sucking him furiously, bobbing her head, hollowing out her cheeks, and using both hands to stroke what she can't fit in her mouth. He runs his fingers through her hair and puts his hand on the back of her head, gently urging her forward and backward in quick motions. He's panting and whispering instructions. "Suck that cock, baby. Yeah, take it real deep." She moans every time he says something, and he praises her with, "Good girl. Just like that."

"Okay," I timidly interject, "we can cut it here."

"Come on," he says, his smile wide and mischievously charming, "just a little bit more. Here, I'll fast forward past the blowjob if you want."

"Yeah, 'cause it's gonna get so much tamer after that," I dryly reply.

"Just watch a couple more minutes." He grins, pressing his index finger to my chin and turning my head so I face the TV again.

I cover my eyes but peek through my fingers as I continue to watch.

After she sucks him off, he lays her down on the bed and kneels between her legs. He takes his enormous cock in his hand and rubs it over her a little bit before plunging into her to the hilt. I'm certainly not unimpressed by the way he moves, more like a wave than a jackhammer. His motions are fluid and smooth, and it looks like it probably feels pretty great. Her moans even sound real, and I like the way he looks into her eyes.

"Seen enough, cupcake?" he teases, hitting pause on a wide shot of him gripping her hips and lifting her up so he can get deeper.

"Yes!" I giggle, refusing to look at him.

"Anything you liked?" he says, rotating my face again and meeting my eyes. "Anything you wanna try?"

"James!" I blush.

"Come on, you've fucked around with dudes before—even though I've made it my fuckin' job to try to stop you. What do you dig?"

"Does any of that matter?" I say, clearly dodging the question.

"Yes, it matters to me. Just tell me. What kind of stuff do you like guys to do to you?"

I sigh and lean back on the couch, my cheeks stinging with embarrassment as I attempt to scowl at him for putting me on the spot.

"Lola, it's me. You can tell me anything, baby," he says warmly. "I'm just curious about it, that's all. I know you haven't fucked anybody, but what's the furthest you've gone? You had a couple of years of high school where I wasn't around to protect you. What'd you let 'em get away with?"

I laugh lightly at that. Of course he would think about it that way. In his mind, every man on earth is waiting with bated breath for the opportunity to catch me off guard so they can nail me. Where he gets these crazy ideas, I'll never know.

"Come on," he playfully pushes. "What's the most you've done?"

"Third, I guess," I weakly answer, my voice quiet and shy.

"Somebody went down on you?" he asks with eyebrows raised in surprise.

"I thought third was…touching," I reply.

"For you, maybe." He shrugs and gives me a cheeky smile. "For dudes I think that falls into the second base category."

"Well, how do you define that scale? What stands for what in your baseball analogy?" I inquire. "I've always learned it as French, feel, finger, fuck. What are you going on?"

"I've heard that one too, but we always said finger counted for feel and that third was actually fellatio," he replies.

"Oh, okay, then second, by that scale." I nod.

"So you let somebody finger you, huh?" he says with overplayed disapproval.

"Two guys, actually," I add with a defiant, smart-ass smirk.

"Two? That kills me, Lo!" He smiles, leaning his head back against the couch like he's devastated. "You liked it so much you had to do it twice?"

"Well, um, no, not really," I timidly respond.

"You didn't like it?" he asks inquisitively.

"No, I mean, it was cool and all, it just wasn't anything to write home about. Nothing too special," I answer.

"So I take it you didn't come," he says.

"I don't think so," I bashfully respond.

"Don't think so? What do you—how could you not know?" he says with bemusement. "Unless…Lola, have you ever had an orgasm?"

"It's getting late and I'm tired," I say, my cheeks flushing beet red as I stand up from the couch.

"Hey, hey," he says, grabbing my wrist and playfully tugging me back down. "Come on, answer my question."

"Does any of this matter in the grand scheme of things?" I say, still not answering. "What does it matter if I have or haven't? That question is so not important."

"It's important to me," he says, trying to be patient and sweet as he coaxes this out of me. He pulls me onto his lap so I'm straddling him, and he tucks my hair behind my ear. "Just tell me, hm?"

I take a deep breath and look down, not wanting to meet his gaze as I subtly shake my head.

"Never?" he asks, shock still plastered across his face.

"No," I murmur.

"Not even by yourself?" he continues to prod.

"No. Jesus Christ! Why are we even talking about this?" I whine.

"You know where you're supposed to touch, right?" he teases.

"I've taken health class, yes," I snap, trying to keep from erupting in embarrassed giggles.

"And you just can't make it happen?"

"No."

"Un-fuckin'-believable!" he loudly exclaims.

"Great, now my best friend who fucks for a living gets a good laugh at the fact that I've never had an orgasm." I roll my eyes with a smirk as I move to get away from him.

"I'm sorry." He snickers, pulling me back and holding me to his lap. "I'm totally sorry. I shouldn't laugh or anything. I'm not trying to make you feel weird about it. I just...wow! I can't fuckin' believe you've never come before! You get so turned on, and it seems like it wouldn't be that hard for you to get there."

As if I wasn't pink enough, now he has to bring up my indiscreet arousal! I vividly recall him pointing out that my nipples got hard very fast when he was kissing my neck. Apparently, he finds this very intriguing.

"Okay, well, that's out there now," I say, rising to stand up.

"Wait, Lo," he says, reaching for my hand and gently stroking my knuckles with his thumb. "Don't get weird about it. I just wanted to know. I'm not judging you or trying to make you feel embarrassed. If anything, I think it's kind of cute. You're so fuckin' innocent, and you have no idea how sexy that is to me."

I almost don't know how to respond. I'm comforted by the fact that he doesn't want me to feel shy about what I've just revealed. I'm simultaneously touched and annoyed that he finds this cute, and I'm just a tad surprised that he's described my naiveté as sexy.

"Don't feel bad for telling me, okay?" he softly requests. "Don't ever feel bad for telling me any sexual stuff. I tell you everything, for fuck's sake, so there's nothing you could say to me that would make me look at you different. You can tell me anything, anytime, anywhere."

I kiss his cheek and hug him. "Thanks for not making me feel super weird about it—even if you were a total shit for laughing when you first cornered me and poked at me until I told you."

He wraps his arms around me lovingly and kisses the top of my head. "Hey, somebody's gotta poke you if you ever want to come."

I sit up and smack him in the shoulder, which makes him laugh hard.

We return to the task at hand and decide to watch *Young Franken-stein*—a regular movie, the kind that doesn't feature gaping orifices and dildos of varying sizes. By the time it's over, I'm feeling pretty tired, so James says I should take the first shower so I can get to bed.

I tie my hair up in a bun, too sleepy to wash and dry it. While I lather up with soap, I think about the fun day I had with James, Chad, and Alejandro on the yacht. Chad said James was into me. I know it's dumb, but it puts a smile on my face even now. James has been "into" a lot of girls, figuratively and literally, and I can't help but feel flattered at the mere possibility that I might be one of them. He finds me attractive, that I know, but is he *into* me?

When I'm all done, I slide back the shower curtain and gasp when I see him standing in the bathroom looking right at me. My hands frantically reach for a towel, and I wrap it around myself as I quickly try to hide my naked body.

"Lo, I've been thinking about what you said," he says with a furrowed brow like he's in deep concentration. "I think we should do it."

"Do it? Do what? Not…you can't mean that…?" My rushed words betray how flustered I feel.

"No, not that we should fuck or anything—unless you want to—but I mean that I think you should let me see if I can make you come, 'cause, baby, you know I'm the man for that job."

I laugh loudly and step out of the shower, tightening the towel across my chest.

"Just let me try it, huh?" He smiles at me in the mirror as I brush my teeth. "I could knock it out in two fuckin' flicks of my tongue."

"No fucking way I'm doing that!" I chuckle.

"Why not? I'm really good at it, not to brag or anything," he playfully boasts.

"Nope, not happening." I shake my head.

I rinse my mouth and then go into the bedroom, slipping my gray, jersey knit nightie over me before pulling my towel off discretely. He follows me and watches as I slide my panties on under the shield of my nightie.

I lift the covers and start crawling into bed when he comes over, catches my ankle and kneels off the side of the bed in front of me.

"Lola, you gotta let me make you come tonight," he says with great conviction. "It's gonna drive me fuckin' insane for years if I don't do it. I can't know that you're walking around never having felt that."

"Seriously?" I ask with surprise. *Can he really mean that?*

"Yes, baby," he says in a smooth, sensual tone. "I want to do it so bad. I, like, *need* to make you come."

"Um—" I pause, weighing this out. I can't deny how much I want it, though I'm slow to nod my head. "Okay, I guess."

"Fuck yeah!" He smiles and makes a triumphant fist pump. "Lie back on the pillows, okay?"

I lie back, and he looks me over.

"It'd be a lot easier if you got naked," he says, smiling, "but I'm guessing you're not about to go for that."

I giggle and shake my head, biting my bottom lip.

"And I'm assuming you're not going to let me go down on you either, are you?"

"No way!" I laugh.

"It'll be more intense that way." He grins enticingly like he's trying to make the ultimate sales pitch. "I bet I could make you come instantly if you'd let me get my mouth on you."

"Absolutely not!" I declare through ridiculous giggles.

"Then we'll just have to do this the middle school way."

"What's the middle school way?" I snicker with raised eyebrows.

"You can keep your clothes on, but open your legs wide so I can get my hand in there easier," he instructs.

"Well, wait, what are you planning to do?" I ask, my eyes wide with curiosity and a little apprehension.

"I'm just gonna rub you on the outside, so don't freak out," he says with a shrug like it's so obvious that I should have known it from the second he proposed this idea.

I gulp and look away.

"I can do it over your panties if you want, but it'll be faster if you let me go direct," he explains.

"I uh…um, I mean…" I don't know how to respond.

"Let's try under the panties and then, if it freaks you out, we can do over," he offers. I nod. "I'm gonna need to get you warmed up a little first, kid, so is it cool with you if I kiss your neck and stuff?"

I swallow hard and take a deep breath. Vivid memories of Dave Keegan's pool party and the incident a few months ago come to mind. Both those times felt hotter than anything I've ever done with anyone else. The man knows how to turn a girl on, I have to hand it to him.

"I mean, it'd be ideal if I could take this off because I know how sensitive your nipples are, and it'd be good to start out there," he explains, tugging at the hem of my nightie.

"Um…" I need to think about that. I want this. Bad. Still, I'm worried that I'll like it too much and that I won't be able to separate this from our friendship. I don't want him to be my boyfriend, but what if this changes that?

"I just want to touch them a little bit," he elaborates. "You know I fuckin' love how hard your nipples get, and I know it feels good for you when I play with them. I wanna do everything that makes you feel good because I need you to let go enough to have an orgasm. A lot of this shit's in your head, so you gotta get really into it. So… shirt off, hmm?"

I pause and think it over. "Yeah, okay." I nod. "But, one thing…"

"Uh-huh?" He smiles. I think he's enjoying this negotiation.

"Can we turn off the lights first?" I timidly ask.

"You want the lights off? Why?" He snickers at my shyness.

"I just...I feel weird about you seeing me with my shirt off," I meekly respond.

"Why? I've seen you in bikinis and stuff. I saw your tits for a couple seconds just now in the bathroom," he says like he's genuinely confused about this.

"I'm just...I'm not pretty, James. Not like those girls in your videos. If you really want me to take my shirt off, that means you're gonna see me. A lot of me. I'm self-conscious because I'm not all silicone and tan like the girls in your movies."

He laughs loudly and shakes his head. "Are you kiddin' me?"

"What?" I smile at his jovial reaction.

"Lola, you're the hottest girl I've ever seen. Why would you ever be self-conscious about anything? You're a knockout, kid," he says with sincerity. "I'm actually totally psyched to see you with your clothes off again. I think you're gorgeous and your body's super sexy."

It's blunt, but I can tell he's being a hundred percent honest. This isn't just some line of bullshit to get me to take my top off; he really means that stuff. It's kind of touching.

I give him a subtle nod, and he sits me up and reaches for the bottom of my nightie. He gently removes it and then looks down at my bare chest for a few seconds before I feel overcome with modesty and cover myself with my hands. When he looks up at me, he's got a big appreciative smile that makes me snicker.

"Very nice, Lo!" he says, giving me a thumbs-up.

I burst into laughter, and he chuckles along with me.

"All right," he says, taking my wrists and nudging my hands down.

"Wait, you're really gonna do this?" I bashfully inquire.

"Yeah, babe," he says. "I can't play with your nipples if I can't get at your titties."

I take a deep breath and nod my head to myself. I'm going to let him do this. I'm going to let James see me completely topless here in his bedroom, even though I know I shouldn't. My mind is coming up with excuses left and right, but I'm already nodding to him.

"Wait!" I interject as I'm suddenly bared to him.

"Yeah?" he asks sweetly like none of this is a big deal at all.

"I can't—I have to turn the lights off. This is too bizarre to do with the room lit up like the goddamn Fourth of July."

He laughs loudly. "You mean the single lamp on the nightstand with the forty watt bulb?" he dryly teases. "Yeah, it's like a stadium in here."

"James," I whine, "just get it dark in here, okay?"

He looks at my pleading face and snickers. "They're just boobs, Lo. I've seen them before—including yours."

I ignore him, and I reach over to turn off the lamp myself. I can't have the lights on. Something about watching him touch me seems too intense. I'll be able to hide my stunned reaction in the cloak of darkness, and I won't have to worry about him seeing how much I like the things he does. From my limited experience with him, I know I'm going to thoroughly enjoy this, and I don't want him to get cocky when he sees my expression.

"Dark enough for you or do you want me to contact someone about shutting off the streetlights?" he jokes, referring to the orange-tinted light coming in from behind the blinds.

"Oh, *ha ha*," I scoff. "A real comedian. You gonna start doing a stand-up routine?"

He laughs and moves closer to me, reaching up for my arms, which I've unconsciously crossed over my breasts again. I'm exposed, but at least I have the cover of darkness.

"No more being self-conscious," he playfully reprimands me. "You're way too hot, and I won't stand for you hating any part of yourself."

I giggle, and I'm glad it's dark because he can't see me blushing.

"You're beautiful, Lo," he whispers, leaning over and kissing my shoulder before letting his lips drift up my neck to that spot right below my ear that always turns me on.

His fingertips brush my sides, and his hands are so big that he can basically cover my ribcage from the front to the back. I draw in a breath as subtly as possible when his hand comes up to rest on my breast. Already, it makes me shiver a little just to have him touching my bare skin this way.

"Goddamnit, I love how fuckin' hard your nipples get!" he says with a grin that I can just make out in the low light.

I laugh loudly and cover my face, peeking out from behind my fingers.

"So fuckin' hot, I swear to God." He nods like this gets his seal of approval.

I'm laughing, and I feel much more at ease when he kisses my neck again. He's sweet and playful, which makes it much easier to relax in such a strange situation. This isn't some lustful impulse; this is just cute, sexy experimentation, and I get a warm feeling at the idea that he's the one doing this to me. James has always shown such respect for my body, and that makes it a lot easier to let my guard down with him.

"Mmm, so fuckin' awesome," he whispers against my neck as he holds my breasts and brushes circles over my nipples with his thumbs. "I fuckin' love your boobs, Lo."

I try to hold it in, but I have to laugh at that one. I hear him laughing too, and I can see the whiteness of his teeth as he smiles broadly before he kisses my collarbones.

"Okay, lie back, babe," he says, rubbing my back and lowering me onto the pillow. "Tell me if I do anything that goes too far for you, okay?"

Before I can respond, his tongue flicks over my nipple, and I inhale sharply. *Wow, something so tiny and it feels so good!*

"Told you your nipples were sensitive," he gloats before he closes his lips around the tip of my left breast.

He's right; my nipples are sensitive, and I've enjoyed this in the past from other guys, but it never felt this good. He's slowly suckling me while his tongue flutters over the very tip of my nipple, and I can't get over how much I like this. I think it's the sensual way he's doing it that makes the biggest difference. He's taking his time, worrying about the quality of each lick instead of the quantity of licks, and this is certainly high quality indeed.

His large hand slips between my legs, and he touches me over my panties.

"Oh, shit," he breathes when he feels the dampness on the fabric. "Yeah, dude, this is only gonna take, like, thirty seconds. You're beyond ready right now."

I giggle and shake my head. This is so surreal, but I love how he's keeping everything so light and humorous.

"Okay, beautiful girl," he says as he looks at me. My eyes have adjusted to the light, and I can see his warm smile. "Prepare yourself for the motherfuckin' real deal," he playfully boasts.

I smile and laugh as his fingers find their way beneath my panties.

I gasp a little when the very tip of his middle finger comes in contact with my clitoris. Right away, this is better than anything anyone has ever done to me before. I'm moaning softly as he starts to gently rub and stroke my most sensitive places, making my hips involuntarily rock with the rhythm of his fingers.

He leans over me, kissing my neck and jaw as he moves his fingers incrementally faster. I unknowingly spread my legs wider, giving him unprecedented access to continue. It's almost instinctual when I slide my hands up his shoulders and run my fingers through his hair as he starts to kiss around my breast again. He takes my nipple in his mouth and sucks it lightly before doing the same on the other side. The combination of sensations is delightful.

I close my eyes, and I can hear myself making soft, breathy moans as I pant. My heart is racing, my hips are moving faster, pushing me more firmly into his fingers, and my whole body feels electrically charged. He makes a hungry groan as he suckles me just a tiny bit harder, and I tangle my fingers into his hair and press him to my breast, nonverbally begging him to keep going.

I know something is about to happen. I can feel it uncoiling deep within me. There's a shiver running up and down my spine, and it's getting stronger with each little touch of his fingertip. I'm close, so close to that famed sensation that is the Holy Grail of all sexual experiences.

He must be able to tell, because he rises up and looks in my eyes, lowering his lips closer to mine and increasing the tempo between my legs.

"Ohhh!" I whimper.

I put my hands on his shoulders and grip onto him because I know I'm about to get swept away by this wave.

"That's right, gorgeous girl," he whispers and runs his nose along mine.

I whimper again and hold his face in my hands as I look in his eyes. He seems absolutely overjoyed with the way my body is starting to unravel. His smile is both loving and proud as I make a series of staccato gasps and my whole body tenses up.

"Yes, baby. Just let it go," he softly whispers, locking eyes with me.

Then it happens. The explosion. I swear to God, I can see sounds and hear colors like I've got synesthesia! I've completely lost control of myself, and my back bows off the bed as my legs tremble and shake.

I'm moaning and whimpering, and all I can do is cling to him and try to process this overload of pleasure. *Oh. My. God.*

"That's perfect, Lola," he murmurs as he continues gently rubbing me.

The sensation keeps rolling on, and I'm gasping and panting as my whole body lights up like a fucking Christmas tree. I pull him closer, and he presses his forehead to mine as I shake and shiver. It must be minutes. It has to be. This is no rogue wave; this is a goddamned tsunami, and the surge keeps coming and coming — no pun intended.

Finally, I yelp when I feel my senses overloading, and he slows to a stop, cupping my sex with his palm as I quake with the aftershocks of that outstanding, spectacular, astonishing, marvelous, astounding experience.

I try to catch my breath, and when I'm finally able to open my eyes, he's hovering above me and looking down with a big, adoring smile.

"Jesus Christ! I think I love you!" I breathlessly exclaim, brushing my fingers through his hair.

He laughs loudly and looks very proud of himself. *He should be!* That was earth-shatteringly good.

"And that's what an orgasm feels like," he says with a grin.

"Yeah, I'm definitely planning to have a lot more of those," I joke. "That's on the agenda for the near future, that's for fucking sure!"

He snickers and kisses my forehead before scooting back and sitting up on the bed.

"Holy fucking shit!" I say in an exaggerated sigh.

That gets a hearty laugh from him, and I could be wrong, but I think he's blushing.

"Fucking hell! How did you learn how to do that?" I exhale.

"Practice," he says with a smart-ass grin, "but I think you're just extra sensitive. It only took you, like, ten seconds to get there. You're really responsive, quite the orgasmic girl."

"Then how come I've never 'responded' to it before?" I raise an eyebrow.

"I dunno." He shrugs before giving me a cocky smile. "Maybe I'm just the shit and I'm an expert at making girls come."

"You say that in jest, but that could very well be true," I reply with a laugh.

"Maybe you've always been too busy being all psycho and insecure, but tonight you let that guard down a little bit and went with it," he proposes.

"That could also be true."

He gives me a playful smirk. "Maybe those idiots you've been with didn't know how to listen to a girl's body and see how she wants to be touched."

"That's very likely, yes."

He grabs my hips and pulls me on top of him so I'm straddling him as he lies back on the bed. "Or maybe I'm a fuckin' sex god and you just got a little taste of my superpowers." He grins, giving me a sexy wink.

I laugh and nod in agreement. Sure, this will stroke his ego, which needs no stroking, but there's a kernel of truth to it too. James has always been able to do this kind of thing to girls and it never seems like it's all that difficult for him, so maybe he really is exceptionally sexually gifted.

"You think that was intense, you gotta try a G-spot orgasm," he says, taking my hips and bucking me a few times. "This is a good position for it because the girl controls the tempo. You can get it as deep as you want and really ride it."

I look down at his body, assessing his words. I can picture him beneath me, the way his abs would tense up as he panted, the way his shoulders and his biceps would flex as he gripped my hips. *Yes, this is probably a position I'd like.*

"Or, if you want, the guy can sit up and you can look into each other's eyes," he says, sitting up on the bed and wrapping his arms around me.

He looks at me intently, but then crosses his eyes to make me laugh.

"Don't let some guy try to convince you to do doggy on the first time," he advises. "It's too impersonal without eye contact, and you're gonna want something more romantic than that. You're a candy-and-roses kinda girl, and candy-and-roses girls don't want to get fucked from behind."

I snicker and nod. He's probably right.

"You'll probably want it like this," he says, whisking me around so I'm on my back and he's lying on top of me. "Put your legs up here for a sec," he says, sliding his hand down my body and pulling my leg so my knee is bent and my thigh is up high against his side. I move the other leg into the same position. "Yeah, like that."

He rocks his pelvis to give me a preview of the position. I note the fluidity of movement in his muscles, the same that I saw on the video. James's motions showcase a polished artistry, like his body was specifically designed for sex—probably why he's such a star.

"I hardly ever get to do this one anymore," he says, continuing to sensually undulate into me. "I'm pretty sure they think it's not very cinematic—not dynamic enough, you know?"

It feels pretty damn dynamic to me, and his crotch is pressing right between my legs as he pantomimes sex in the missionary position.

My lips part, and I can't contain a tiny moan.

"Oh, sorry." He smiles with surprise. "Still pretty sensitive down there, huh?"

"The way your jeans are hitting me...it's really doing something for me," I bashfully admit.

"I'm gonna turn you into a wanton, horny, ravenous sex goddess," he says, rocking firmly into me with each word before he stills.

"Oh, fuck, you are such an asshole, winding me up like this," I say, chuckling as I try to block out how good that feels.

He gives me that mischievous smile and licks his fingers before sliding his hand between my legs. He looks right in my eyes with a cocky grin as he starts rubbing me again, but this time at a teasingly slow pace.

"Am I an asshole now, Lola?" He smirks. "I'm only an asshole if I turn you on but I never pay it off."

"Ohhhh...seriously, James, that feels so good it's insane," I say through a half moan.

"Nice! I like this." He chuckles, and a triumphant smile spreads over his lips. "Now I know how to shut you up when you mouth off to me."

Even though I'm getting incredibly turned on, I laugh at his remark.

"You start giving me shit, I give you an orgasm," he jokes.

"I think that'll work the opposite of how you want," I say, my voice sounding progressively aroused as he rubs me. "It's Pavlovian conditioning. You'd basically be rewarding me for giving you shit."

"Hmm, maybe you're right," he says with a smart-ass grin as he takes his hand away.

I whine loudly, and he laughs.

"It would appear that you want some more," he teases with an eyebrow raised.

"It would appear that way, yes," I say, attempting to sound sassy even though I'm willing to scream and beg for him to keep going.

"What an interesting turn of events indeed," he says with an exaggerated accent like he's Sherlock fucking Holmes.

"Come on!" I whine.

"The girl that was so reluctant to even take her shirt off is suddenly desperate for another orgasm," he continues in this silly English character. "My, my, how the tables have turned."

I grab his hand and put it back between my legs, and he raises his eyebrows like he's surprised and impressed by my aggressiveness.

"You always have to get what you want, eh, Lola?" He shakes his head, giving me an overdone tsk-tsk of disapproval.

I nod and give him my best adorable smile, opening my legs wider as he starts to rub me again.

"I'll make you come…under one condition," he says.

"Okay." I nod for him to go on.

"You have to let me kiss your neck and hold you and spoon you all night if I want to."

I snicker. *Such a cute demand.* "Agreed."

"And you have to keep your clothes off the whole time," he adds with that patented devilish grin.

"I knew there was a catch!" I laugh and point to him accusingly.

"I just…I really like it," he says, looking down at my bare breasts. "Your tits are sexy as hell, Lola, and I wish I got to see 'em more often."

I blush and cover my face, which makes him smile.

"Oh, Lola's Boobs," he says into my chest, "I wish we knew each other better."

I crack up laughing.

"What's that you say?" he jokes, putting his ear to my right breast. "You wish you could come out to play more often but Lola doesn't let you? Well, that's a shame."

I'm cackling with laughter.

"So will you?" He looks at me with a cheerful grin.

"Will I what?"

"Let me play with your boobs all night?"

"James!" I squawk.

"How about if I just look at them, then?" he bargains.

"You're fucking crazy!" I laugh.

"Can I persuade you?" He flirtatiously smirks as he teases me with his fingers.

He rubs me a little faster than before, and I can't hold back my moans. My neck arches back as it starts to build, and my hips begin rocking again. Right when I'm really getting into it, he takes his hand away.

"Oh, for fuck's sake!" I sigh in exasperation.

He laughs loudly and raises his eyebrows. "Well?" he asks expectantly.

"All right, all right!" I giggle. "I'll leave my clothes off, just don't stop doing that again, okay?"

He snickers and nods his head before he gives me a sweet, tender kiss on the forehead and looks right in my eyes. He resumes his motions, and it can't be more than thirty seconds before he sends me over the edge.

"Fuck!" I exhale as I catch my breath. "Can you do that to me every day for the next, like, fifty years?"

He throws back his head with laughter. "You really like it that much?" he says proudly.

"Fuck yes! I totally do!" I reply honestly.

"All right." He nods matter-of-factly. "How about you lose the panties, I give you three more tonight, and then I get to cuddle you while you sleep?"

"Six more tonight," I counter as he hooks his fingers into the waistband of my panties and slides them down my legs.

"Four," he says, chuckling.

"Five." I pretend to scowl.

"Deal." He nods, holding out his hand so we can shake on it.

Two hours later, I feel like I'm going to pass out. He caved and decided to ignite me eight more times, and now my body is exhausted and I feel like I'm floating on a cloud.

"You seem awfully sleepy." He smirks as he looks me over. "It looks like I might've worn you out."

"Mm-hmm," I reply in my content and dreamy state.

"I can put your little ass to sleep with this shit," he playfully boasts. "You go from zero to ten, and you're ready to crash."

"I would fight you on that, but you're right," I drowsily murmur.

"What was that?" he asks with wide eyes. "I think I just heard you say I was right. Mark this day on the calendar, everyone!"

I giggle and lightly smack his shoulder.

"See, now comes the part I like the most," he says softly as he takes his shirt off and reaches for the zipper on his jeans.

He's taking his clothes off, and at first I wonder if perhaps he wants to have sex. Even though I have no experience with it, I'm surprised by how comfortable I'd be with the idea of having sex with James right now. I'm already naked, and it would be so easy to go for it. Plus, if he can do that with his fingers, imagine what he could do if we really did have sex tonight. Still, I'm way too exhausted to work up the necessary energy for that.

He strips down to his underwear and scoots me on the bed so my legs are slightly askew.

He sits between my thighs and looks down at me. If his eyes are anything like mine, his vision has completely adjusted to the dark and he can see every inch of my body clear as day. I don't really care anymore, though. I'm tired, and I've been thoroughly pleasured, so I can't get self-conscious right now.

"The things I would do to you," he murmurs, running his palm from low on my stomach up to the middle of my chest.

"Like what?" I giggle, opening my legs a little wider.

"So you want to tease me, huh? That's the little game you're going to play tonight?"

"Why, whatever do you mean? I certainly have no idea what you're talking about," I feign innocence.

"I'd take you like this, too—just like this," he says, lifting my hips and rocking me up against him so that only my shoulders are still on the bed. "Then I'd probably lower you down and get right up on you so I could look at your beautiful face when you came." He crawls forward and lies down on top of me. "I'd want it this way with you," he whispers, running his nose along mine.

I love James's tender side. It's a hidden aspect of his personality that's never been seen by Internet viewers and random girls he's slept with. He can be so incredibly warm and caring, so gentle and loving, but he doesn't really show that to anybody but me. I'm the same way with him. He's the only guy who's ever seen this new sexual side I've adopted in recent months.

"I'd like it like this with you, and I think you'd really like it too," he whispers, kissing across my cheeks.

"I already like it," I softly reply, wrapping my legs and arms around him to embrace him with my whole body.

"I love this, Lo," he murmurs as he slides down a bit so he can nuzzle into my neck.

I feel so content and relaxed with him on me like this, blanketing my body with his warmth. I find myself starting to doze off, and he kisses my neck a couple times before raising up off of me. He runs his nose along mine, and then I feel his lips brush against my cheek on a path to my mouth. Our lips touch for a brief instant, and I get goose bumps. It's very light, hardly a kiss, but it's clear that he'd like to kiss me. In truth, I'd really like for him to kiss me, but we can't do that. It's an unwritten rule between us. Kissing makes this all real, it introduces a genuine intimacy, real emotion, and neither of us wants to go there.

"Come on into my arms, beautiful girl," he whispers as he pulls me to him.

I rest my head on his chest, and he wraps his arm around my back, stroking my bare shoulder with the tip of his thumb. His other hand brushes my hair off my forehead and caresses the side of my cheek.

"Goodnight, Lola," he says, kissing the top of my head as I snuggle into him.

"'Night, James," I sleepily whisper, turning my head to give him a sweet kiss in the middle of his chest.

Chapter 25

James

I slowly start to wake up and I feel warmth all over me. Soft kisses drift all over my face, and I feel smooth skin pressing against my chest. I open my eyes to see that Lola's on top of me, her lips gently brushing across my cheek as she straddles me. She's holding herself up with her hands on either side of my shoulders, and her long hair is soft as it drifts over me in those gorgeous waves I've always thought were so sexy. She looks like an angel. A beautiful, soft, sexy, naked angel.

I smile like I've just won a Powerball jackpot. Lola's naked and kissing me awake. *This is livin', man.* I'd do this shit all day, every day if I could.

My hands slide up her thighs and onto her hips before I stroke her lower back and then wrap my arms around her.

"Hi." She softly smiles as she pulls her head back to look at me.

"Dude, this is the best fuckin' wake-up call of all time." I grin at her, and she laughs in this angelic giggle that sounds magical.

My eyelids feel heavy, but it's not because I'm tired; it's because I'm horny. This is getting me hot. She's so fuckin' beautiful and so naked! I keep thinking about last night and those pretty sounds she made. I loved doing that to her. I'd do it again a zillion times if she'd let me.

"I figured I should wake you up, since I'm leaving this afternoon and I want to maximize our time together," she says, her voice seductive and smooth.

"I take it you had something in mind." I grin, sliding my hands up her ribs and caressing her perfect tits. Her nipples instantly firm up. *So fuckin' sexy!*

"Oh, you mean this?" She smiles innocently, looking down at her bare skin pressed into mine.

"Mm-hmm." I nod. "And this too," I add, caressing her cheek. "You're giving me that I-wanna-fuck look."

"I can't help it," she says, giggling. "It just felt so good when you touched me, and I want it all the time."

"Fuck! That's sexy as hell." I laugh to myself, very amused by this sudden horny turn to her personality.

She blushes, and she gives me a shy smile, but there's a whole ocean of sensuality behind it. She's such a flirt sometimes, and I can never tell if she's aware of it or if she's just a natural at turning me on.

"I just like it a lot," she sweetly whispers as she leans onto me and starts kissing my neck. *Fuck!* Her lips are amazing. "It was the best feeling—nothing else even remotely compares to that."

I can feel my breathing getting heavier. I want her so bad right now it's not even funny! The only thing separating us is the fabric of my boxer briefs. That's it. Just a layer of cotton dividing me from being inside her.

"Okay, I got something new for you, if you're up for it," I propose.

"Yeah?"

"How about we spend the morning finding your G-spot?" I grin.

"Inside?" Her eyes are wide, and she looks excited.

"Yeah." I nod. "I want to put my fingers inside you, but I'll only do it if that's cool with you."

She bites her bottom lip, and I can see her internal struggle. She wants this really bad; it's totally clear from the way she's subtly grinding against my dick, but I think she's a little scared too.

"It can just be this once," I volunteer. "We don't ever have to do it again if you don't want to."

She pauses, and a sexy smile spreads across her lips. "Okay."

"Sweet!" I grin, which makes her laugh.

I wrap my arms around her and press her against me so I can kiss her neck in that spot behind her ear that turns her on. I let my hands run up and down her little back, gently caressing her skin. She likes it, and I can tell because her hips rock a little bit more. I don't think she realizes she's doing it. I think it's autopilot and her body's just super primed to fuck. This girl could be a sex goddess, I swear. It amazes me that she's never done it even though her body can switch on like this.

"Up here," I whisper, lifting her a little bit and sliding her forward.

She catches my drift, and soon she's hovering over me while I kiss, lick and suck on her nipples. *Christ!* I love this beyond belief, and I think I might be even more turned on than she is. *Fuck, man! What this girl's body does to me!*

"Mmm," she exhales in a soft moan.

"You like this, baby?" I whisper against her skin.

"Yeah," she breathes. "I really like it."

"Me too," I reply, moving my hands around her and letting them fall on the small of her back just above her ass.

Her back curves a little, bringing her boobs closer to me. I move back and forth between them, flicking my tongue over her nipples before I take them between my lips and suck them. That's what seems to get her going the most. I always knew her nipples were super sensitive, and I love knowing there's something I can do that will get her hot so quickly like this.

"Lo," I say, nudging her back down so we're at eye level, "you ready for more?"

"Uh-huh." She nods, her breath already faster.

"Lick my fingers, baby," I say, turning up the sensuality.

This is probably the boldest thing I've asked her to do, even though the request doesn't seem to be too much. The way that I said it — that's what gives off the extremely sexual vibe. It was almost like a command, like the kind of thing I'd tell some other girl, and she'd nod and happily obey me. Lola usually doesn't like that bossy shit, though, and she's not exactly one to be told what to do.

I almost can't believe it when she looks into my eyes, takes my right hand from her hip, and brings it to her lips, then runs her tongue up and down my fingers. I nearly moan when she takes my index and middle finger in her mouth and sucks a little bit. *Holy fuckin' shit!* Lola's so sexy. She's become this sensual, horny, ultra-hot seductress. I broke through her innocent shell and let her libido run free. I. Fucking. Love this shit!

"Mmm, now?" she asks as she continues to suck off my fingers and make me wish she'd use that talented little mouth on my cock.

"Okay." I nod, too horny to form a real sentence.

I'm so turned on. I'm so motherfuckin' turned on right now! She can tell, too, because she gives me a little smile that says she's got me—which she totally does. At this point, I'd probably blow my load if she even so much as looked at my dick. Nobody's ever gotten me like this before. I can't even control myself. No amount of breathing and trying to get my shit together can put a damper on how much I want her right now.

I reach between her legs and rub her clit for a moment. She moans the second I touch it, and I love looking up at her and watching her while I make her feel good.

"I'm gonna put my fingers inside you," I whisper to her, sounding all hungry and aggressive. It came out way more lewd than I thought it would.

"Do it," she breathes, her hips rolling as I keep rubbing circles over her clit.

Her mouth forms an O shape, and she closes her eyes when I let the tip of my finger slip between her folds and into her. *Oh, my God!* She's so wet. *Holy shit!* She's wet and tight, and I've never felt anything so perfect. I can say with certainty that whoever gets to bang Lola is in for a fuckin' treat because no girls I've been with have felt this good. The way it would feel to be inside her…I'd love that more than words can even describe. I'm picturing it right now, actually—her on top of me like this, riding my cock into a dozen orgasms until she collapses onto me because she can't hold herself up anymore.

"That feels…so…good," she pants as I start to move my finger inside her.

The look on her face is unimaginably beautiful. She loves this. I can tell right away that this feels better than what we did before—and she came really hard before, so this must be incredible.

"Can you take another one?" I ask, using my other finger to trace a line down from her clit to her entrance.

"Let's try," she replies, her voice taking on that husky tone of a girl who's on the bullet train to pleasure town.

"Tell me if it hurts and I'll stop, okay?" I say, and she nods.

She's tight as hell, but she's so wet that it's easier for my finger to slide into her. I feel her tense a little, but not like it's painful, more like she's getting used to this new feeling. From her reaction, I can guess that the other two guys who fingered her never actually penetrated her. In a way, that makes me feel kind of honored. As of this moment, I'm the only guy who's ever been inside her—even though it's just my fingers.

She gasps when I slowly stroke her G-spot, and she contracts in a few quick flutters. She's getting there. She's getting there fast.

"Oh! James!" she moans as I keep going.

Hearing her moan my name like that might be the sexiest thing I've ever heard. She's totally naked, she's on top of me, I've got my fingers inside her, and she moaning my fuckin' name now. I have to commit this to memory because it could very well be the greatest thing I'll ever get a chance to do.

"You're so beautiful, Lola," I whisper before my brain has a chance to filter the thought.

She looks down at me and smiles through her panting and moaning. I tell her she's gorgeous all the time, but I feel like she really absorbed it just now. She knows I'm not bullshitting. I really do think she's the most beautiful girl on the planet.

"Mmm!" she exhales, her whole body starting to curve back.

"Put your hands right here," I say, instructing her to brace herself on my stomach. "Work your hips, baby. Let yourself go."

She puts her palms on me and starts working her body in this wave motion that amazes me. *How has she never fucked anyone?* The way she moves is like a pro, like she just knows how to ride it to get the most pleasure.

Speaking of riding, that's all I'm thinking about right now: her on top of me riding something besides my fingers. I've got my hand between her legs, but she's also grinding against me a little bit, and I can feel how hard I am on the back of my hand as I rub her spot.

"Oh! Oh, yes!" she says in a whimper.

It's starting. I've only gotten her off a few times, but I know it's starting. Her body is an open book, and all this stuff seems to happen completely on instinct for her. Her nipples get really hard, her pupils dilate a little bit, she starts breathing deeper, her hips make these little motions like she's begging me to be inside her — now I also know that she gets really wet and she tightens up a lot just before she comes.

"Yes, baby," I whisper to her, putting my free hand against the middle of her chest like I can feel her heart. "Let it go, Lola. Come for me, beautiful girl."

She does. This time we don't have to be hidden in darkness like we were last night. I take her in, watching the expression on her face and enjoying the way the muscles in her firm little stomach flex and expand while she shivers. All that is gorgeous, and that's not even counting how she feels inside when she pulses against my fingers. I can completely guarantee that fucking Lola would be a dream come true.

"James!" she cries out and collapses onto me, her body still shaking as she pants into my chest.

"That was so beautiful, Lo," I say, feeling almost as pleased as her. "You're so beautiful, my gorgeous angel. You're my special little treasure."

I hold her in my arms, and I almost get choked up, which is weird. I feel like we just shared something major, something way beyond the physical boundary we just crossed. It's kind of like everything got blocked out for a minute and the only thing that mattered to me was making her feel good. I don't normally get that way with girls. Sure, I always want them to get off, but I'm usually trying to get something out of it too, so this kind of selfless experience is sort of weird for me. I wanted her to feel good, and I didn't give a shit about what it was like from my end of the deal. All I cared about was her, and now all I want to do is hold her while she comes down from it. This just feels so…intimate.

"That was so intense," she whispers, her breath hot against my chest.

"I know, baby," I say, wrapping my arms around her tighter and kissing into her hair. "I felt it too."

I know it was intense for her, but the weird part is that it was so intense for me. I didn't even do anything, but I feel that kind of relaxed sensation you get after you come really hard. Just holding her like this…it's done something to me, and I feel different.

"You're so perfect, Lo," I whisper to her, trailing my fingers up and down her back. "You're so special. Everything about you is beautiful."

She lifts herself up on shaky arms and looks in my eyes, giving me a smile that could light up the whole city.

This is definitely a moment. Something's happening right now. The way she's looking at me and the way it makes me feel, all fluttery and warm…shit's taking place that goes way over my head, and I can't pinpoint what it is, but it's there. I feel it.

I tuck her hair behind her ear and then stroke my fingers down the back of her neck. I feel weird about it, but I really want to kiss her right now. In fact, I'd like to stay in bed and kiss her for the rest of the day until I have to drive her to the airport. *Who does that? Who wants to be in bed with a hot, bare-ass naked chick and just kiss her?* Something's wrong with me if I'm thinking like this.

"James…I…that was," she says like something's gone weird with her too. *What happened to us just now?*

I tilt her head toward me, and I slowly close my eyes as I touch her forehead to mine. "You are the most perfect human being in the world," I whisper softly to her. "You're the most amazing person, and you're beautiful, and I wish you lived here because I'd do this forever." *Christ!* This sounds like the kind of thing you say to a girl before you propose to her, like the spiel that comes before telling her you love her. But that's not…unless…*do I love her?*

"You're so warm." She giggles as she presses into me and nuzzles under my neck.

"You're so hot," I reply, my face fixed in a perma-smile.

That makes her laugh, and I'm happy to lighten things up a bit. We were heading into some uncharted territory there for a minute, and it kind of freaked me out to consider some of those feelings I had toward her.

"I want to take a shower," she says, lifting up on her arms again so she's hovering over me and looking like some shit religious people would describe when they talk about heaven.

"Want me to join you?" I throw out there with a raised eyebrow. Considering how shy she was yesterday, I seriously doubt she'll do it. But hey, worth a try, right?

I can't really hide my total surprise when she pauses, gives me a sexy smile and then nods her head. "Yes, I think that'd be nice."

"You're fucking with me, aren't you?" I smirk.

"Nope." She shakes her head. "I wanna shower with you, James," she adorably replies, biting her bottom lip in that way that makes me crazy for her.

I close my eyes and take a deep breath. I can hear her snickering. "That is, hands down, the best thing you've ever said to me."

She laughs loudly and sits up all the way, still straddling me and giving me a view of her bare body. The way her hair falls over her boobs reminds me of a mermaid.

"You just don't know!" I chuckle as I sit up and wrap my arms around her. "You have no fuckin' clue what this does to me!"

"I have some idea." She grins, looking down at my crotch.

"You make me harder than I've ever been in my fuckin' life!" I admit.

She tries to hold it in, but she nearly snorts when she bursts into laughter. *Yeah, I get it.* It wasn't exactly the smoothest compliment. It makes me laugh too. I just said that to my best friend. I just blurted out that she gets my dick hard, and I told her that right after we had this sweet little moment. I'm sure I could have phrased it better, but she fries my circuits and I'm way too honest with her.

"Do you want me to do something about that?" she asks, sliding her hand down my stomach. "That's one thing I have done before."

My mouth opens a little bit, and I let out a deep breath. Even the slightest touch of her fingertips feels good.

"Maybe I could return the favor," she continues.

I swallow hard and close my eyes, trying to get my shit together. I can't even describe how bad I want her, but I'm worried about it. If she so much as touches my dick, I'm going to end up fucking her. I know it. If she's naked *and* I'm naked, it will happen. I won't be able to control myself. We're too close, and it would be too easy to go for it.

"I don't think we should," I say against my libido's screaming pleas.

"Are you sure?"

"Yeah." I nod. "Lo, I can barely hold back as it is. Don't make fun of me, but I want you so bad right now that it hurts, and I'm gonna go fuckin' werewolf on you and frenzy fuck you if we keep going."

She bites her lip to keep from laughing.

"You're naked, and you're like three inches from my dick. There is not a goddamn thing I want more than to just grab your hips and fuckin' plunge into you," I continue to say, despite the intelligent part of my brain telling me to shut the fuck up. "I want to fuck you until you scream so loud the neighbors call the cops. I want to make you come so hard you faint. I want to be inside you for hours. I want you to miss your flight and stay here riding my dick for, like, the next eight days."

"Goddamn!" She cackles loudly as her expression changes to amused surprise. "That's graphic."

"I can't help it," I say, chuckling. "You do crazy shit to me. You make me get filthy. The things I want to do to you right now...it's so bad I don't even want to tell you about it."

She completely cracks up, taking my face in her hands and planting a big kiss on my forehead. "I guess we should cool it down, then. I don't want you to lose it and go all ravenous on me."

"I fuckin' would, too!" I chuckle. "Christ! The things I would do to you—it'd be totally obscene."

"You'd defile me?" She laughs, raising an eyebrow at me.

"I'd completely defile you," I tease. "It would get totally dirty, Lo, really vulgar stuff. And I'd never stop going, either. I'd fuck you so good it'd be burned into your brain for the rest of your life. Any time you fucked somebody else, you'd be like, 'Damn, this is nowhere near as good as when James did it,' because I'd do it so good that nobody could ever compare."

"Shit!" She giggles and sits back like she's assessing me. "You've thought this through."

"You have no idea." I chuckle.

"I think you just like talking nasty to me."

"I do like it." I grin and pull her closer, touching our foreheads together.

"All right, dirty boy, let's shower," she says, patting my stomach and sliding off of me.

I miss the feel of her the second she's away. I'm kind of horrified at myself, at how horny I am for her right now. She's Lola! She's my best friend, my little sweetheart. Even though she's proven that she has a sexy side that could boil my blood right out of my body, I shouldn't think such lewd shit about her.

"Come on," she says, walking happily naked into the bathroom.

I'm out of bed in ten seconds, and I follow after her like a fuckin' puppy. *Shit!* She totally has me now—not that she didn't before, not that she hasn't since the day I met her. I'd do anything for this girl, but now she knows it. I'm never going to hear the end of this if my friends find out. I'm supposed to be the ladies' man, the love-'em-and-leave-'em guy who gets any chick he wants and acts all alpha male all the time. Now a girl—a tiny, petite, pretty, innocent girl—has me wrapped around her little finger.

It makes me smile a little bit, though, because I know she likes it and I like anything that makes her happy. Lola's seen sides of me that I don't show to anyone. I've cried in front of her, got into screaming fights with her, and then come crawling back to grovel and apologize because she was right all along—she's almost always right. I've gone crazy, primal protective over her, and I've gotten all paranoid because of her. She just taps into my most base impulses, and everything I do is cranked to eleven when it comes to her.

She turns on the water and peeks over her shoulder at me. She knows exactly what she's doing. I've completely lost the upper hand—if I ever even had it in the first place, that is.

My eyes feel all hooded with lust as I watch her rinse her hair, the water flowing down her body in all the places I'd like to touch her. *Shit! This is really bad.* I'm fuckin' obsessed with her.

"Can I wash your hair?" I ask her. *What kind of a request is that? How pussy whipped am I and I haven't even had her pussy? Fuck! Fuck! Fuck!*

"Uh-huh." She nods, reaching up to run her fingers through that gorgeous hair. The way her stomach elongates makes me crazy. I don't think I've ever wanted anyone more than I want her right now.

I grab the shampoo and lather up her long hair, massaging her scalp. I hate myself for how much I love this. After I smooth in the conditioner, I take the shower gel and lather up my hands, rubbing her shoulders and back until she's relaxed and breathing deeply. I wash the rest of her, but I try to avoid her boobs, since I can't risk touching them if we're both naked in here and I know I could easily hike her up against the wall and fuck her until my lungs give out.

She rinses out the conditioner and then trades places with me so I'm under the water. She grabs the bottle of shower gel and starts pouring some out on her hands, looking up into my eyes in this sexy way that makes my smile turn more flirtatious.

I inhale a sharp breath when she runs her hands over my chest, onto my shoulders, down my back, and around onto my abs. Her little fingers are talented, and she's fuckin' caressing me in a way that has my heart pounding. It's not necessarily sexual—she's not going for my dick or anything—but it's sexy. It's kind of sensual, but innocent at the same time.

"You freaked out that you're naked with me?" I grin at her. "You were such a dork about it last night, but now you're a fuckin' Playboy Bunny prancing around here and teasing me."

"Teasing you?" She raises her eyebrows like she's surprised. "How am I teasing you?"

"Are you fuckin' kidding me?" I laugh. "How are you *not* teasing me?"

"Because I'm naked and taking a shower with you and washing your body with my bare hands?" She smirks, running her palms over my chest.

"Yeah, that would be it." I nod. "I don't think best friends do shit like that."

"No," she says, and her voice takes on a new, sensual quality, "they don't."

What does that mean? The way she said it was all soft and seductive, but she doesn't elaborate on it. There was more to it, though. I feel like there were a whole bunch of other words hidden under the surface of what she said. She couldn't possibly mean…does she want to be more than friends?

That thought is both awesome and terrifying at the same time. I don't doubt that Lola would be an awesome girlfriend, but I don't think I could be an awesome boyfriend. I'd probably end up fucking some other chick and pissing her off, because that's kind of what I do. I'm good as a friend with benefits, good as a fuck buddy or a one-night stand, but I'd be shitty to date because I have the tendency to fuck things up with people who care about me. Just ask my dad, who all but flat-out told me I wasn't worth a shit when he was kicking me out of the house for doing porn. I know it sounds totally emo, but I don't deserve for somebody to have feelings for me that go that deep. I especially don't deserve for Lola to feel that way about me. She's a zillion times better than I deserve—than anyone deserves, really.

We finish showering, and she starts combing out her hair with a towel wrapped around her body. It's the first time all morning that I haven't been able to stare at her tits, and I miss them already.

"I'm gonna make us some breakfast," I say, kissing the top of her head.

I head out into the kitchen and start cracking some eggs and preparing French toast for us. Breakfast food is fast and easy, but I like to add my own little flare to it to make it more gourmet. The omelets I'm making, for example, have an assortment of veggies and spices to give them a little more flavor. It's cool to be cooking for Lola again. I missed it. I used to love cooking dinner for her when we lived back home. She'd eat at my house a lot or I'd go over to her place and make stuff for her and her mom. I loved the way she'd scarf it down and then tell me she felt like her belly would explode from how full she was.

She comes into the kitchen, but she's fully clothed and she's pouting a little bit. She stands against the counter and holds something up. It's a black G-string with sparkly stars on it.

"Why was this on the floor by your bed?" she asks, clearly not happy about the discovery.

"It's from last week," I reply, not really sure what to do in this situation.

"Whose skanky-ass thong is this?" she says like she's even more pissed off.

"Lexi…or maybe Tara," I answer truthfully.

"You don't know which one?" She's not pleased. Definitely not.

"Last week, we all did a shoot together, and we were still hyped up so they came over here, since my place is close to the studio," I attempt to explain.

"You had a fucking ménage with those two bitchy girls last week?" she says. She sounds like she's hurt, and I don't know what to do.

"Yeah, dude." I shrug, still not sure of the best course of action. "Why are you getting weird about it?"

"I…I'm not," she replies, stumbling a little bit. She shuts up after that and then goes to sit down at the breakfast bar that looks over the counter.

"Eggs are almost ready, and I got some turkey bacon for you, since I know you don't like the real thing." I smile, motioning to the stove.

"Okay," she says, but her voice is all deflated.

"Lo, what's going on?" I ask her, stopping what I'm doing to come around the counter and stand in front of her.

She pauses, and I can see her brow starting to furrow. She's still pissed. "Did you at least change your fucking sheets before you had me in your bed? I'd hate to think I slept on the same sheets where you fucked those nasty-ass bitches."

"Whoa! What?" I say, stepping back. *Where the fuck did that come from?* "You're pissed about Lexi and Tara?"

"No," she says, clearly meaning yes.

"Why would you be mad about that?" I ask her. "You know what my job is; you know that I do that shit all the time. Fuck, I've told you about almost every chick I've banged, and you've never once flipped out like this. What's the deal, kid?"

"Nothing." She shrugs, but she won't look me in the eye.

"Nah, I'm not gonna let you just shut it down like that," I say, taking her face in my hands and making her look at me. "Why are you pissed?"

"You make me feel like a jealous girlfriend," she murmurs. "I don't like feeling like I'm some whiny girl who bitches when you fuck somebody else, but that's how this makes me feel."

"Well, don't feel like that." I shrug. *Isn't this perfectly obvious?* "You're getting all crazy like I cheated on you or something. Fucking them isn't cheating. How the fuck could I cheat? I'm not your boyfriend."

Her lip shakes, and I can tell that really hurt her feelings. I feel like an asshole.

"Wait, that sounded mean. I'm sorry," I immediately apologize. "I just—that's not how I meant to say that."

"It's okay." She shrugs and hops off the barstool. "You're right."

She starts shuffling back to the bedroom, but I catch her elbow and turn her around. "I'm sorry, baby," I say to her. "I really am, okay? I didn't mean for that to sound so harsh. I just meant that we're best friends and that you never usually get all weird about me and other girls. Talk to me. Tell me what's going on here."

"I don't know," she says and her voice trembles a little.

"It's 'cause of what we did, isn't it?" I nod, putting my arms around her to comfort her. That's what happened. She let loose and shit got real, so now she's all jumbled up inside about how she feels. She likes me, and I mean "like" likes me.

"It's not that," she says, totally lying. "I'm just bummed about having to go back to school."

"No, you're not," I cut right to it. "You're bummed because you felt something for me. You're freaked out because something happened, and now you don't know how you feel about me."

"How would you know that?" she timidly responds.

"Because I feel that way about you all the time," I say.

"What?" She looks up at me with confusion.

"Yeah, dude." I smile warmly as I brush her hair behind her ear. "I like you so much, Lola, and it makes me get all weird when I think about you being with other dudes—even just being friends with other guys. I told you, you're my treasure, kid, and I don't want you to open yourself up to anybody else."

"Yet you can still do it whenever you want to?" She pouts.

"I just…I can separate it out, I guess," I reply. "I can take how I feel about you and put it someplace else, someplace away from the girls I want to fuck or the girls I work with."

"I can't," she whispers so quietly I can barely hear it.

"I know," I say, pulling her into my chest and holding her close. "I was worried about this. You're a romance kind of girl, and you can't randomly fuck around with somebody without feeling something deeper."

"That's probably true," she says with a resigned sigh.

"I shouldn't have even started it, really, because I was worried this would happen and I'd end up hurting your feelings. I just started thinking about it, and I wanted it so bad. I've never done anything like that with you, and I got so obsessed with the idea that I didn't think about the consequences. I just…I'm really sorry," I say, kissing the top of her head.

She takes a deep breath, and I feel her relax a bit. "This is your fault," she says with a little smile. "You're so good that it made me lose my mind. It's like *Ghostbusters*. You crossed the streams, and now I'm all fucked up and confused."

"Hey," I say, chuckling, "I'm confused too. I've known you since you were six years old and you were just naked on top of me. You're not supposed to get a hard-on thinking of your best friend, but you turn me on all the time, and I could have blown my load in my fuckin' boxers when I watched you come this morning."

She giggles and shakes her head.

"This confuses the shit out of me because I shouldn't want it as bad as I do—and I really fuckin' do. I should not get this horny for my best friend, but you do that to me, and I have no idea why, how or what to do about it, so I just let it slide," I elaborate.

"So it's not just me who felt it?" She shyly smiles.

"Hell, no!" I laugh. "I wasn't lying when I told you I wanted to do all kinds of nasty shit with you. You don't think it fucks my head up to want to bang my best friend? I've practically, like, sworn an oath not to let anybody fuck you who doesn't deserve you, and then what the fuck happens when I'm the one who's trying to fuck you? I've, like, violated everything I stood for, for fuck's sake!"

She laughs and wraps her arms around my hips, resting her cheek on my chest. "We really shook shit up, didn't we?"

"Yes, yes, we did," I say.

"So this should be the beginning and end of all this," she says. "Probably need to put the brakes on any further sex stuff or else we'll be royally fucked up for years to come."

"I totally don't want to do that—because you're sexy as fuck and I love getting to do sexual shit with you—but you're right." I smile at her as I hold her face in my hands.

"Okay," she sighs. "Best friends only, from now on, then?"

"Word." I grin, holding out my pinky for her to pinky swear me.

She hooks her finger in mine and gives me a nod.

"Now let's eat some fuckin' breakfast. I'm super hungry."

"Me, too," she says, going with it when I take her hand and lead her back to the kitchen.

Chapter 26
Lola

James and I are standing just outside the security screening area at LAX. My bag is checked, my boarding pass is printed, and all my liquids over three ounces have been packed away with my toiletries bag. I'm departing in just under a half hour for the long trip back to my dorm all the way on the other side of the country. My heart hurts already from how far I'll be from James.

"I hate this," I say, trying my very hardest not to cry.

I know it would be stupid to cry. I'll probably see him again in three months or less, so I shouldn't be sniveling about leaving. Still, parting ways with him this time will be a lot harder because of what we did. I feel closer to him now, almost attached to him, and it's like ripping off a Band-Aid to head back to reality like this.

"I'm gonna miss you like crazy." He reaches up and rests his hand on the back of my neck.

"Oh, dude, you have no idea how much I'm gonna miss you!" I reply. "You're here with sun and palm trees. I'm going to the east coast. In winter. To go write thesis papers and take exams and shit."

He laughs and tucks my hair behind my ear. "You ever thought about going to school out here? UCLA can be very nice, I hear."

"After this trip, I might consider it," I say, only half joking. I'd love to be closer to him, but I got into a great school, and I'm sure a bunch of my credits wouldn't transfer, so everything would be complicated.

"All right," he says, "well, needless to say, I love you, and I'm crazy about you, and I'm gonna think about you constantly and count down the days until I can cuddle you in my bed again."

"That better be soon, either at your place or out at my school. I'd love to see how my roommate, Rachael, reacts when there's a big, burly hunk sleeping in my little-ass dorm bed with me wrapped up around him like a fucking Burmese python."

He grins and gives me a wink. "I'll show you a python," he jokes.

I laugh loudly and give him a playful smack on the shoulder.

I should go. The security line is long, and those people can fuck up your whole day if they decide you're worthy of a random screening. I hike my bag back up on my shoulder and gaze longingly into James's eyes.

"Wait," he says softly, "before you go, I have to do something."

"Okay."

"Close your eyes," he instructs.

"Why?"

"Do you trust me, Lola?"

"Yes."

"Then close your fuckin' eyes," he says, chuckling.

I do as he says, trying to attune my other senses to what he's trying to do. I smell his shampoo mixed with his trademark virile, masculine scent—a combo that makes me inwardly swoon. Just so male. And so hot.

I keep my eyes closed when I feel his lips brush against mine in the most tender, sweet, soft little peck I've ever experienced.

My eyes slowly open, and he's staring down at me with this reverent, appreciative, loving gaze that makes my heart swell.

"I just wanted to do that before we stopped the sex stuff for good," he says.

My God! How I'd like to throw my arms around him and lock him in a kiss like something out of a movie. He's stunningly beautiful, standing in front of me in jeans and an olive green T-shirt that does wonders for his tan skin and clings to his spectacular pecs. His long hair falls in perfect waves at his shoulders, he's got a little bit of stubble that brings out the delicious shape of his pouty lips, and his hazel eyes practically sparkle as he looks at me.

He's not my boyfriend. He's not my boyfriend. He's not my boyfriend. It's probably good that I'm leaving because I'd never be able to focus on that mantra with him standing in front of me. I've got functioning eyes and no amount of mental willpower could overtake what I see: a gorgeous, breathtaking, stunningly beautiful man who just gave me a little kiss. A man who's just as confused as I am about what our little escapade meant. A man who cares about me, who wants to protect me, who cooks for me and makes me laugh, and has all the makings of a perfect boyfriend. But also a man who's not my boyfriend and could never really be my boyfriend—or anyone's boyfriend, for that matter. James has everything a girl could ever want, except that monogamy gene that tells him to keep his dick out of slutty porn stars. A sad fact of life, I guess.

"Bye, kid," he says softly to me, his fingertips caressing the side of my face.

I turn to go to security, but I snap back around and grab his hand. "Wait!" I say. "One more."

I stand on my tiptoes, and he bends down so I can place an affectionate, close-lipped kiss on his mouth.

"Okay," I say, feeling my cheeks flush, "now I can go."

"You're the greatest ever, Lola." He smiles and gives me a wink.

"Right back at you, stud." I smile back, blowing him a kiss and heading off to the TSA line.

When I finally get to my window seat on the plane, I think back on the weekend and on my friendship with James. He means more to me than anyone I know, but I should never combine that with how attractive I find him because it'll make me fall madly in love with him, and that can only lead to disappointment. He's never disappointed me as a friend, has always been loyal and caring, so I shouldn't fuck that up by expecting more from him than he can give.

The way I freaked out in the kitchen this morning was wrong. I know James. I know what he is. Finding those panties should have come as no shock to me. I should heed the advice of Liza Minnelli in *Cabaret*: a tiger can't be a lamb. James practically radiates sexuality, and women lose their minds over him like they're overdosing on pheromones or something. The fact that he had a three-way with two porn stars a few days before I arrived isn't even news. It's nothing I wouldn't have already guessed, so it was dumb to have a shit fit over it. He didn't do anything wrong because I'm not his girlfriend, and I don't hold dominion over who he screws in his free time. I need to accept that and move past it, because I love him so much and he's my best friend. I can't harbor any resentment toward him for doing what he always does: getting laid.

I have class to look forward to, a new school, new friends, new opportunities. My future's ahead of me, and I know James will always be a big part of it, but it might be nice to do some growing up. Maybe flirting with some other guys will give me a chance to stop hopelessly dreaming of a relationship with my best friend, who just so happens to be incapable of monogamy. James is in my heart forever, but I need to do what he said. I need to separate it out and put the part of me that adores him far away from the part of me that's so sexually drawn to him. Never the two shall meet. They just can't. It would end in a fucking disaster.

When the flight attendant announces we're at cruising altitude, I recline my chair back and decide to listen to my new iPod. Though James and I may be far apart, we're always together. As long as I don't let my lingering emotions get in the way, we can be together forever, the very best and tightest of friends. Sure, maybe we won't get to fool around anymore, but being best friends is definitely good enough for me.

Acknowledgments

First and foremost, I'd like to thank every single person who read my self-published work. It's been an absolute delight to see people enjoying these characters as much as I do. You all gave me the confidence to finally take my writing beyond the confines of my laptop and out into the world. James and Lola's story would have never continued past *First Dance* if it weren't for the support and encouragement of my early readers.

Thank you to Micha, Lisa, Elizabeth, Traci, Meredith, and everyone at Omnific for believing in my writing. Thanks to Erin, Ben, and PS for being subjected to my endless brainstorming. A gigantic thank-you goes out to Kyle for getting the wheels in motion for me like a Tom-Ford-wearing, mad-connection-having angel.

About the Author

Bianca Giovanni was born and raised in Boulder, Colorado. She grew up with a single mother and Italian grandmother, who was an avid reader. She is a graduate of The George Washington University where she focused on film theory. She has had a love of writing since childhood, but self-published her first short stories in 2012. Bianca's strong female characters and witty dialogue have struck a chord with readers and lead to her popularity on self-publishing platforms. She currently resides in Denver, Colorado, where she can often be found jotting down story ideas in a notebook.

Young Adult

The Ember series: *Ember & Iridescent* by Carol Oates
Breaking Point by Jess Bowen
Life, Liberty, and Pursuit by Susan Kaye Quinn
The Embrace series: *Embrace & Hold Tight* by Cherie Colyer
Destiny's Fire by Trisha Wolfe
The Reaper series: *Reaping Me Softly & UnReap My Heart* by Kate
Evangelista

Erotic Romance

The Keyhole series: *Becoming sage* (book one) by Kasi Alexander
The Keyhole series: *Saving sunni* (book two) by Kasi & Reggie Alexander
The Winemaker's Dinner: *Appetizers & Entrée* by Dr. Ivan Rusilko &
Everly Drummond
The Winemaker's Dinner: *Dessert* by Dr. Ivan Rusilko
Client N° 5 by Joy Fulcher

Paranormal Romance

The Light series: *Seers of Light, Whisper of Light, & Circle of Light*
by Jennifer DeLucy
The Hanaford Park series: *Eve of Samhain & Pleasures Untold* by Lisa Sanchez
Immortal Awakening by KC Randall
The Seraphim series: *Crushed Seraphim & Bittersweet Seraphim*
by Debra Anastasia
The Guardian's Wild Child by Feather Stone
Grave Refrain by Sarah M. Glover
Divinity by Patricia Leever
Blood Vine series: *Blood Vine & Blood Entangled* by Amber Belldene
Divine Temptation by Nicki Elson
Love in the Time of the Dead by Tera Shanley

Historical Romance

Cat O' Nine Tails by Patricia Leever
Burning Embers by Hannah Fielding
Good Ground by Tracy Winegar

← ••→ Romantic Suspense ← ••→

Whirlwind by Robin DeJarnett
The CONduct Series: *With Good Behavior* & *Bad Behavior* &
On Best Behavior by Jennifer Lane
Indivisible by Jessica McQuinn
Between the Lies by Alison Oburia

← ••→ Anthologies ← ••→

A Valentine Anthology including short stories by
Alice Clayton ("With a Double Oven"),
Jennifer DeLucy ("Magnus of Pfelt, Conquering Viking Lord"),
Nicki Elson ("I Don't Do Valentine's Day"),
Jessica McQuinn ("Better Than One Dead Rose and a Monkey Card"),
Victoria Michaels ("Home to Jackson"), and
Alison Oburia ("The Bridge")

← ••→ Singles and Novellas ← ••→

It's Only Kinky the First Time (Keyhole series) by Kasi Alexander
Learning the Ropes (Keyhole series) by Kasi & Reggie Alexander
The Winemaker's Dinner: RSVP by Dr. Ivan Rusilko
The Winemaker's Dinner: No Reservations by Everly Drummond
Big Guns by Jessica McQuinn
Concessions by Robin DeJarnett
Starstruck by Lisa Sanchez
New Flame by BJ Thornton
Shackled by Debra Anastasia
Swim Recruit by Jennifer Lane
Sway by Nicki Elson
Full Speed Ahead by Susan Kaye Quinn
The Second Sunrise by Hannah Downing
The Summer Prince by Carol Oates
Whatever it Takes by Sarah M. Glover
Clarity (A *Divinity* prequel single) by Patricia Leever
A Christmas Wish (A *Cocktails & Dreams* single) by Autumn Markus
Late Night with Andres by Debra Anastasia

CPSIA information can be obtained at www.ICGtesting.com
Printed in the USA
LVOW08s0000230114

370546LV00001B/23/P